# FREEZING

*One of the most exciting crime and mystery series debuts of the year. Think Kathy Reichs and Patricia Cornwell*

When a bundle of frozen body parts tumbles out the rear door of a van on a Los Angeles freeway, FBI agent Scott Houston knows just where to go for an off-the-record analysis: Agency 32/1, a non-profit missing persons identification resource center run by forensic anthropologists Jayne Hall and Steelie Lander. Jayne and Steelie quickly determine that the remains are human, though from several women. But Scott's call has unintended consequences for the two women, putting their lives in jeopardy, as their unique skills uncover evidence leading directly to the killer...

*Titles by Clea Koff*

*Non-fiction*
THE BONE WOMAN


*The Jayne and Steelie Mystery Series*
FREEZING *
PASSING *


* *available from Severn House*

# FREEZING

Clea Koff

**Severn House Large Print**
London & New York

This first large print edition published 2013
in Great Britain and the USA by
SEVERN HOUSE PUBLISHERS LTD of
9-15 High Street, Sutton, Surrey, SM1 1DF.
First world regular print edition published 2011 by
Severn House Publishers Ltd., London and New York.

British Library Cataloguing in Publication Data

Koff, Clea.
  Freezing.
  1. Women forensic anthropologists--California--Los
  Angeles--Fiction. 2. Dead--Identification--Fiction.
  3. United States. Federal Bureau of Investigation--
  Fiction. 4. Murder--Investigation--United States--
  Fiction. 5. Suspense fiction. 6. Large type books.
  I. Title
  813.6-dc23

  ISBN-13: 978-0-7278-9980-4

Severn House Publishers support The Forest Stewardship Council
[FSC], the leading international forest certification organisation. All
our titles that are printed on Greenpeace-approved FSC-certified paper
carry the FSC logo.

MIX
Paper from
responsible sources
FSC® C018575

Printed and bound in Great Britain by the
MPG Books Group, Bodmin, Cornwall.

*For LMH*

# 2005

# DAY ONE

## Tuesday

# ONE

The tang of warming eucalyptus intensified with the breeze and Jayne took her eyes off the California Highway Patrol officer to locate the shimmering trees half a block away where they flanked the 101 Freeway. She looked back at the officer. He was listening to the static-bound information emanating from his radio while his eyes traveled over the Jeep's roll bar, dipped into the back on to the twin toolboxes, then returned to Steelie's slim frame in the driver's seat, her hand resting casually on the gear stick but her expression hidden by the peak of a faded pink baseball cap.

'You're the scientists?' The CHP officer put the question even as he beckoned their escort.

A motorcycle rumbled to life a few feet away and its driver pulled in front of them, keeping a foot on the ground as he looked back, lower face serious under a helmet and sunglasses. Steelie gave a loose salute and the motorcycle moved forward.

They followed the bike's zigzag around the Highway Patrol sedans that had made a maze of the Sunkist building's parking lot. Near the northwest corner, the CHP bike peeled off, leaving them facing a wall of dark blue Chevrolet Suburbans. Steelie halted the Jeep. The Suburbans were stationary but their engines were humming and their headlights were on. Both women waited, expecting to see some movement from behind the heavily tinted windows. Nothing happened.

Steelie kept her own engine running. 'If this was Buenos Aires circa 1978, we'd be running for our lives right about now.'

Jayne murmured agreement. After a moment, she pushed her sunglasses into her hair to constrain waves that had been whipped into something unruly when the open-topped Jeep had been bucking over surface joins on the freeway, then she leaned down to put double knots in her bootlaces.

Steelie abruptly turned off the engine. 'I see your man.'

Jayne paused on her second lace but refrained from sitting up. 'He's not my man.'

'Well, he's on his way over and ... looks to me like he's still sporting dark blond hair over a furrowed brow over green eyes over a smirk atop five feet eleven inches of I-don't-know-what's-under-that-suit-but-I'll-take-it.'

Amused, Jayne straightened up, assuming Steelie was exaggerating. She wasn't. At a

8

distance, Special Agent Scott Houston appeared unchanged from when they'd last seen him at Quantico five years earlier. Jayne glanced at Steelie, who was taking off her cap; her short, choppy haircut exposed how the silver amongst the blonde was no longer relegated to the wisps above her ears that had generated the nickname when she was much younger. For her part, Jayne felt sixty-five, not thirty-five and figured she had some of the outward changes to go with it. Suddenly self-conscious, she alighted from the Jeep just as Scott reached its front bumper; close enough for her to catch his quick assessment of her from head to toe. They didn't speak as they shook hands slowly.

'Not bad,' he finally said.

Surprised, she smiled. 'You're not looking so bad yourself.'

His mouth almost twitched into a grin. 'I meant how fast you made it here. Speeding, were you, Steelie?'

He finally released Jayne's hand and turned to Steelie, who was coming around the car.

'You want our help or not, Houston?' She clasped his hand briefly.

He smiled. 'Follow me. I'll introduce you to the team.'

Jayne and Steelie walked behind him with their toolboxes over to the far side of the Suburbans where a huddle of four men broke up, lowering clipboards and clearing throats. Three of them were dressed like commandos and Scott introduced them as the 'Critters' from the Federal Bureau of Investigation's Critical Stabiliza-

9

tion and Recovery Unit, there to maintain chain of custody for any evidence collected that day. Scott then addressed his team, inclining his head toward the women.

'Jayne Hall and Steelie Lander. They run Agency 32/1, an outfit that does forensic profiles of missing persons, matching them up with unidentified bodies or living Does. I called them in because they're forensic anthro-pologists and they do dental as well. Steelie here's a triple threat 'cause she's also a lawyer, so watch your P's and Q's. These are the people who're going to tell us if what we've got is human, so we defer to them at the scene. OK?'

There were polite nods all round, then Scott said he would take a minute to brief the new-comers. The Critters cleared the area but the one man Scott hadn't yet introduced kept his stance, feet spread, one hand held over the other in front of his body, causing the fabric of his suit to pull slightly over muscular arms. Jayne noticed his skin was almost as brown as her own, but his hair was dark and straight, and his eyes – she averted her own. He had been looking at her looking at him.

Scott said: 'My partner, Special Agent Ramos.'

Jayne started. 'You're Eric? Eric Ramos?'

He stepped forward to shake her hand. 'Uh-oh, what's he been saying about me?'

'No, I mean ... it's a pleasure to meet you.'

'In that case, Scott,' Eric glanced at him as he turned to greet Steelie. 'I'll get you your money later.'

'All right, let's get started,' Scott said. 'We're

10

dealing with a single vehicle accident around five this a.m. on the 101 right here behind us. A guy's car takes out part of the side railing. Guy tries to get out of a DUI charge by telling Highway Patrol he rear-ended a van, then had to swerve to avoid a body.'

'A body lying on the freeway?' Jayne asked.

'No, that's the thing. Guy says the body came out of the van he hit. Happened to have noticed the van earlier because it had a peach on the license plate and this guy just had a bellyful of peach schnapps.'

'Peach plate,' Steelie mused. 'Georgia?'

'Got it in one. So, there was no sign of a body but CHP reports that the side railing scraped off part of the front of this guy's car. Anything could have dropped down under the freeway because it's one of the sections with a berm sloping off it on the north side. Lots of vegetation, creating a basic ravine situation. They secured the area as soon as their flashlights picked up what they thought were BP's.'

Jayne glanced toward the ravine. 'How many body parts are we talking about?'

Eric answered her. 'We don't know yet.'

'OK,' said Steelie slowly. 'I don't want to seem uninterested but why were you so insistent on calling us in? Why not Rudin or Sweetzer? This is their beat.'

'Coroner's office can't spare Rudin because of the crematorium investigation and they said Sweetzer's on her honeymoon. But ... there's another reason.' Scott crossed his arms and took a deep breath, only to look up at the sky.

11

Jayne looked to Eric. He was focused on a tarmac fissure at her feet.

Scott exhaled his story like a confession. 'Eric and I have some open cases from Georgia involving body parts. All female, none yet identified. We believe they're related to the disappearance of a number of prostitutes in and around Atlanta. We figured it for one serial killer, not a bunch of Johns who just didn't want to pay the sex workers.'

Jayne scanned Scott's face. 'You never told me about this case.'

He looked away.

Eric took up the slack. 'Look, our boss wasn't convinced by our reading of the facts so he scaled back our investigation. Finding this perp became the Holy Grail for us. Then we got transferred to LA and that killer's still out there.'

Steelie asked, 'What makes you think the material in the ravine is related to your Georgia cases?'

'If the stuff is human, then it's the MO of dismemberment in combination with the type of vehicle: multiple witnesses recalled the missing Atlanta women last being seen getting into a van.'

Scott added, 'When CHP notified us this morning that there was a van wearing Georgia plates involved in this mess, we made it Federal and put on our thinking caps.' He finally met Jayne's eyes. 'Thus the early morning call to you.'

Jayne nodded slowly. 'So you want us to confirm human, non-human, sex? What else? Because this isn't our area anymore. We're dealing with families, not bodies.'

'Ever noticed how the wick goes all the way through a candle?' Scott asked.

She frowned at the apparent non sequitur.

He re-started, 'A candle couldn't burn if the wick didn't go all the way through. That's why you can burn it from either end.'

'Is that supposed to mean something in this context?'

Eric cut in. 'He's trying to say that we're all doing the same thing, just starting at different ends. You're trying to make ID's by starting with missing persons; we're starting with their bodies. And I've heard from Scott that you two have done more than your fair share of body work with the UN. If anyone's qualified to check out this site, it's you guys.'

'So,' Scott said. 'Can we do this?'

Jayne and Steelie nodded and Scott called over one of the Critters who arrived holding some flat nylon straps with clips on the ends. He spoke with a deep voice when he identified himself as Agent Weiss. 'When we get over to the site, you'll see that the best way to get up there is for me to winch you up. Can I get you two fitted out?' He unfurled the straps to show they were fixed into a harness that resembled underpants.

Steelie stepped forward to get into the rig as the others watched and she leaned on Weiss' shoulder for balance. 'Y'know, Scott, you didn't have to go to all this trouble just to see me in some underwear.'

Eric choked back a surprised laugh. 'Hang on.

13

How long have you guys known each other?'

Steelie replied, 'Since Houston here was still in training pants.'

'Not training,' Scott corrected. 'Trainee. And it was a uniform.'

'It was a training gun, though, right?'

Eric looked over at his partner. 'Is she talking about the red ones we use at Quantico?'

'Before your time, Ramos.' He looked at Jayne. 'Can't you rein her in?'

'No,' Jayne said, stepping into her own harness. 'I can't.'

But by now Steelie had Eric's attention. 'When Jayne and I were at Quantico, we watched a classmate of Scott's run a semi-covert op to steal his gun.'

His eyes widened as he looked at Scott. 'From the back of your pants?'

'She didn't succeed,' Scott downplayed. 'And then I stole hers.'

'Yeah!' Steelie rejoined. 'And she yelled at him from the other side of the bar like it was NASA Control. "Houston? We got a problem." So then he—'

'Eric doesn't need the rest of that story,' Scott interrupted. 'You ready, Jayne?'

They followed a CHP officer to the edge of the parking lot and clambered over a low concrete wall to descend into the ravine. They hiked along the bottom for a short distance. Past the Sunkist property line the ravine narrowed and became more overgrown; eucalyptus, vinca, shreds of plastic bags, all sprouting with equal vigor. It was darker and cooler because the sun

14

hadn't filtered down yet. The group fell silent.

The officer slowed and called back to them, pointing to the left where the berm led up to the freeway. 'The material's up there. We marked a wide perimeter with flags. The slope is steep and it is slippery.' He stepped to the side, using the trunk of a small tree as a handhold.

Jayne and Steelie hung back while the Critters moved in to do their work. Then Scott turned to the anthropologists and said, 'OK, 32/1, tell us what we got.'

The two women moved to the front of the group, the clicks of the power buttons on their flashlights echoed by clicks on others as people followed their lead. Ten seconds passed as they looked up the berm from below. Brown leaves, wet leaves, wet tissue exhibiting pale, red blotches.

'Well, it's human. I can tell you that from here,' declared Jayne.

'In that case,' Scott said, 'I authorize you to take a closer look.'

Weiss clipped their harnesses to a rappelling rope and checked all the connections. Once they were lined up with Jayne in front, he started winching and she and Steelie climbed the slope. As soon as they were parallel to the body parts, they leaned toward them at various angles.

Steelie called down to the others. 'We're not going to touch anything because you guys will have to detail-photo this first, OK?'

'Ten-four, ma'am,' came the reply.

'OK,' Jayne murmured to Steelie. 'I'm seeing two arms, present from the shoulder down, all fingers present. A chunk of thigh and knee ... left. You seeing the same thing?'

'Yeah, plus I've got another chunk of torso down here. Everything's wet.'

'Is it just wet around the BP's? Or is that condensation?'

They both looked around. Everything else was dry and dusty, like Southern California should be in the summer.

'What's the deal?' asked Jayne. 'The parts aren't fresh but they don't look like they're decomping either.'

'They're not,' Steelie replied. 'Listen. Do you hear that?' She held her hand up and Jayne stopped moving, cocking her head to the side.

In between the rushes of sound that accompanied the passing traffic on the freeway above them, there was a distinct sound. *Sip, sip ... sip ... sip, sip*. Then, before their eyes, out of the tissue visible in the cross-section of the exposed left knee, came a droplet. It was a watery red shimmer, hanging, then dropping from the tissue on to the bed of leaves below.

'Not decomping...' said Steelie. 'Defrosting.'

They straightened up.

Jayne called out, 'Houston.'

'Yo,' came his voice from below.

'We got a problem.' She wasn't smiling.

# TWO

Scott watched Steelie's Jeep leave the Sunkist parking lot as he wrapped up the call on his cell phone. He summoned his team from where they were talking to Highway Patrol.

'OK, we've got the green light from Quantico to process this scene.' He held up his hand as two of the Critters began to move toward the open rear doors of their vehicle. 'Hang on. After we get the material, it's going to the LA County coroner, not Virginia, so bag it for local transport, not shipment.'

Eric looked like he wanted to ask a question but Agent Sparks got in first. 'You want us to stick to the perimeter CHP established?'

Scott asked Weiss, 'What'd you see when you put up the rappelling line?'

'The body parts look like they were thrown down from above. Maybe they've rolled a bit but I didn't see signs that this was the dismemberment site.' Weiss gestured an invitation to the Critter to his left, who was holding a stack of plastic photo markers with surgical-gloved hands.

Lee nodded. 'I haven't seen anything beyond the immediate area where they're dripping. And CHP kept their perimeter well wide of that. I wouldn't go wider.'

'All right,' Scott said. 'Let's use their perimeter line and note that. But Lee, I want you to photo-doc outside the perimeter as well.'

'You got it.'

Scott headed back to the ravine. Eric walked briskly to catch up and fall into step beside him.

'You told Quantico this might be related to the Georgia cases?'

'Yes,' Scott replied.

'So...'

'So, they're not biting.'

'Did you explain about the cuts?'

Scott nodded.

Eric continued. 'I think you should climb up and take a look yourself.'

Scott climbed over the wall in a swift movement and carried on toward the ravine. 'I was about to do just that.'

Jayne swore as she unlocked the door of the low-slung brick building while balancing two Styrofoam cups of coffee and the bag of donuts. She'd just registered how bright the sign above the door was: *Agency 32/1*, emphatically illuminated by both daylight and spotlight.

The Agency wasn't much to look at but it had a good view: the back-end of Dodger Stadium and surrounds – low hills of eucalyptus and oleander sectioned by midsummer's nut-brown scrubland. If you left the stadium and went to the Agency as the crow flies, you'd cross the 5 Freeway, the Los Angeles River, the rail yards, and San Fernando Road before landing in the front parking lot. Just five spaces, two marked *Reserved* and three marked *Visitor*. One reserved space was home to Steelie's Jeep, the other, Jayne's old cream-colored Ford truck.

'I forgot to turn off the lights earlier,' Jayne called out to Steelie, who was approaching with their toolboxes.

'The real question is –' Steelie exchanged the boxes for the donut bag and peered inside with a practiced eye – 'did you remember to get me a lemon-filled?'

'Is today Tuesday?'

They went into the building, Jayne crossing in front of the counter where their volunteer receptionist would sit when she arrived at nine a.m. Carol was a retired grief counselor who claimed she would rather sit all day at the Agency than at home. She dealt with phone calls, incoming and outgoing mail, file creation, petty cash, tea, and the watering of the one plant: a big aloe named Fitzgerald.

Jayne passed through the double doors just beyond reception to go into her office, aware of Steelie trotting past her other door, which opened to the hall and led to kitchen, bathroom, and laboratory. She sat down at her desk and swiveled her chair to switch on the computer to the left, the lamp in the center, pull a legal pad and pen from the right, and, from all the way behind her, pull one file out at random from the cabinets that flanked the wall. Every morning, she looked at one file fresh, with no muddle from the day and no emotional muddle with the file.

The file: the missing person. Each 32/1 file described someone who had gone missing, but this wasn't a missing person report. It was a family history, a story told by those who knew the missing person and remembered falls from first bike rides or someone's favorite candy. Jayne and Steelie had translated those falls and candy into a database of healed fractures on bone and cavities in teeth, all in the hopes of identifying the 40,000 dead bodies that languished in coroners' offices throughout the country. But Jayne didn't start with data in the morning. This was about the stories, in case a fresh look made something jump out.

The file she pulled today had a sleeve inside the front cover. In the sleeve were photographs: a smiling twenty-two year old. Jayne automatically zeroed-in on the teeth: left central incisor – tooth #9 – was slightly twisted. It gave the woman an earnest look and would help identify her if she was lying in the morgue, dead. Unable to say her name, her bones and teeth would speak for her. Jayne flipped to the dental chart at the back of the file just to check that #9's mesial torsion was noted. It was.

She was several pages into the transcript of the interview she'd conducted with the missing woman's parents seven months earlier when she heard first the bells hanging from a string on the front door, then Carol's crisp, 'Morning all,' which seemed to encompass not just Steelie and Jayne but the missing person files too.

Jayne walked to her doorway to see the plump, white-haired woman putting her canvas bag on the front counter. 'Thanks for coming in, Carol.'

'It's been nine months. You can stop thanking me.' Carol waved her hand in dismissal.

Steelie had arrived to greet Carol and Jayne turned back to her office, thinking about the grant applications for the Agency's third year of funding, which included a modest salary for their receptionist. It was too late to adjust the requests for the second year and she hoped Carol would keep accepting lunch five days a week as some compensation. She picked up the transcript again.

Steelie came to stand in front of her desk. 'Which one have you got today?'

'The girl from Tarzana.' Jayne waited expectantly.

Steelie put a finger to her lips, then pointed at the file. 'Bulbous frontal, twisted front tooth, missing from her job at ... Victoria's Secret?'

'Jesus. I don't know how you do it. We've got a hundred case files and you can always remember details like that.'

Steelie bowed as she walked backwards toward the hall.

Jayne called after her, 'Was it X-rays in the package that came yesterday?'

Steelie nodded. 'Just getting to them now.'

A few minutes later, Steelie's voice called out from the intercom on the desk telephone.

Jayne activated the microphone. 'Steelie, you can only be in one of two other rooms in this tiny building. Why are you using the intercom?'

'Why did we buy phones with intercoms if not to use them?'

As usual, she had a point. 'OK, what is it?'

'Can you come down to the lab? There's something here you should see.'

Jayne walked down the hall and turned into the last doorway on the right. Steelie was at the end of the room, at the base of a U formed by countertop on three sides. She was perched on a stool, looking at an X-ray clipped to the large wall-mounted light box, papers spread out on to the countertop below. Jayne came up to stand at the counter and looked at the film.

It was a radiograph of a man's head, taken from the left side. The bony parts were milky-white, as were the teeth, though the metallic fillings were bright white where the metal had blocked the light from passing through the X-ray film. Something else was stark white but in an unexpected place. Jayne leaned in, her eyes traveling above the eye sockets, perhaps between them; an inch or so back from the forehead. She turned to look at Steelie.

'These *are* antemortem films, right?'

'Yep.'

'OK.' Jayne paused. 'So he's got a bullet in his head.'

'That's what I came up with.'

'What case is this?'

'Thomas Cullen.'

'From Twenty-nine Palms?'

'The same.'

'Well, I remember interviewing his folks. They didn't mention that he had a bullet in his head.' She turned to Steelie. 'Are you thinking war wound or something?'

22

'Too young for Vietnam, AWOL for Afghanistan and Iraq.'

'What about Desert Storm?'

Steelie swung back to the X-ray, pulling herself closer to the counter and pointing at the film with the eraser end of a pencil. 'Actually, here's what I'm thinking: from the angle of the bullet I'd say he shot himself through the roof of the mouth but he didn't count on the ol' sphenoid being there, let alone being so convoluted, and the bullet lodges. Pain associated with shot is numbed by shock at still being alive. Never even tells his family he tried it.'

'Is there a shot of the maxillae?'

'Not in this batch. I reckon the doc took these to see where the bullet was and determine if they were going to dig it out.'

Jayne's eyes widened. 'They *had* to leave it.'

'Probably.'

'And it would make him identifiable as hell.'

'Yep.' Steelie was warming to the subject. 'According to the file, Cullen's parents only referred to a dentist, not a doctor, when they put in the missing person report. It wasn't until they came to see us that they started to look for medical X-rays. Didn't even think they'd find any. So ... since the dental hasn't made the match yet, I think we should put out an ACB.'

An ACB was an All Coroners Bulletin. 32/1 had developed it to notify coroners with unidentified bodies when there was new information about highly identifiable characteristics on missing persons; details that couldn't have been included in the original police report and there-

23

fore wouldn't be in the FBI's national database, NCIC. The ACB was in its pilot phase, with strict usage guidelines the Agency had established in concert with coroners nationwide.

'This'll be the first one. We'll have to follow protocol to the letter, Steelie.'

'I know the rules. Unknown or suspicious circumstances only.' She indicated a manila folder on the counter. 'I've got the Cullen file right here. I'll check it out.'

The lights suddenly dimmed and the lab computer behind them turned off, then restarted itself.

'Shit. Brownout,' they said simultaneously.

'We've got to get a generator, Jayne.'

'I know. They say it's going to be a long, hot summer.'

'It's LA. It's always a long, hot summer,' Steelie dead-panned. 'You said our budget's strapped?'

Jayne pushed off the counter. 'We'd have to raise the cash separately unless I'm reading the charity rules incorrectly. Maybe you can have a look also.'

When Carol announced Scott Houston on Line 1 later, Jayne answered the phone at her desk before she took her eyes off the sentence she was reading, which made her sound distracted.

'Scott. How are you?'

'Good, but you sound tired. We get you up too early this morning?'

'Very funny. What's up?'

'Well, when was the last time you ate?'

'What are you, my mother? I'm not *that* tired.'

24

'Actually, I was trying to ask you to lunch.'

'Oh.' Jayne looked at her watch but couldn't take anything in. 'Is it lunchtime already?'

'Is that a ladylike way of saying, "No, thanks"?'

'Only a more gentlemanly invitation would get you a ladylike response.' Jayne was focusing now.

'Oh ho! I'll send round an embossed card with gold edging next time.'

'Yeah, I'd like to see the words "In-N-Out Burger" in calligraphy.'

'I can do better than that. Cal Plaza.'

'Downtown?'

'Why not? It's only ten minutes from your shop.'

'I know. I mean, Cal Plaza's great but you moved to LA, like, a week ago. I'm surprised you've even heard of it.'

'Hey, I get out,' he protested.

She wondered with whom.

He spoke into her silence. 'Is that a yes?'

'Yeah.'

'OK, I'll be by around noon.'

'With Eric?'

'Nope, Eric will be eating with the Critters at the site.'

'They're still there, then?'

'You fishing, Jayne?'

'No. I'm not asking you to divulge—'

'Relax! I'll tell you all about it at lunch.'

When Jayne returned to the lab, Steelie was just hitting the *Print* key on the computer. Jayne sat on a neighboring stool. 'Scott's going to bring me up to speed on the BP case.'

'Cool. When?'

'Noon.'

'A lunch date,' Steelie chirped.

'No one used that word.'

'Wait, "lunch" or "date"?'

Jayne gave her a quelling look.

Steelie relented. 'I've got something more interesting than Agent Houston right here.' She whipped the paper out of the printer tray and handed it to Jayne.

It was the ACB. It looked serious and official:

### ALL CORONERS BULLETIN
Dear Coroner/Medical Examiner,
**In the matter of CULLEN, Thomas**
DOB 03-01-1959, NCIC# M-004517592

Please be informed that the aforementioned individual sustained GSW to palate and sphenoid with projectile remaining lodged in sphenoid and visible on attached LEFT radiograph dated 04-15-1992. For further information, contact:

Steelie Lander

'That looks good,' Jayne said. 'What were Cullen's circs in the end?'

'The cops logged him in as unknown. He had asked for a few days off work, didn't return, car found at John Wayne Airport. I think he went to do the same thing as in '92 but with something more reliable than a handgun. Pills, maybe.'

'Go on.'

'He flies up to Alaska, to see the ex.'

'What ex?'

'It's in your interview transcript: the girlfriend who left him in '91 and the reason I think he tried this number.' Steelie tapped the X-ray image of the bullet.

'OK.'

'He tootles up there, says goodbye or what-have-you, takes his pills, and suddenly he's Alaska's problem.'

'Could be.'

'Well, whatever happened to him, if he's been found and they've done a craniotomy – or even if an Anthro pulled the maxillae to X-ray the teeth – they would've been clued into the old bullet. Even if he's alive and has amnesia, this X-ray is key. The fact that the police didn't know he had a bullet in his head when they did his misper report warrants the ACB.'

'No argument from me. You have the checklist for the protocol?'

'Right here.'

'OK, let's sign it so you can get this sent out.'

As they finished up, they heard Carol talking to someone at reception.

'That'll be your lunch,' Steelie commented.

'If it is, he's early.'

The two of them walked to the front of the building. Scott was leaning on Carol's counter. Their receptionist was finishing a sentence with, '...afford it on my salary.'

Steelie interrupted in a warning tone. 'Don't try to tempt Carol away with your government wages, Houston.'

He stepped back from the counter with his hands raised, palms out. 'I would never do that to the Agency. You should know that about me.'

'Yes,' Carol began. 'Agent Houston and I—'

'Please call me Scott.'

'Very well. Scott and I were just comparing the V6 and the V8 when used in the four-wheel-drive Chevrolet Suburban.'

He looked at Jayne and Steelie. 'You guys knew that Carol rode shotgun when her mom drove the Alaska Highway just after it opened in the forties?'

'In a wood-panel Suburban,' Carol added with pride.

Scott leaned toward her again. 'I look forward to continuing our discussion another time.'

Jayne thought their receptionist was on the verge of patting her hair demurely, so she propelled Scott out the front door and into the heat of the day.

# THREE

The mist of California Plaza's fountains kept its amphitheater of granite steps cool even when the Santa Ana winds were blowing hot over Los Angeles. Every riser supported a person's back and every flat surface was a perch for buttocks and take-out sushi. Scott and Jayne had opted for hot dogs from a deli and they sat at the top step with their backs to Angel's Flight, the funicular that used to carry people up and down Bunker Hill for 25 cents. All talking had been deferred in favor of eating, so there was just the hum of others' conversation, the occasional outburst of distant laughter, and the unpredictable *ha-sisssss-fwap* of the fountains' geyser-like water jets falling back to the granite floor far below them.

Jayne popped the last bit of ketchup-drenched bun into her mouth and mumbled, 'Now, *that* was a good idea.'

Scott murmured agreement as he wiped his mouth and held a hand out for her paper hot dog boat. Stacking it with his, he stood up and walk-ed to a trashcan.

Jayne started to relax in the sun, admiring the openness of the plaza, until she noticed how this position on the steps, which Scott had subtly chosen, was in the only section not covered by close CCTV. Most of the cameras were mounted on the buildings clear across the way, focused on the entryways of boutiques and cell phone stores. She looked around for Scott and found him striding back, scanning the perimeter of the amphitheater.

When he was next to her again, she said, 'All right, give me the skinny on the body parts and tell me why we had to come to the best spot in Downtown to not get overheard.'

'Worked that out, eh?'

'Spill.'

Scott leaned forward, his elbows on his knees and lowered his voice. 'OK, the Bureau's direct-ed us to move the freeway body parts over to the LA County coroner's office, where you know they're going to the bottom of their list—'

'Wait. How come they'll go to the coroner? I thought that once the FBI has a case, that's it.'

'Well, the boys in Virginia don't want another bunch of body parts to deal with, especially when those parts don't include a head. Not without the locals at least trying to ID them first. We get to keep the investigation into the vehicle because that could go interstate but we've been directed to move the body parts to Mission Road ASAP.'

Jayne immediately thought of the Automated Fingerprint Identification System. 'Can't you at least check the fingerprints through AFIS? Fingers were present on both hands.'

Scott seemed to glance over his shoulder. 'I climbed up to the body parts and had a look at

30

the cuts. They're precise. All at anatomical locations to make dismemberment easier. We know these parts were dislodged accidentally due to the drunk rear-ending the van but whoever's been carrying them around in a freezer is a pro. I don't think he'd be sloppy enough to leave us fingertips if he thought they could ID the vic through a database every cop accesses daily.'

'I noticed the precision of the cuts, too,' Jayne said thoughtfully. 'You wouldn't try AFIS anyway?'

'You know that fingerprint matching only works when the victim's fingerprints are already on the system for another reason, like a criminal record, right? I would try it but the Bureau would be on me like a fly on shit if I started accessing AFIS for a case I've been told isn't the Bureau's. So AFIS has to be initiated by the coroner when *he* gets the case.'

'Which will be when the bottom of their list makes its way to the top.'

'Exactly. But I think your agency can help.'

She looked at him and waited. They were sitting so close that she could see hazel flecks in the green of his irises. The proximity was seriously testing her long-held resolve to remain platonic with the most attractive man she'd ever met until she could figure out how to make herself 'whole' and thus available to him.

He was standing up. 'Let's go over here.'

Curious, Jayne followed him across to the metal railing that overlooked Bunker Hill, glancing down the grassy slope at its homeless habitués lying on the lawn in clusters of two and

31

three, making her think of a Manet scene. She'd never stood at this exposed railing without having a breeze whistle in her ears, so she leaned toward Scott to hear him better, bumping into him, for only an instant, but his shoulder left a warm memory on hers.

'My theory is that those body parts have been held a long time, maybe years. They seemed to be freezer-burnt, not just frozen, so I'm betting there aren't any active investigations into those victims as missing persons. That's if there were any in the first place. I think that if those vics have family looking for them, they'll either have been to your agency, or they will be.'

'You want us to check our database?' Jayne asked. 'That's no problem. Just give us the autopsy or anthro report when it's ready.'

'I was thinking that maybe you could do an anthropology exam yourself and then check it against your files.'

Jayne looked back at him in surprise. 'But the coroner's going to want to do an autopsy. You can't precede that with anthro. And Steelie and I don't work for LA County.'

'What if you did an external, non-invasive sort of ... preliminary exam?'

'Wait a minute, Scott. What is this?' When he looked away, she continued, 'You know, ever since Eric said that solving this case had become your Holy Grail, I've been trying to work out why you never mentioned it to me. We must've talked tons of times while—'

'I couldn't.'

She exclaimed. 'I *do* know the meaning of sub

32

judice, you know. I wouldn't compromise a case. But, whatever.'

'No, Jayne, I meant I literally could not tell you. After certain ... things happened with the case, Eric and I decided our phones weren't safe. We communicated in person or by private messaging between our BlackBerrys. Plus, we had to fly under the radar so our boss couldn't see the number of hours we were putting in on leads he considered dead ends. There were only two other agents in the office we could trust with what we were doing and I didn't talk to anyone by phone on this. Not anyone, OK?'

She took in his expression: earnest, concerned. She wanted to ask him what those 'things' were that 'happened' but that could wait. 'OK, so tell me about the situation here. Do you have the same constraints you had in Georgia?'

'Theoretically? No. New office, new supervisor. But if the body parts we saw this morning are related to the case in Georgia, we need to know ASAP. Has a Georgia serial killer gone mobile? Does California need to be on alert? Are there any clues on the Ventura Freeway that will help us solve the cases in Georgia? To get leads to answer those questions, we need ID's for the body parts.'

'It sounds like you want us to do this external exam just because you don't want to wait for the coroner's office. Or is there something more?'

'Listen, superficially, those body parts have characteristics that look like one of my cases, so I think of them as part of my case; doesn't matter that they turned up in LA not Atlanta. I'm ready to ID them, then the Bureau takes it out of my hands and gives it to people who've got so many bodies to ID, they've become statistics.' He tilted his head back and forth as though getting a kink out of his neck. 'Maybe I don't like that so much.'

She almost laughed. 'That doesn't sound like "maybe".'

'Yeah, well, Eric pointed out that it's no coincidence that "bureaucracy" and "Bureau" share the same Latin root.' He paused. 'Look, we've been told to make the transfer as soon as possible. In my experience, that means we've got two days with the body parts in our custody. Can you do an exam and a report for me in that time?'

'Could you provide X-ray facilities?'

'Sure.'

She thought about this. Then she asked, 'How will this be cleared?'

'Don't have to clear it; the material's in our custody.'

'You've got cold storage?'

He nodded. 'Big enough for this case anyway.'

Jayne was silent for another moment, looking into the distance toward the ivory bulk of County-USC Hospital and the summer-drawn smog blanket above East LA. She felt small against the spread of the city and the thought of how many millions of people it took to make that haze by driving cars, smoking cigarettes, manning factories, wielding leaf blowers. Living. Then she thought about the paupers' graves the county funded to bury the overflow bodies that had never been identified. She thought about the body parts from the freeway ending up there, with only some taxpayer-funded strangers to say a few words for them.

'OK, count us in,' she said.

# FOUR

Jayne knew she was the first one back at the Agency when Scott dropped her off because Carol's 'Out to Lunch' sign was still hanging on the front door. The phone started to ring as she walked in. She picked it up at Carol's desk.

'This is Ron from A1 Electrics?'

Jayne wondered if he was asking her or telling her. She sat down in Carol's chair. 'How can I help you?'

'Yeah, I'm calling about the generator?'

'The generator?'

'Yeah!' Chewing gum snapped and clicked. 'I've got a  uh ... two-stroke Give-All generator with shut-off switch to deliver and I just need to confirm your address.'

'I don't know what you're talking about.'

'Oh, if you're worried about the installation, that's all included.' He sounded pleased.

'That's nice but I didn't order a generator and neither has anyone else at this address, to my knowledge.'

'Well, ma'am, I've got the receipt right here.'

'So who ordered it?'

'Let's see –' *snap-snap-pop* – 'I don't have a name on the requisition sheet but there's a note about angles.'

'ANGLES? Is it an acronym?'

'Or, "angels"? "Angels flight"?'

'What?' Jayne stood up so abruptly she almost yanked the phone off the desk by its cord as she looked to see if Scott was still in the parking lot.

'You still there, ma'am? It *is* all paid for.'

She straightened the phone. 'Ron. I'm going to put you on hold for a minute.'

She punched the hold button and dialed out on another line.

'Houston.' He was on speakerphone and she could hear ambient noise in the background.

'Scott, I've got a guy on the other line asking me where I want my new generator. You know anything about this?'

'No-o-o.'

'No?' Jayne was incredulous and her words came out like bullets. 'I find that very hard to believe because he just told me that it's for "angels flight". Now that's too much coincidence in my book.'

'Let's say I do know something about it. Why are you so angry?'

'You can't just turn up here and start giving me gifts!'

'Let me reassure you right now that I don't think the way to a woman's heart is through gas-powered machinery. It's for the Agency.'

Jayne was too hot under the collar to feel mortified. 'I know *that*! What I meant was, you can't just give me gifts for the Agency. We're governed by 501C3 regulations. And, dammit Scott, I can take care of this place myself!'

'Well, that's not what Steelie said to Eric in relation to this.'

Jayne faltered. 'Steelie?'

'Yeah. She got to talking with Eric about the brownouts, mentioned your office needs a generator but doesn't have the funds, and Eric decided to organize a donation to the Agency. All by the book.'

Before Jayne could muster a response, Scott continued. 'Plus, we don't want your computers going down while you're working on anything related to our discussion at Angels Flight.'

'I see. Well, in that case, thank you. We'll send you a donation receipt. Or send it to Eric...' She petered out.

'Take your time, Hall.' He sounded amused. 'Ten-four.'

Jayne reflected on Scott's mellow response to the fact that she'd completely jumped the gun before she remembered gum-chewing Ron on Line 1. She pressed the button to retrieve him and politely organized the delivery of the generator for Wednesday.

She'd only been back at her desk for a few minutes when she heard Carol and Steelie enter the building. Jayne walked out her side door to meet them in the hall.

Steelie asked, 'Good lunch?'

Jayne followed them into the small kitchen where they were putting leftovers in the fridge. 'We need to be at the FBI's Wilshire office tomorrow at eleven.'

She explained Scott's theory about the body parts and his desire for a preliminary report.

Steelie sounded doubtful. 'And the coroner's office isn't going to have a problem with this?'

'Apparently not.'

Carol looked at the two anthropologists. 'If Scott's got it cleared on his end and you're not compromising a future autopsy, you won't be interfering with the wheels of justice turning down at the coroner's office. Maybe you'll even grease them a little. That fits into the Agency's mission, in my view.'

The bells on the front door rang out. Carol said, 'I'll go.'

As she padded away, Jayne addressed Steelie. 'Your loose lips have won us a generator.'

'No way.'

'Yeah. Eric and Scott have ordered one for the Agency.'

'Wow.' Steelie's broad smile collapsed when she caught Jayne's expression. 'Don't tell me you did one of your don't-think-me-ungrateful-but-we-can-do-it-ourselves numbers on them? Oh, you didn't!' Steelie threw up her hands. 'Y'know, not everyone is paternalistic or even chauvinistic—'

She broke off when the sound of a sob traveled back from the front of the building and then motioned with her head that she'd be in the lab. Jayne went into her office through the hall door and was relieved that the double French doors to Reception were closed; Carol's doing, no doubt. She didn't want to interrupt what the doors' mottled glass panels allowed her to make out. Carol, in full grief-counselor mode, had sat down next to the visitor. The crying, which had

39

started as though a dam had burst, was subsiding, but Jayne sensed that the force of the tears had been only dammed up again, not spent. And was it ever?

It was possible that the visitor wouldn't stay for an interview on the first visit. Sometimes it was enough for family members to come in the front door and deal with what that represented. They'd reached the stage where they were considering the possibility that their missing relative had been found, but found dead. They returned when they felt stronger.

A darkening across the room made her look up. The visitor was leaving. A knock on the door a moment later was Carol.

'That was Solana,' she said, sitting in the chair opposite the desk. 'Here about her son Roberto, missing for six months. She was referred by the Alstons in Pasadena.'

'Some referral. We haven't been able to find their daughter.'

'Well, you'll be interested in what Solana said, then. She started working for the Alstons as a housekeeper a few months ago. At some point, they asked her to live in. She said she couldn't and then broke down. They were busy reassuring her that she wouldn't lose her job but then she explained about Roberto and how she didn't want to be away from home for any twenty-four hour period in case he came back and she wasn't there.'

Jayne nodded.

'That's when they told her about how Kate had disappeared and how the Agency had helped them focus their energies and given them hope of some sort of answer. She agreed to pay us a visit but, as you would have heard, it took a lot out of her.'

'Do you think she'll come back?'

Carol considered this as she stood up. 'I don't know. It's taken her weeks just to come inside, having driven past a few times. But I gave her one of our brochures to take home.'

Jayne could hear her humming quietly as she returned to her desk.

Scott walked into the office he and Eric shared on the fourth floor of the FBI building and saw his partner on the phone. He wondered if information was coming in from a law enforcement officer who'd seen their Be On the Look Out notice for a van matching the description of the one hit by the drunk on the 101 Freeway. He set one of the cups he was carrying down on Eric's desk.

Eric hung up the phone and turned to face him. 'That was Detective Schrader over in LAPD Robbery Homicide.'

'He call you?' Scott winced as he scalded the roof of his mouth on the coffee.

'She, and I called 'cause I got to thinking: we've got the BOLO out for the van but if the perp's decided to stop so he can disguise it, we don't just have to wait for a hit on the BOLO. We can go out and track him down.'

'Body shops?'

'The *right* body shops.'

'Did the D give you their watch list?'

'Yeah. She gave me eighteen shops that have come to their attention for handling stolen vehicles.'

'What radius from the body parts?'

'I asked for a five-mile radius from the nearest freeway exit to the north, which was ... uh, Van Nuys Boulevard. We can expand it if we have to.'

'Chances are the perp wasn't driving too far once he realized he lost his load out the back door.' Scott was already getting up and he grinned at Eric, who was trying to get some coffee down and fast. 'You ready?'

Eric swallowed. 'Just remember whose brilliant idea this was.'

'You want a gold star? I'll give you one if we get a lead on the van.'

'Yeah, I've heard that before,' Eric grumbled but he was getting up with alacrity and the two agents left the office.

Steelie didn't leave the lab all afternoon. Carol did crossword puzzles at her desk until 4 p.m. when she watered Fitzgerald and then made tea for everyone else. Jayne pulled together the material they'd take to the FBI office: biometric forms, sliding calipers, rulers. Then she checked the Agency email account.

There were seven new messages in the Inbox since she'd last checked: three were spam, two were lurid spam, one was from the server warning account-holders that old messages would be deleted, and one was from a family looking for a missing relative they believed was alive.

The last email was of a type that the Agency received with regularity: relatives of missing persons had learned about 32/1's forensic profiles, saw no point in having coroners' freezers scoured for their relatives, but still got in contact for any scrap of information that might lead them down a new path to find that relative.

The standard Agency response would include a list of resources and links for organizations like People Search and the National Center for Missing and Exploited Children. No mention would be made of the Doe Network or coroners' Internet bulletin boards with photos of unidentified bodies. Jayne typed the response, thinking that it was time to simply write a template for responses sent to these particular inquiries. She pulled a 32/1 brochure from a drawer and drew a couple of phrases from it for the conclusion of the message.

*If you don't find the answers you're looking for at any of these sources, don't forget there are other places you can look. Agency 32/1 exists to help identify all unidentified people, including living people who can't identify themselves due to trauma or disease. A visit to the Agency means a chance for you to talk about your daughter as you know her: a vibrant, living person. We do the rest. If she has been found, she will be counting on you to tell her story.*

Carol came to the doorway. 'It's just going on five, so I'll take your cup and then I'll be going.'

'Thanks, Carol. See you tomorrow.'

Jayne did a quick Internet news search about the missing girl's case before she hit *Send*. There were five articles from *The Birch Herald*, the paper local to the girl's neighborhood in Wisconsin. The first three were dated just after she disappeared while walking home from her summer job at the Dairy Queen. She was fifteen and her name was Amy Ledbetter. One quote from her mother read, 'If she'd worked at that Golden Clog Tourist Center on the highway, I might have been worried. But this was right here in town.' The other two articles were dated a year apart, one for each anniversary of the girl's disappearance. It looked like the *Herald* was about due for a third one. Jayne sent the message to the Ledbetters and the Inbox refreshed.

There was a new message and she smiled as she read it. She went to the lab where she found Steelie hunched over her keyboard.

'You won't believe who just sent us an email.'

Steelie's eyes didn't leave the screen. 'Who?'

'Gene.'

'As in, India Tango One?'

'His call sign was India Tango Five, as you well know.'

'But he was Number One in his own mind. Probably still is.'

'Well, you'll have a chance to see for yourself because he's flying into LA and suggested we all get together for dinner.'

'I'll be busy.'

'You don't even know what day it's going to be!'

'If it involves Gene and dinner...'

'He's not with the FBI anymore,' Jayne offered.

44

Steelie looked at her. 'Oh? What's he doing now?'

'Didn't say.'

'Well, whatever it is, I'm sure he's still Number One.' Steelie turned back to the computer.

Jayne looked over her shoulder at the screen. 'How's it going?'

'I posted the ACB on to the network and it's reading fine. Now we just need a reply from someone.'

All the electrical equipment hummed, faded, and came back to life as another brownout swept over the neighborhood.

'Hope you weren't working on anything important,' Jayne said, with irony.

'Just bring me that generator. In fact –' Steelie stretched her arms above her head – 'let's take that as a sign and get out of here.'

'Yeah. Let's lock up.'

Jayne replied to Gene's email, then the two women moved through the building, turning off lights and locking the safe that held X-rays and original photographs that would later be returned to families. At the front, they closed the venetian blinds over the windows, flipped the switch for the sign outside, and activated the alarm.

'Keep watch, Fitz,' Steelie said to the office plant as she stepped out the door and locked it behind her.

It was still hot outside but the light was mellowing, the sun beginning to consider a descent somewhere behind Griffith Park's looming hills. Steelie and Jayne were both heading in that direction; Jayne to her apartment facing the

45

Silver Lake Reservoir and Steelie to her cottage in Atwater Village.

They pulled out of the Agency's parking lot, one vehicle white and rumbling, the other dark and nimble, to join commuters for whom San Fernando Road was just a way to avoid a particularly hairy part of the 5 Freeway. They were halted next to each other at the first traffic light and Jayne could hear Steelie's radio, tuned to the all-news station: *'It's slow-and-go on the Golden State Freeway this evening, folks...'* She smiled at her friend before the light turned green.

# FIVE

Scott drove East on Beverly Boulevard, frustrated that none of the body shops on Eric's list had so far generated a lead on the van. One shop owner merited a second visit; that was on for tomorrow. He turned on the radio and then glanced at it as he registered a female voice that evoked Hollywood movies from the 1940s. He could hear two other people's voices, both wholly American, one apparently a chef and the other seemed to be a landscaper, which fit with what Jayne had told him about the regulars on a particular LA radio program. This had to be 'Weekends with Prentis'. He upped the volume for his introduction to Jayne's mother, who was requesting that a caller put her question.

*Caller*: 'Hi, Marie? Or any of your guests today, I know we're all supposed to be doing xeriscapic gardens these days but do you ever find that your yucca tree, well ... disappoints?'
*Marie*: 'Oh, chop it down, darling. And eat its roots for dinner.'

Scott heard the caller's astonished gasp as he glanced in his rearview mirror to change lanes. The small white car behind him indicated at the same time and Scott accelerated to get in front. The studio guests were chiming in.

*Andrew*: 'I'd recommend dry white wine to go with yucca, however you cook it.'
*Jess*: 'The main thing to remember with xeriscapic gardens is that once they're established, *don't* water them. I take it you've been watering your yucca?'
*Caller*: 'Well ... yes. You see, it's right next to the azalea, which just *loves* water, so it's hard to integrate the, um, Mexican yucca.'
*Marie*: 'Listeners, we must all remember that it's *xeriscapic*, not xenophobic, that we're aiming for in these troubled times. And that goes for the Rose Garden as well.'

Theme music and a voice advising that this episode of 'Weekends with Prentis' had been a repeat drowned out any other comments Marie might have had, leaving Scott trying to picture a woman who would tread so close to the political edge on a show that was ostensibly about food and plants. But Jayne had told him that her mother's ability to cast a spell over people had, so far, kept her out of trouble. Apparently, the spell wasn't just due to her looks, which Jayne had described as 'like Catherine Deneuve, but browner'. Scott remembered how Jayne's voice had sounded on the phone when she'd said that; rueful humor laced with a wistfulness that betrayed how unaware Jayne was that she could have been describing her own looks.

Realizing he'd almost missed his turn, Scott

48

hung a quick right on to Spring and continued down to the light at 2nd Street. He noticed the white car was still behind him and making the same right turn. Now it was pulling over to the curb and two Skid Row residents were approaching it. Scott's traffic light clicked to green, so he pulled left, made his way to his building and turned into the underground parking lot, the gate lifting and then closing behind him.

As he went up the elevator to the fifth floor, his thoughts picked up where they'd left off: how good it had been to see Jayne in the flesh, not just hear her voice coming down the phone line. The physical attraction mattered and it had produced the same pull he'd experienced the night they'd first met in Quantico's noisy basement bar, to the point that he'd almost forgotten he was at a crime scene with Eric and a convoy of Critters. Eric. Scott smirked as he got out of the elevator. His partner had picked up on something right away, though he'd held off raising it until Scott had been on the verge of leaving to meet Jayne for lunch.

Scott unlocked the door to his apartment and went in, activating down-lights as he walked into the kitchen. He stepped around the packing boxes on the floor so he could pull out lasagna from the freezer and turn on the oven. Then he leaned against the counter, remembering how Eric had tried to arrange his face into an appropriate expression after he'd overheard Scott ask Jayne to lunch.

Eric had opened with: 'So. How long has this

49

been going on?'

Scott had tried to sound blank. 'Nothing's going on.'

'Then it's been a whole lotta nothing.' Eric paused. 'Was it going on while you were with Mindy?'

'*Mad* Mindy?'

'Was she that one?'

'Yes, she was.'

'OK, Callista then. Or whoever you brought to Angie's fortieth. Was it going on then?'

When Scott didn't answer, Eric burst into laughter and slapped his thigh. 'I don't believe it! Jayne's been the one this whole time? Y'know, I always wondered why you dated such lightweights. It was weird, man. Angie and I used to talk about it – oh shit, Angie! I can't wait to tell her!'

Scott pointed at him. 'Don't tell Angie anything. Plus, Mindy and Callista – and Helen for that matter, who was a rebound thing and you know it – were *not* lightweights when it came to my wallet.'

'That's because you kept giving them consolation prizes every time you missed barbecues or bowling or whatever those kind of chicks plan.'

'Tapas ... for couples.'

'Spare me. Anyway, it's not your wallet that's in danger with Jayne.'

'What's that supposed to mean?'

Eric shook his head. 'I've never seen you look at someone the way you looked at her this morning. And I've seen you look at a lot of people.'

Scott frowned. 'How did I look at her?'

'It was a little ... wolfish.'

Scott grimaced. 'That can't be good.'

'Yeah, you might want to work on that.'

A CHP officer had walked in their direction just then and Scott had levered himself into the driver's seat of the Suburban. Eric leaned on the door so Scott couldn't close it and lowered his voice to a confidential tone. 'So why haven't you been seeing her this whole time? And why didn't you tell me about her?'

'Precisely so we wouldn't have this conversation.'

'Man, you need this conversation if you haven't made a move on her yet. Five years? Really? You're lucky she's still around – and available.'

Scott's face must have betrayed him because Eric asked, with incredulity, 'You don't even know if she's single?'

Scott covered looking away by putting the keys in the ignition. The car sounded a warning.

Eric shook his head. 'You *really* need this conversation.'

'I'm handling it.' Scott made to close the door.

Eric stepped away and said, 'Just try not to screw up lunch. We've got a case riding on this.'

Scott pulled a bottle of water from the under-counter fridge in his kitchen, grabbed a fork from a box, then used a dishtowel to take the now hot lasagna in its foil pan over to the leather armchair, turned to get a view of the *Los Angeles Times* building through the wall of west-facing windows. He put his feet up on the footrest and ate from the pan.

He took in a mouthful of cold water and let it rest against the roof of his mouth where he'd scalded it earlier. He really was glad that the reunion with Jayne had been over this freeway case. If he'd seen her any sooner after transferring to LA or met her over dinner, he would have been over-eager, pushing for an answer to the question on his mind ever since his transfer notice: what kind of relationship would they have after several years of long-distance companionship, flirtation, and restrained intimacy? He swallowed and then looked at the *Times* building. It was a confirmation: he was finally in LA. And if the case slowed things down with Jayne and kept him from acting 'wolfish', then maybe that was a good thing.

Jayne pulled her truck close to the top of the driveway fronting the redwood two-story building that housed her apartment. She climbed the concrete staircase on the left side of the building, rising above a neat lawn that held its own under an ancient fir tree. The only neighbor was downstairs and his front door was on the other side so Jayne enjoyed the sense of privacy and ownership she felt every time she ascended to her door, which was why she'd finally bought some terracotta pots for the landing and filled them with plants.

She had lived there for five years after moving out of her graduate student apartment in Westwood and refusing the tempting offer of a cottage at the end of her mother's sprawling garden. Across the street, the Silver Lake Reservoir began immediately after tall redwoods and the sidewalk. The reservoir was a clear space in LA that no one could build on and so drew a faithful crowd of joggers and dog-walkers to its edge every day. Some of the faces were familiar to Jayne but she didn't know anyone's name.

She was expecting her mother to drop by, so she left the front door open to the screen as she put together a light supper in the kitchen, which overlooked the open-plan main room. When Marie arrived fifteen minutes later, she just called out, 'Yoo-hoo!' and swept in through the doorway. Her gold silk shirt was mirrored in golden powder glinting at the base of her throat while bronze highlights emphasized a hairstyle usually achieved only on photo shoots by using large fans. Her every move produced a melody as bangles met and dangling earrings swayed.

After hugging Jayne, Marie went back to look at the porch. 'Darling, has it ever occurred to you that you'd get more dates if you kept something other than cacti by your front door?'

'Is that advice about gardening or relationships, Mom?'

'You should have something like gaura pinks. Or maybe gaura lindheimeri – you know, the white ones. Just a few pots, uneven in number.'

'What, so I can find the man who has just one similar pot and say, "You ... complete me"?' She faked a swoon as she crossed to the kitchen to finish preparing their roast chicken and avocado sandwiches.

'You're so irreverent, darling. That also keeps people away.'

53

Jayne cut the sandwiches into triangles. 'This gaura. Is it the wispy one you planted all over your garden?'

'You've noticed!'

'Then, no thanks. Too feminine.'

'What's wrong with a little femininity these days?' Marie asked as she cast an apparently critical eye around the main room.

'Nothing, for you. It's just not my style.' Jayne walked over with the plate of sandwiches and a wooden salad bowl. She handed Marie the salad and ushered her on to the deck facing the reservoir. The table was covered in a white tablecloth, which was decorated with numerous tea lights and drying rose petals.

As they sat down, Marie fluttered her fingers over the petals. 'I thought you said feminine wasn't your style?'

Jayne smiled, pushing bits of avocado back into her sandwich. 'I just like winding you up. Have some iced tea.'

Marie folded some butter lettuce and speared it neatly with her fork. 'Steelie said you're seeing Scott.' In went the lettuce.

'Not "seeing", Mom – I've seen him. We've all seen him.'

'Now, just a minute. The last time I set you up with someone – that perfectly nice teacher *and* a Venezuelan – you stated that you'd rather spend an hour on the phone with Scott Houston than five more minutes with *el profesor*. I remember that quite distinctly.'

Jayne regarded her mother. 'Let me get the strawberries.'

Marie called after her. 'And now this Houston is here in LA.'

'So?' Jayne brought out the tray holding bowls of berries and a jug of cream.

'So! I didn't raise you to be a five o'clock fish.' Marie fixed Jayne with her 'severe' look, which consisted of one arched eyebrow while she tilted her chin up. 'You remember the five o'clock—'

'Yes, yes. The fish that's been sitting out all day at market and no one wants to buy old fish or whatever. I told you I don't like the commodification of women inherent in that metaphor. It's ridiculous. I'm not a piece of seafood. Nor am I on a shelf.'

'You're up on this deck, Jayne! Most evenings, all weekend. You're hiding up here with I don't know what memories from some mass grave or other haunting you, and you've given yourself nothing for comfort other than...' She gestured wildly. 'Than spiky cactus plants!'

Jayne looked out at the reservoir. Its surface was rippled in its best imitation of a lake. Night was falling and she could see through the fir trees to the hills on the other side where the lights of invisible houses sparkled orange-yellow and white.

Marie touched her hand, then began to fold and re-fold her napkin. 'I worry about you,' she said softly.

'I know.'

'You don't talk to me about everything you saw when you were out with the UN and I know why: you've got Steelie. But even she thinks you need someone here at home, as it all falls into perspective. You both spent a decade helping to uncover war crimes, for heaven's sake, and *now* you've gone on to do something that drains you. Maybe in a different way, but it drains.'

Jayne shrugged, looking up at her mother. 'It is draining sometimes. But it feeds me, too. I like what I do.' The candles on the table flickered in the breeze, threatening to go out but then flaring back up triumphantly.

'Even if it breaks your heart almost every day?'

'Other people's hearts are broken already, before they come to us. It's not *my* heart breaking. It's just an empathetic sort of ... heart-stretching.'

Marie poured cream over the berries. 'And from what you've said, Scott is almost the perfect person for you to spend time with. You seem to have interests and sensibilities in common. He might not have been on the same forensic missions as you but he understands what went on over there.'

'You think I should be with someone who's got the same fodder for nightmares as I have, is that it?' Jayne was stacking slices of strawberry on her fork.

Marie paused. 'Have the nightmares started again?'

'Not really, they're just infrequent, that's all. Can I finish your berries?'

Marie pushed over her half-eaten bowl of fruit. 'Why don't you come up to my place when things get bad?'

'That's just running away.'

'I thought you'd say that, which is why I brought you this.' Marie pulled a small plastic bag from under the table and handed it over. The bag was emblazoned with the name *Rite Aid,* the local pharmacy.

Jayne pulled out the package inside: night-lights, pack of two. She smiled. 'Thanks.'

They sat in companionable silence until the wind picked up enough to blow out the candles. 'You want coffee?'

'No, darling, I've got to go. I'm judging the student exhibits at the Garden Expo in Pasadena tomorrow, so it's an early night for me.'

Jayne saw her mother down to the driveway where Marie's sleek, sky-blue Mercedes 450SL was parked behind her truck. As she walked back up the stairs to her door, she looked at the much-maligned cacti and laughed to herself. They did look like sentries; totally unapproachable and silent.

After Jayne cleared up, she locked the sliding door and went to bed, banishing all thoughts of real people as she pressed the *Play* button on the cassette deck resting on her bedside table.

She didn't hear the man on her front doorstep when he smashed one of the cactus pots. The measured reading of *Gaudy Night* had taken her into a rare dreamless sleep.

# DAY TWO

## Wednesday

# SIX

Eric's voice was quiet. 'Here he comes.' He stepped away from the door of the Suburban to allow Scott to get out. They had been waiting for the owner of the body shop on Magnolia Boulevard, Al Corso, to finish locking his office so they could question him a second time. When Corso saw them advancing, he came to a standstill and threw out his hands, causing his nylon briefcase to wave around.

'What? You not done with me yet?' His tone was aggressive and resigned all at once. 'I answered all your questions, didn't I?'

'Yeah,' said Eric, resting an arm on his shoulders and pulling him toward the Suburban. 'We just didn't like your answers so much, Corso. Thought we'd give you another chance.'

They reached the vehicle and Scott opened the back door. Corso looked at each of them, then his shoulders slumped and he got in. Eric hopped in next to him while Scott got in the driver's seat and closed the door. The door locks thunked closed.

Eric used a friendly tone. 'Mr Corso, are you familiar with the term "obstruction"?'

The body shop owner held up his hands. 'Look, I told you what I know.'

'No ... you told us you had a van in here for bodywork but that you didn't get its license plate number.'

'That was true!'

'But you remembered that it was a California plate?'

'Yeah?' Corso sounded tentative.

Eric punched him lightly on the shoulder. 'Don't get nervous, Corso! I'm just reminding everyone of what you said when we interviewed you.'

The man tried to laugh but he looked nervous.

'So it was a California plate but you didn't get the number,' Eric rejoined.

'Uh-huh.'

'And you said that you couldn't remember if it was a vanity plate or a regular one.'

'So?'

'I wondered if you knowing that we're looking for this van because it's at the center of a Federal murder investigation might help jog your memory?' Eric smiled at him.

Corso's voice came out at a slightly higher octave. 'Murder?'

Scott leaned around from the front seat. 'And not just murder. We have evidence to suggest that the guy driving the van cut people up into pieces.'

'I-I-I didn't know about any murder! The guy

didn't look like a murderer.'

Eric was calm. 'The guy who brought the van in.'

'Yeah. I told you, he was just a nobody, maybe forty years old, nothing weird about him.'

'And he paid cash.'

'Everyone pays cash!'

'Let's talk about the other cash.'

'What other cash?!'

'Come on, Corso. We know he paid you hush money. And don't pretend you haven't been in this business long enough to note the plates even before you start working on the cars. Come on. How else do you think we found you? LAPD gave us your number 'cause you've handled stolen cars.'

'But this one *wasn't* stolen.'

'How do you know?'

Corso looked crestfallen; he'd walked straight into the trap Eric had laid. He sighed. 'OK, fine, look. Look. I've got a contact at the DMV. He checks plates for me because of all the problems I had with the cops. I've been trying to go straight, OK? I only just got the place out of Chapter Eleven.' He appealed to Eric.

'I don't want to hear your bankruptcy sob story, Corso. Tell us about the plate on the van or we'll be telling LAPD that you're hacking into Department of Motor Vehicles files.'

'OK, OK! The plate was like I said, California. It was clean.' He unzipped his briefcase and pulled out a sheet of paper. He ran a finger down the page, then read out a license plate number.

Eric nodded at Scott, who was writing it down.

'So if it was clean, why the hush money?'

Corso shrugged. 'I don't know. The guy just pulled out the cash – three hundred dollars – and I knew exactly what it was for. I didn't want to take it but he said, "Remember, I know where you live."' Corso looked indignant. 'I took the money, OK? I've got kids to feed, a mortgage.'

'Get out, Corso.' Eric's words were punctuated by the sound of the door locks lifting.

'Wait! What about the LAPD? What's going to happen?'

'Just get out.'

Corso looked at Scott for a reprieve but he was focused on his cell phone. The body shop owner got out of the car, shoulders still slumped, clutching the unzipped briefcase to his chest.

Scott spoke as he dialed. 'I'm calling the plate in.'

Eric moved up to the passenger seat and read the notes Scott was making on a pad.

As soon as Scott ended his call, Eric asked, 'The van's registered to a woman?'

'Well, the plate that Corso gave us is registered to this woman. But he didn't check that the van actually went with the plate. Lance just ran the woman's name through NCIC. No convictions, no arrests. Allegedly living at an address in Woodland Hills since 1990.'

'You thinking the perp comes out here from Georgia and borrows her plate to cover his tracks after he gets hit on the freeway?'

Scott looked grim as he turned the ignition key. 'All I know is, this is the only van we've found that matches the drunk's vague description *and* needed repair to its back doors since Monday.'

The FBI office on Wilshire was in a multi-story building constructed in the 1970s when concrete blocks and tinted, deeply inset windows were in vogue. Only the barricades at the front curb hinted that a warren of government offices lay behind the unremarkable exterior. Inside, Elevator Number 2 was moving silently upwards, carrying Steelie, Jayne, and Special Agent Weiss.

Weiss had cleared the anthropologists through Security after they arrived from the visitor parking lot but as the elevator reached and passed the fourth floor, where Scott and Eric's office was located, Jayne and Steelie exchanged a look.

Steelie cleared her throat, watching the floor numbers go higher. 'Uh, where are we going, Weiss?'

'I'm afraid that's classified, ma'am.' He smiled at her as the elevator doors opened. It was the tenth floor.

He ushered them into a foyer with four doors marked 'Restricted Access'. A wall-mounted keypad flanked each one. Weiss punched a code on the one directly ahead. A buzzer sounded and he opened the door for them. 'Welcome to Critter Central.'

Jayne went first into the large, windowless room whose rows of fluorescent tube lights gave it the feel of a clinical space. The foreground was a workspace; metal desks, filing cabinets, and bookshelves filled with forensic science reference texts. The back of the room was set up as a wet lab with fume hoods and countertop.

Steelie sounded impressed: 'So *this* is where you guys hang out?'

Weiss nodded. 'Tony Lee, who did the photography out by the freeway, is just through that door, in the cool room.'

'What goes on here, exactly?' asked Jayne.

'We do collection of trace evidence, some analysis.'

Agent Lee emerged from the door at the end of the room. He was wearing blue scrubs and had two reddish stripes across his cheeks where the elastic straps on a filter mask must have pulled tight. There was another stripe across his forehead and his dark hair looked flattened. He raised a hand in greeting.

'Hey, 31/1. Been expecting you.'

Weiss said, 'I'll leave you to it, then,' and departed.

Steelie and Jayne followed Lee into an anteroom that was divided by a bench and had lockers on one side. At one end, there was a sink with a mirror above it next to a door marked 'Restroom'. Adjacent to that were two swinging doors, each with a porthole.

Tony explained, 'We'll do the examination in the cool room itself because we're trying to keep the material as cold as possible on account of the coroner needing it next. Here's the protective gear. I'd suit up over your own clothes – you'll need them for warmth. The shoe covers are here.' He gestured to a container by the entrance to the cool room.

'And the glasses are inside this box.' He put

his hand on a wall-mounted cabinet holding Plexiglas safety glasses on a series of hooks, all illuminated by a soft ultraviolet glow.

'I'm here to run the fluoroscope for you, capture whatever images you want, take photos, and move the material if necessary.'

'Basically cater to our every need,' joked Steelie.

'Exactly.'

Jayne was glad Steelie had made the joke. She was beginning to feel tense about seeing the body parts out of the natural environment by the freeway where the leaves and detritus had masked the brutality of the cuts. The clinical setting would make the body parts look more like a dismembered body – one body in particular, one *person* in particular: Benni – *no, don't think of him, don't even conjure up his name.* Jayne felt Steelie nudge her and she took the mask Steelie was holding out, shaking her head in response to the question in her friend's eyes.

She pulled up her hood and followed the others into the cool room, another windowless space whose chill was a shock. Most of the overhead lights were switched off but a panel illuminated the center of the room above the fluoroscope. The fluoroscope's neck was cantilevered parallel to the floor, making the portable X-ray machine resemble an out-of-commission oil derrick. The body parts were in black body bags, each bag on its own gurney, and lined up next to the fluoroscope.

'Sorry for the "CSI" effect with the lights,' Tony said, only slightly muffled through his mask, 'just trying to keep radiant heat to a minimum but let me know if you need more light.'

He pulled the nearest gurney towards the fluoroscope and unzipped the body bag. It held the severed leg.

The pale flesh was damp and had defrosted. Blood pooled darkly in the recesses of the body bag. Jayne was relieved that her first instinct was to move closer to get a better look. She and Steelie positioned themselves on either side of the gurney, while Tony stayed by the fluoroscope.

'The cut goes through the femoral shaft,' commented Steelie. 'Looks like midway up the thigh.'

'And the other cut's just under the patella,' Jayne murmured.

'Trying to avoid sawing through bone again?'

'Maybe. Can't tell which cut he tried first.'

'How much of the patella have we got?'

'I don't think he even nicked it. Take a look.' Jayne moved to the right to examine the proximal cut, while Steelie bent down to look at the patella, its tip just visible amongst the ligaments and fat of the knee.

'We don't have much to go on for sex,' said Steelie.

'Not when we can't expose the femur to do a mid-shaft circumference.'

'Even that's just an indication.'

There was silence as the anthropologists looked at the leg, tilting their heads this way and that.

Tony cleared his throat. 'The thigh's not

shaved. Would that indicate male?'

'Possible, but not reliable,' replied Jayne, her eyes still on the leg. 'Not all women shave their thighs and plenty of men do, like swimmers and cyclists. If you can take photos of each cut and from above, we can move on to the fluoro.'

'No problem.' He went into action, the re-charge of the camera's flash whining as he took two shots from each vantage point, the latter requiring a stepladder that he wheeled over from the corner. Before turning on the fluoroscope, Tony brought over three lead vests and they all slipped the heavy material over their heads, adjusting them by the shoulder sections until the vests could rest there without too much discomfort.

Tony turned two switches on the fluoroscope and began pushing and pulling the lens head over the severed leg on the gurney. An X-ray image of everything in the lens' path beamed out of a monitor on an adjoining trolley.

Jayne asked, 'Can you bring it in a slow sweep from one end to the other?'

The anthropologists' eyes flicked between the partial leg and the fluoroscope screen, trying to orient the gradations of grey that represented bone and tissue.

They all noticed that the cut at the top of the femur didn't reveal any shards of metal or metallic fragments, as might have been expected from forceful cutting action. Steelie asked Tony about the apparent absence of trace evidence.

'Yeah,' he replied. 'There are indications that the perp washed the body parts after he'd done the cutting.'

As the fluoroscope traveled down the thigh, faint, lighter marks were visible at the distal end of the femur.

'Hold it there, just above the knee,' said Steelie. 'Lines of fusion?' She looked questioningly at Jayne, who was staring at the screen.

'Looks like it. Move it down a fraction, Tony ... and back up?'

He pushed the lens to where it had been a moment before.

Steelie said, 'Lines of fusion.'

'I'll be damned,' breathed Jayne.

'Talk to me, 31/1,' said Tony, glancing back and forth at each woman.

Steelie pointed at the monitor. 'See those lines at the top of the knee? That's where the epiphysis, or growth plate, is in the process of fusing to the shaft of the femur. Fusion happens at standard ages across populations and sexes. So, because we can see that line, we know you've got a teenager or someone in their early twenties, regardless of sex.'

He made a low whistle.

'Make a print of what you've got on the screen now,' Jayne said. 'Then can you flip the leg over so we can see the same region from the posterior?'

'What label do you want?'

'Distal left femoral epiphysis.'

'Can you spell that?'

'Left femur will be fine,' Steelie clarified.

Jayne looked at the fluoroscope screen and felt a surge of excitement to see that pale jagged line.

67

An identifying marker to narrow the search. A start.

Tony tapped buttons at a keyboard beneath the screen, then raised the fluoroscope's neck to make space to turn over the leg.

He handled the leg carefully, supporting it at each end, barely raising it off of the gurney before laying it back down. He put it on a section of body bag that wasn't bloody, then removed one of his two layers of gloves and returned to maneuver the fluoroscope towards the back side of the knee.

Similar pale lines were again visible on the fluoroscope screen, this time clearer without the patella in the foreground.

'I think it's either close to fully fused or it finished fusing not long before death, and that's why we can still see the line,' said Steelie. 'Another shot, Tony.'

He worked with the machine, then asked, 'Want to take it from the top again?'

'Yep,' said Steelie, 'then let's move on to the next bag.'

Nothing remarkable came up on this second pass. Tony re-bagged the leg and Steelie and Jayne watched him discard his dirty gloves and double-glove again with clean ones. Tony then switched that gurney for the next one. Jayne was no longer apprehensive about how the contents of the next body bag would affect her. She had moved on to thinking about the person who made the cuts and did the killing. She was thinking about bringing them down.

* * *

Scott and Eric barely talked until they were at the base of Jeffdale Avenue in Woodland Hills. The street didn't extend far up the slope before making a sharp turn but the matching pastel split-level houses gave it a sense of suburban uniformity. 3180 Jeffdale was on the left side of the street. The double garage door was closed but there was an oil mark in the driveway concrete as though a vehicle that leaked fluids usually sat there.

'OK,' said Scott, his eyes on the oil stain. 'It's either in the garage or it's on the road right now. Let's get a look in the garage first.'

'Then you're on the front and I'm on back duty?'

Scott nodded and jutted his chin at the glove box in front of Eric. Eric unlocked it and removed two guns in their holsters and two pieces of small electronic equipment. They strapped the gear on to their waistbands. Before they got out of the car, they put on FBI-marked windbreakers that covered their waistlines.

They approached the side of the garage and looked in the window. The glass was dusty and had cobwebs in the corners but the van inside was clearly visible. It was white with a blue stripe down the side and sported a roof rack.

Eric nodded to Scott and they put in the single earpieces that would allow them to communicate with each other through transmitters once they were separated. Eric started moving quietly down the side of the house. Scott waited until Eric said he was in position by a rear entrance, then he stepped out from the side of the house and rang the front doorbell.

The woman who eventually answered the door looked like she'd been sleeping. Her strawberry-blonde hair was pushed up at the crown and the cut-off denim shorts she wore were creased. Scott waited for her to stop yawning in his face before he opened up his badge wallet.

'Ma'am, Special Agent Houston, FBI. Are you Tracey Ellen Redding?'

'Yeah.'

'Does anyone besides you reside at this address, ma'am?'

'No ... I've got a friend here visiting, though.'

'Is he or she at home with you right now?'

'No. Why?'

'Ma'am, could I step inside and speak with you, please?'

She shrugged, apparently uninterested. 'Sure.'

The woman turned, leaving the door open behind her, and walked through the house, her flip-flops slapping against the floor tiles.

Scott followed her to the kitchen, noting the rear entrance to the house, which was a sliding glass door from a patio. The sliding door was also visible from the kitchen counter where the woman was pouring herself a glass of flat Coca-Cola out of a two-liter bottle.

Lighting a cigarette, she asked, 'What's this about?'

'Is the van parked in the garage yours, Ms Redding?'

'Yeah. I own it. It's paid off.'

'And have you been fully cognizant of its whereabouts for the past several days?'

She squinted at him through a haze of smoke. 'You asking if I know where it was?'

Scott nodded.

'Sure I know. I mean, I let Sky use it the other day, but I know where he was.'

'Who is Sky?'

'My friend who's visiting.'

'Were you aware that the van was recently involved in an accident that required repair work, Ms Redding?'

For the first time, the woman looked more alert and exhaled the smoke faster than she had been up to that point. 'No...'

She looked at the kitchen cabinets as though she could see through them into the garage, then shook her head. 'I think you're wrong about that. Sky would have told me.'

'Where is Sky at the moment?'

She hesitated, then took a deep drag on her cigarette. 'Actually, I don't know where he is. I was taking a nap before you rang the doorbell and woke me up.'

She stubbed the cigarette out in a small plate that held some toast crumbs. 'He could be any-where. He takes walks in the hills.' She gestured with her hand as though waving away flies.

Just then Scott's earpiece reverberated and he heard Eric say, 'FBI. Identify yourself, Sir,' then a grunt followed by, 'Code Four!'

This meant Eric was OK but Scott didn't like what he'd heard. He ran to the sliding door while pulling his gun from its holster. He opened the door, quickly put his head out, pulled it back in and then stepped out fully, holding the gun at the

71

ready by his shoulder.

Eric was between a rangy evergreen bush and the stucco wall of the house, his knee squarely in the center of the back of a man who was face-down in the dirt, struggling and cursing. Eric was already handcuffing him so Scott holstered his own gun. He turned to locate the woman. She was coming to the door, eyes wide.

'Sky?' She looked at the man Eric was pulling to his feet. 'Why didn't you tell me you were in an accident in my van? Huh?'

The man she was addressing was spitting dirt out of his mouth, his face red with anger and exertion. His hair was pale next to the red of his forehead and the veins of his neck were twitch-ing above the collar of his NASCAR logo T-shirt. 'Shut up! For once, woman, shut your trap.' He spat once more, directing the spittle to the wall of the house but some of it flew toward the woman.

She ran to him, got on tiptoe, and slapped him hard across the face. He reared back into Eric, who instinctively shoved him forward.

'Bitch!' The man tried to kick out with his legs but she was too quick for him and was running inside the house, shouting that he would find his things on the front lawn.

'Enough!' Scott's voice was authoritative and the man stopped struggling in Eric's hold but he still looked angry. 'What's your name?' Scott demanded.

The man focused on Scott. The whites of his eyes were bloodshot and when he spoke, the ripe smell of alcohol wafted into the air.

72

'Sky Horton.'

'You got any aliases, Mr Horton?'

The man shook his head.

'What about time inside? We're going to check on that, so you may as well speak up instead of looking like you're trying to hide something.'

This set the man off but now his tone was aggrieved. 'Listen, I know I should have reported it but I don't have the money to pay the damages and it isn't even my van. It's not like I hurt anyone for Chrissakes!'

Eric spoke. 'Should have reported what?'

'The accident.' The man tried to twist to see Eric's face. 'That's why you're here, right? Did the City call you?'

'Tell us what happened.'

'I backed into the traffic light, OK?' He looked at Scott. 'It was a tight turn and I was in a hurry. I didn't even realize the thing was there until I hit it and the light came down with a God-awful crash. I almost swore it moved while I was turning!' He tried to twist again.

The agents locked eyes, then Scott spoke. 'Mr Horton, we're going to need you to accompany us to our office for questioning.'

'I'm owning up to it, man! I'll pay the City! Can we work something out?'

'Right now,' replied Eric, 'you're looking at a charge of assaulting an identified Federal Agent and that's just for starters. We'll cover the rest of this at our office once we've examined the van. Move forward.'

# SEVEN

Tony Lee had brought out the torso and Jayne was finding it more frustrating than the leg. Whoever had made the cuts had aimed just below the ribcage but just above the pelvis, avoiding cutting through bone even on the spine, where the cuts had been squeezed in between vertebrae. The flesh didn't yield any clues; no scars, no tattoos, no perimortem bruising. When Tony turned it over, there were some moles and beauty marks on the back, along with some hair towards the base, but not enough secondary sex characteristics to even start a sex determination. Tony photographed everything before turning on the fluoroscope.

On X-ray, the epiphyses of the vertebrae were clearly fused.

'OK, fusion puts this one easily over seventeen and more likely over twenty-five,' said Steelie. 'So we're still at an MNI of one.'

'MNI,' Tony repeated. 'Minimum number of individuals?'

'Yeah,' Jayne answered. 'So far, you can't say you have more than one person here but I suspect that the leg's a youngster, while the torso's over twenty-five. But let's move on to the next bag before we make grand pronouncements.'

74

Jayne caught Steelie's look and knew what it meant: there wasn't enough information yet for them to reliably compare these body parts with any 32/1 profiles.

Tony was switching over the gurneys and unzipping the third body bag. It was the left arm and hand. Here, the cut was above the humeral head, allowing a careful disarticulation of the shoulder joint.

'If the person who cut this nicked anything, it would have been the scapula. The humerus itself looks unscathed,' commented Steelie.

Jayne asked, 'You notice how much cleaner these cuts are than the other parts we've seen so far?'

'Want a photo of that?' asked Tony.

'You read my mind.' Jayne stepped back to give him room at the gurney's edge.

Next was the fluoroscopy. The humeral head looked small on the screen, female. But Steelie and Jayne wanted a better estimate and asked Tony for a shot of it so they could measure it with calipers.

In pulling the fluoroscope down the length of the arm, they had to stop twice to take shots of old, healed fractures. One mid-shaft on the humerus, the other close to the wrist on the ulna.

'Defense wounds?' asked Tony, as he typed in a label for the second shot.

'Looks like it,' replied Jayne.

'The ulna's got a classic parry fracture.' Steelie demonstrated the defensive pose by holding one arm out diagonally in front of her chest, and then her face, trying to imitate the position the ulna

75

would have been in when hit. 'Nasty.'

'Badly healed, too,' said Jayne.

Tony looked at the hand with its chipped burgundy nail polish. 'Are you thinking this is a different person to the leg and torso?'

'Well, all the epiphyses of the arm bones are fully united, so we're looking at someone older than their mid-twenties,' began Steelie. 'Plus, those sunspots on the forearm suggest an older person. We might be able to narrow it down by looking at the structure of the bone on the X-ray prints you give us.'

'Which isn't something we do all that often,' added Jayne. 'Usually, we deal with X-rays taken at a known age and don't need to examine internal structures.'

'But since we don't have much to go on with this material, we'll try everything we can,' Steelie rounded out.

'OK. Want to move on to the other arm?' He looked at her expectantly, one hand on the gurney.

'Sure.'

As Tony switched the gurneys for the last time, Jayne felt deflated. They weren't getting very far. All the parts appeared to be female, all had pale skin, all were post-pubescent and therefore it was more difficult to discriminate between them, especially within the parameters of their non-invasive examination. Body parts that might give a clear indication of age, like the pelvis or the teeth, were not in this batch. Jayne felt her hopes for an identification of any of the victims fading. She suddenly felt weighed down by her lead vest. She shifted it and stretched her back uncomfortably.

Tony was moving as though he wasn't wearing a lead vest, exposing the right arm in the body bag with efficient movements. The arm lay slightly sideways in the bag so he moved it parallel to the edges of the gurney. His gloved hand momentarily supported the fingers with their polished nails and Jayne had a sudden, violent image of a dead woman being led in a waltz. She looked at the ceiling to banish the image from her mind, causing her mask to pull on the skin under her cheeks. This brought her back to reality. She was mildly tired from this kind of concentration and the standing, and the cold was getting to her. Gruesome images fed on her fatigue, she knew that already. *Just one more body part*, she told herself.

She looked down when she thought Tony had photographed the arm from every angle. It was a right arm and appeared, superficially, to be the match for the left arm they had just examined. Tony drew the fluoroscope down along the severed limb, pausing briefly to take a shot of the small humeral head. Then the fluoroscope's lens resumed its journey, Tony carefully keeping it in line with the arm, and Jayne's mind began to drift on to where they'd get the reference material to improve the age estimate for both humerii.

'Jesus *Christ*!'

Steelie's exclamation made Tony freeze and Jayne jump. She looked at Steelie, who was staring at the fluoroscope screen. Jayne immediately followed her lead. And there it was, the thing the killer couldn't have known about – unless he had an X-ray machine.

The surgical plate was screwed into the humerus at about midshaft. It would have been applied by a surgeon, could have an identifying number, and might just lead an investigator to that surgeon's patient records. *Surgical plate as homing pigeon*, Jayne thought, and then immediately realized they wouldn't find this woman's identity in the Agency's files. They didn't have a single client who had reported a missing woman with a plate in an arm, nor had they received any X-rays that showed plates on examination. But it was the first real lead on the identity of this woman and thus the first real lead on her killer.

Tony was looking at the screen. 'I guess this is a good thing?'

Steelie's voice sounded excited. 'You just got yourself a lead, Tony.'

Eric walked into his office and sat down heavily at his desk. Scott looked at him, eyebrows raised.

Eric shook his head.

'Everything checked out?' Scott asked.

'Yeah. The City confirms that well after our van got hit on the freeway yesterday morning, someone put a traffic light out of commission at Winnetka and Hatteras. They had traces of white paint on the light post and had just started searching for the vehicle that did the damage. The Critters have examined the Redding woman's van. No suspect biological traces, no work

78

on the van besides the body work on the back doors.' He looked at Scott. 'What did you get from Redding on interview?'

'She alibied him, under caution, for the time the van we're looking for was hit on the freeway. And given how mad she is at him, I think it's a safe bet she wouldn't cover for him if he wasn't actually there.'

'So we're back to square one.'

'Not exactly.'

Eric looked interested.

'Let's expand your body shop theory. We started with the ones that have handled hot cars but if it's our perp from Georgia, he doesn't know which shop to go to out here in California, does he? He picks whatever is convenient from the freeway and figures that, with enough incentive, he can keep the shop quiet.' Scott pulled a printout closer to him. 'I've got twelve more body shops we can check in that radius you set up around the accident site. There's hope for your gold star yet.'

Eric had stood up to scan the list over Scott's shoulder when someone knocked on their open door. Weiss was waiting for their attention.

'Heard you guys were in the building. Thought you should get this from 31/1 direct.'

At his summons, Jayne and Steelie appeared, the latter carrying a toolbox. Eric gestured for her to take his empty chair while everyone greeted each other.

'You found something?' Scott asked.

Jayne announced, 'There's a surgical plate in one of the arms.'

79

Neither agent reacted at first. Then Eric put the question. 'What does that mean for the case? Do you know who she is?'

Steelie smiled. *'We* don't know but you're probably gonna know. Tony's working on it now, up in your lab.'

Jayne explained, 'If the plate is batch-stamped or coded in any way, and you add that it's screwed into the right humerus of a woman between the ages of twenty-five and forty, say, then you guys are about as close as you're going to get to a shortlist of people who had this procedure done off of that batch of plates.'

'You'll notice there are a couple of *ifs* in that statement, though,' cautioned Steelie.

'And there's another way we can search, right?' Eric commented. 'Using the National Crime Information Center database, we could generate a shortlist of all missing women in that age range with a plate in the right arm.'

'That, too,' agreed Jayne.

*'If* she's been reported missing,' countered Steelie. 'And *if* the person who reported her knew about her surgery or put the cops on to the medical records, and if the records then actually got uploaded into NCIC. And we know that doesn't always fly.'

Scott looked thoughtful. 'Was there a scar? Like, from when she had surgery to put the plate in?'

Steelie smacked her forehead lightly and turned to stare at Jayne. 'Of course! We got so carried away by the plate, we forgot about the scar. Of course there's a scar.'

80

'So,' Eric concluded. 'We can do a simple search on "scar, upper right arm" and forget about the person who put in the misper report knowing what kind of surgery or accident led to the scar?'

Jayne commented to Steelie, 'And you always had a low opinion of these law enforcement types.'

Scott rocked back in his chair and grinned at Eric before saying to Jayne, 'He just wants the gold star I promised him.'

She raised her eyebrows. 'Is that what they taught you at Quantico? Carrot and stick?'

He paused, locking eyes with her, then said, 'Well, you've been there—'

Steelie cut in. 'No, we were only there for a week giving our two cents on NCIC 2000. At the time, your main object of study appeared to be a beer bottle.'

Scott dragged his eyes away from Jayne to respond to Steelie. 'Then you wouldn't know that the Bureau stalwarts who teach us think the only place for a carrot is in a side salad – shredded.'

'And even then, it's suspicious,' Eric added.

Scott grinned at him. 'Plenty of stick around, though.' He stood up. 'And we should escort you out before our boss comes in here wielding his.'

# EIGHT

Jayne went into the Agency's laboratory to put away the biometric equipment they'd used to measure the X-ray images Tony Lee had printed at Critter Central. Steelie was booting up the lab computer. After it whirred to life and executed a few beeps, she said, 'Check it out. Our first message via the All Coroner's Bulletin. From a coroner in Anchorage about Thomas Cullen.'

Jayne pulled up a stool and read the couple of paragraphs, whose font was all capitals. Then she translated, 'The coroner's saying that they have a John Doe with a projectile in the sphenoid but they have his cause of death down as GSW with that bullet as the projectile that caused death? So ... they don't think it's Cullen but they're notifying us as a courtesy?'

Steelie nodded. 'Looks like they ascribed the bullet to a more recent gunshot, not an old bullet that was sitting in his head for years.'

Jayne pushed back from the desk and frowned. 'But how could they confuse the two?'

Steelie shrugged. 'Maybe they didn't. Maybe it's not Thomas Cullen but rather some guy who *actually* died from shooting himself the same way.'

Jayne looked back at the coroner's message.

'It's a decent match on the identifiers though ... Caucasoid male, forty years plus or minus five, five-foot-nine plus or minus two, dark brown head hair, eyes brown, picked up in 1998...'

'So he's a forty-year-old white guy with brown hair and eyes, no known scars, marks or tattoos. No wonder they've never had any hits in NCIC; there's almost nothing there to discriminate between him and thousands of other missing men. Doesn't mean it's Cullen, that's all I'm saying. They could be right and it's a different guy.'

'Send them another message.'

'I'm going to. I will encourage them, in polite language, to compare any X-rays they've got with the one we digitized. They haven't done that yet.'

Jayne got up. 'OK, I'm going to write up the report on the BP's for Scott and Eric. Let me know if you hear anything.'

By the time Steelie came to Jayne's office, she was tidying the papers on her desk at the end of the day.

'Did you get an acknowledgment from Tony on our report?'

'Yes and he said he'd make sure Scott and Eric saw it when they got back.'

'Which was when?'

'God knows.'

Steelie perched on the edge of the desk. 'So where are you meeting Gene tonight?'

'They put him up at the Omni—'

'Who's "they"?'

'His company, I guess. So I'm picking him

up—'

'He doesn't have a rental?'

'No...' She waited for Steelie to interrupt again but she didn't. 'And we're going to eat in Little Tokyo.'

'Which restaurant?'

Jayne stopped pulling the papers together. 'I don't know. We agreed to walk around, see what takes our fancy. If you're so curious, why don't you come too?'

Steelie gave a little shudder. 'I hear your cry for help and yet I am not moved.' She went out the door, then stuck her head back around it. 'But call me when you get home afterwards.'

Jayne nodded. She finished at her desk, closed up the building, and left. At home, she changed clothes and put on mascara and lip gloss, realizing that the last time she'd seen Gene, they'd been at Kigali Airport in Rwanda almost a decade earlier. She'd still had a pair of well-used leather gloves sticking out of the back pocket of her cargo pants even though she and Steelie were leaving the mission in a matter of hours. He'd been wearing dusty boots, on his way to UN HQ, staying in the mission for another six months as he'd joined the team late, on loan from the FBI Lab. She belatedly wondered if she'd recognize him now and was glad he'd suggested the rear entrance of the hotel, which was quieter and he'd be easier to spot. Glancing at her watch, she picked up her bag and went out to her truck, making a mental note to stop by the Home Depot eventually to purchase new plants for her porch. She would have to do more than just sweep up the mess of broken pottery left by bumbling critters the night before.

The traffic on Sunset was still heavy but the evening's milder temperatures were layering in and Jayne drove with the windows down, listening to an Oscar Peterson compilation but not minding hearing music from nearby cars as they idled next to each other along the boulevard. Keeping to surface streets, she turned right on Grand, passed the new cathedral, and made her way to Olive, starting the descent toward the heart of Downtown.

She pulled into the Omni Hotel's curved driveway, its facade looming skyward, dwarfing the people gathered at the curb. A young valet made eye contact with her, raising his hand interrogatively but she shook her head as she drove past him slowly, scanning faces. When she had made the full circuit of the driveway, she pulled to the curb in front of a taxi and twisted in her seat to look for Gene out the back window. Just then, her passenger door swung open and a man dressed entirely in beige leapt in beside her as she pulled her bag to safety.

'Christ, Gene, you gave me a fright!'

'Sorry, I was afraid you were going to drive off without me.'

He leaned over the bench seat and gave her an awkward sideways hug, the zipper of his windbreaker scraping against her cheek. When they released each other, she looked at him and was glad he'd spotted her because she might not have recognized him after all. His blond hair was turning white and his cheeks seemed to droop, which changed the shape of his face altogether. His long body was still lanky, which gave him a certain youthfulness but his pale eyes were as penetrating as ever, their dot-like pupils making it seem as though he were focused on and displeased with whatever he was looking at. But his smile transformed everything, as it always had.

'So, how the hell are ya, Jayne Hall?'

His exuberance was infectious and she laughed. 'Not bad, thanks. How was your flight?'

'Hey, when it's business class, it's always good.'

She gave him an admiring glance. 'Nice.' She pulled away from the hotel and headed back the way she came, then turned right on Tom Bradley Boulevard toward Little Tokyo. 'So, what brings you here in business class?'

'I've been working for an electronics company that's now looking to open a West Coast office. Sent me out here to take a couple of meetings, get the lay of the land. I won't bore you with the details.'

'But when did you leave the FBI Lab?'

'Years ago.'

'I didn't know.'

'Hey, how much of your life do you want to spend dealing with crime and criminals?'

She glanced at him with interest. 'You miss anything from those days?'

'Nope! The job I have now is dull and that's the way I like it. I can get my excitement elsewhere. Seeing you and Steelie is the highlight of this trip. Speaking of which, is she meeting us at the restaurant?'

Jayne was parking at a meter. She raised her voice over the passing traffic as she got out of the truck. 'She couldn't come tonight. Pretty busy this week.'

Gene waited until she'd joined him on the sidewalk. 'She still mad at me, then?'

She gave him an embarrassed grin and started walking.

'Argh!' He threw his hands up in the air and caught up with her. 'How long can someone hold a grudge for God's sake! It's been almost ten years.'

'She's like an elephant; she never forgets.'

'And now you two are running this charity. How's that going?'

'It's good. Early days yet.'

'How long since your doors opened?'

They'd crossed into Little Tokyo's center and were walking past bubble tea cafes and clothing shops. 'It's been about a year now.'

'I only had a second to glance at your website but you're trying to work on the backlog of bodies?'

'Yeah.'

'Pretty ambitious.'

She shot him a look. 'What, just because it's a big job, we shouldn't bother?'

'You know it's not just a big job, Jayne; it's damn near insurmountable.'

She didn't like the way he made air quotes with his fingers around "big job", like she hadn't assessed the nature of the problem correctly. She wanted to say, *Well, with attitudes like that ...* She voiced, 'Depends on how you look at it.'

'You're saying the glass is half full, not half empty.'

'Yeah.'

'Bullshit.'

She stopped walking and turned to look up at his face, remembering how he had a way of making her feel the height differential was just symbolic of his actual superiority. She was suddenly glad Steelie wasn't there. It would save her from having to post bail after Steelie was arrested for grievous bodily harm from punching Gene in the mouth.

'It's not bullshit, Gene. Perspective makes a difference and if that means people like us keep trying to put names to bodies – particularly the difficult to identify – then that's a good thing.'

Jayne felt like his eyes were boring right through her but then he broke into a grin.

'That must be the face your sponsors see when you're asking for grants.'

She couldn't tell if that was a compliment and didn't get a chance to ask because the host of the restaurant they had unwittingly stopped in front of asked if they'd like to see the menu. He was holding out a large, vinyl-covered book that Jayne accepted.

They stepped closer to the doorway to get light to read by and walked into the scent of food. She and Gene looked at each other in silent agreement.

They let the host lead them to a table set in a front window. There were a few other diners at tables partially obscured by ficus trees and ferns in pots. The lights were low, and the atmosphere was muted as people focused on their food.

She and Gene shared several dishes, telling old stories and arguing good-naturedly over details.

As they finished up, he asked, 'Remember when you fell down the ravine in Rulindo?'

'Oh, we can laugh about it now but you guys left me down there way too long.'

'We knew you were OK.'

'I could have broken my ankle!'

'But you didn't.'

'I think I did sprain it or something. It's never been the same.'

'Really? You should get it checked out.'

Jayne smiled. 'A bit late for that, don't you think?'

'You, ah, ever get checked out by a psych?'

'Why? Did you?'

'When I got back to DC. But you didn't answer my question.'

'No, I never saw anyone.'

'Still could.'

'I suppose.' She paused. 'Did it help you? I mean, not that you needed help per se.'

Gene thought for a moment. 'It helped me get some clarity about what I wanted to spend my life doing. Working in Rwanda kinda opened things up for me.'

'How do you mean?'

'I guess I felt some freedom there. When I got back home, I decided to pursue it; give myself permission to enjoy life, not stay enslaved to my government job and the road to a pension.' He tapped his cup thoughtfully and then smiled up at her. 'You charge by the hour or what?'

89

Jayne smiled back.

Gene continued. 'And you? What happened for you after the Kigali mission?'

'More missions. Mostly in the so-called Balkan Hot Spots.'

'That's right. I think I got news of you and Steelie every now and then. All mass graves?'

She nodded. 'Barring a few multiples and a few places where we expected bodies but didn't find any. Carcasses of animals maybe, but no people.' She looked out the window. 'Those were the worst. Thinking you were going to find them and then you didn't and you know they're still waiting for you. Even now, while we're sitting at this table in this window, they're still waiting for us.' She wasn't looking at anything now; her perspective had internalized. 'Or people like us.'

'But that's why you started the Agency, right?'

'Different bodies but yeah, that's true.' She looked at him with a small smile.

'Hey,' Gene laughed. 'I actually *do* charge. By the minute.' He looked at his watch. 'That'll be seventy-five cents, lady. Next!' He called out as though to a waiting patient but the host thought he was summoning the bill and hurried over to put it on the table.

Jayne tried to smother her laughter.

Gene took the bill. 'I got it.'

Eric pulled out of the driveway of yet another body shop and nodded at the manager who was waiting to close the gate after the Suburban. Eric watched him in the rear-view mirror and said,

'Someone's not too happy we held him back after class.'

Scott was flipping through pages in his notebook. 'He was nervous, wasn't he?'

'For a guy whose business is supposed to be on the up-and-up.' Eric was driving with some haste along the broad boulevards in Van Nuys.

Now Scott was almost talking to himself. 'How could he flatly deny they've ever had a vehicle in there from Georgia?'

Eric pulled in to park next to a Tommy's Burger stand. He looked at Scott meaningfully.

Scott was still musing. 'Wouldn't you expect someone to say, "I don't remember; let me check my files"?'

Eric kept his eyes on his partner while lowering the windows until the car filled with the scent of grilling food. Scott finally appeared to get the message because he threw his notebook on the dash and got out of the vehicle. Within two minutes, they were standing at the counter with food in front of them.

Before eating, Scott pulled out his cell phone but didn't dial.

Eric chewed some of his chilli burger. 'Why don't you just call her?'

'What? Who?'

'You don't look innocent, Scott. You can't *do* innocent.'

Scott took a deep breath, stretched his arms over his head, arched his back, twisted his torso, and exhaled.

Eric looked at him. 'I'm trying to eat here and you're acting like it's the warm up for the long jump.'

Scott re-holstered his phone and took a deliberately large bite of his meal.

Eric wasn't finished. 'What are you worried about – with Jayne, I mean?'

Scott shrugged, then swallowed. 'I'm not worried. I just don't want to start something while we're working together.'

'That didn't stop you with Mindy.'

'Yeah and look how that turned out.'

'And Jayne isn't married to the Bureau anyway, so I don't buy that excuse on any level. Nor does it explain what you've been doing for the past five years.' Eric took the time to chew. 'You want me to find out if she's dating someone? I'll ask her. I'll ask Steelie.'

Scott was fierce: 'Don't.'

'Jesus. I won't but Jayne's not...'

Scott looked at him. 'Not what? My type? I know that already.'

'No, that's not what I'm getting at. I'm saying I don't think she's necessarily easy to read.'

'I know.' Scott took a bite of food and then talked through the mouthful. 'I can't believe I'm taking advice from a guy who was married and divorced before he was thirty.'

'I just got married too young. Now, in your case, that *definitely* won't be an issue.'

Jayne turned on her phone as she and Gene strolled slowly back to her truck in the manner of people who'd eaten well and to satisfaction. She looked at the phone even though it hadn't chirped to signify new voicemail. She wasn't sure why she imagined she would have missed a call from Scott. He was on her mind as she thought about how soon they might have an evening like this. They'd had dinner together on the phone often enough. Scott eating at his desk in Atlanta, having stayed late on a case, while Jayne was at home, feeling giddy whenever his calls came after she'd showered so she'd be at her table in just a nightshirt. He'd only ever asked her once what she was wearing but it wasn't one of those nights and she was too honest for her own good, thereby missing, she had always felt, the chance to go down a different path with him. But she'd never forgotten that he'd asked.

Gene broke into her silence as they got into the truck. 'If you're not too tired, I wouldn't mind seeing this place of yours.'

Her mind hadn't shifted gears yet. 'My apartment?'

'Sure ... that too.'

'Oh!'

He laughed and Jayne pulled out from the curb, telling herself to pay attention. 'Sorry, I—'

'Don't apologize. Seriously, I wouldn't mind seeing your office *and* your apartment. I'd like to see these places that are giving you so much therapy.'

Jayne suddenly turned right on Main Street. 'All right,' she said brightly. 'We'll swing by the office, then have coffee on my deck.'

Gene nodded and settled back on the seat, his elbow resting on the open windowsill, the night air brushing his hair off his forehead.

They passed Olvera Street, catching snippets

93

of mariachi music and laughter from around the massive magnolia tree that marked the entrance to the enchantingly historic, if touristy, birthplace of LA. Jayne made the dog-leg turn to follow Hill Street through Chinatown, hitting every green light and bypassing the buses disgorging passengers in front of the alleys full of market stalls selling everything from suitcases to cell phone covers under a canopy of papermâché lanterns. She accelerated on to the 110 Freeway near Dodger Stadium and the LA Police Academy and crested the hill, passing through the short tunnels to emerge with a view of the transmission tower lights twinkling atop the San Gabriel Mountains on the other side of the valley.

She exited at Figueroa, navigated to San Fernando Road and drove fast along the four lanes, past the small trailer park, the old baseball diamond, and the tire repair shop. On the other side of the road, the rail lines and the LA River paralleled her route. The trough cut by the river made the air even cooler here. Eventually, she slowed to turn into the Agency parking lot. The light above the front door was on and the security lights on the corner of the building were illuminating the front and side.

'So, this is it?' Gene asked, getting out of the truck and stretching his long legs.

Jayne unlocked the front door and entered to disable the alarm using the security code on the nearby panel. She turned on the lights as she let him in. He looked around appreciatively.

'Nice.' He walked over to the reception coun-

94

ter and picked up one of the Agency brochures. 'Can I have one of these?'

'Sure. Wanna see the rest of it?' She went into the next room and turned on the desk lamp. 'This is my office. I do the interviews with families and friends of the mispers in here.'

'Thus the sofas and tissues.'

'Are you being flippant?'

'That came out wrong. You do the interviews and then, what, you do the profile off of them?'

'In part, and in part off any documentation we can get our hands on.'

Jayne walked down the hall, then realized Gene hadn't followed her. She turned back to find him. He was looking at the filing cabinets behind her desk.

'Are these all your cases?'

'Yes.'

'How many do you have?'

'About a hundred.'

'And how many have you matched up to bodies?'

'Seven so far.'

'Not very many.'

'Yeah, but if one of those seven was, say, your father, would that matter? Those seven count for a lot.'

'True. Sorry, I keep applying the business models we use at my company and I guess they don't really apply. So where do you keep the closed files?'

She pointed at the top drawer of one of the cabinets and then watched as Gene walked over as though to open it.

'We keep them locked for obvious reasons,' she said.

'I was just interested. Must look kinda empty. You got any plans to fill it up faster?'

'Well, if you'd follow me, Mr Enthusiasm.'

This time he did follow her, past the kitchen to turn into the lab across from the bathroom.

'This is where Steelie does the odontograms and the biometrics and we digitize relevant photos. It's basically an anthro report done off of antemortem instead of the body.'

Gene was turning round, looking at different items on the counters and walls.

'And this,' Jayne said, pointing at a computer terminal at one end of the counter, 'is where Steelie runs the All Coroners Bulletin, which is one of our best tools to speed up the rate with which we close cases and fill that file drawer.'

He looked curious. 'How does that work?'

'Basically, if we come across particularly identifiable characteristics that weren't included on the original missing person report, we get to notify coroners with unidentified bodies through this dedicated network.'

He whistled. 'That's pretty good.'

He looked preoccupied for a moment then asked quickly, 'You made any ID's through it yet?'

'No, but before you spread any more of your good cheer, I'm calling the glass half full on this one.'

'Yeah, you might be right about that.' He looked at the computer and lapsed into silence.

Jayne said, 'I'll just go to the ladies' and then we'll head over to my place.'

When she came out, she looked into the lab but there was no sign of Gene. She shut off the lights there and moved forward to her office. She found him sitting at her desk, revolving slowly in her chair.

He smiled at her. 'I can see why you keep going.'

'Oh?'

'You've broken the big problem down into smaller pieces, haven't you? I bet you do a lot of compartmentalizing.'

'I don't know about that. But I do like it if I can tell when something's over, when a job's done.'

'What about in the rest of your life?'

'What about it?'

'Do you compartmentalize there, too?'

'I don't know! Come on, let's go.'

Fifteen minutes later, she and Gene were walking through the front door of her apartment. While he used the bathroom, she put on the kettle and wiped down the table on the deck. When Gene emerged, she indicated the coffee fixings.

'How do you take it?'

He called back to her as he walked over to the bookshelves. 'Black, thanks.'

As she put the grounds into the press, she watched him, noticing how his height was even more obvious now that he was in her house. He was reaching for a book on a high shelf that she needed a footstool to reach. He flicked through the book and then returned it to the shelf.

'No books on forensics?'

'They're all at the Agency. I rarely want to look at them when I get home.'

He turned and looked at her with a surprised smile. 'You have limits when it comes to forensics? I'm shocked.'

Jayne poured hot water over the coffee. 'All I'm saying is, Spitz and Fisher isn't my first choice for bedtime reading.'

'So you *do* compartmentalize.'

'What is it with your fascination as to whether or not I compartmentalize, as you put it?' She carried the tray of coffee and cups out to the deck.

Gene followed her out. 'I'm just curious about how you keep on with the forensics and still seem to have a normal life. I wasn't very successful at it.'

They settled down at the table and Jayne sugared her coffee. 'Well, I never worked for the Bureau for one thing, and I *never* said I have a normal life.'

'But you're expecting a hot date soon, right?'

'Gene!' Jayne spat coffee in her surprise.

He grinned at her. 'Hey, people who've done the type of work we've done sometimes have trouble finding someone who "gets" them. And I take it from your reaction that you don't get a lot of hot dates.'

'I didn't say that.' Jayne wiped her mouth.

'You missed a spot.' Gene leaned over and presumptuously wiped his thumb beneath her lower lip. 'I was really just trying to find out if you had a boyfriend right now. The way you checked your phone earlier...?'

'No. I mean ... no.'

'Ri-ight.' He sounded unconvinced.

'OK,' Jayne countered. 'Since you're so smug, why haven't you mentioned your fabulous wife and kids back at your massive condo with attached two-car garage?'

Gene inclined his head. 'Because it's a house – my mom's house, incidentally – not a condo, with a one-car garage that's filled with other stuff so there's no room for the car. No wife, but there've been some ... dalliances.'

'Well, I bet your garage has everything labeled and organized because you like to compart-mentalize, just as you allege I do. Am I right?'

He looked thoughtful, then admitted, 'Pretty much.'

'Yeah, I bet your mom loves having you around.'

'Actually, she passed away.'

'Oh, I'm sorry.'

Gene shook his head. 'No, it was for the best. Alzheimer's.'

'Oh.'

'Trust me, you don't want to live with some-one who has that kind of dementia. She didn't know who she was most of the time and she sure as hell didn't know who I was by the end. It's pretty weird, I gotta tell ya, to have your own mother not recognize you. Makes you wonder who *you* are.'

'Shit, Gene,' Jayne breathed.

He shook his head and smiled lightly. 'She's been gone a few years now. And I worked out who I am.'

A car passed below them on the street, its occupants singing loudly along with their stereo. Their voices died away with the air and were replaced with the sound of cricket calls.

Gene drained his cup and stood. 'I should probably get going.'

'I'll drive you back.'

'No need. You look tired.'

'It's no trouble...'

'Seriously, no need. But you said you had a copy of that photo we took at Kigali Airport?'

'Right, I do. Give me a second to find it.'

They went indoors and she left Gene there while she went outside and down the stairs to her storage room off the driveway. It took a few minutes to find the right box and she carried the whole thing back upstairs.

He met her at the door and they went through the box together on the dining table, looking at photos from Bosnia. Streets of shelled houses in Broko, carts of ripe peppers for sale on the shoulder of the road to Tuzla, a bright new gas station on the highway to the Croatian coast. When they came to the photos from Rwanda, the Kigali Airport shot was near the top. Jayne put the duplicate in an envelope and gave it to him. They walked to the front door.

'I'll keep in touch,' he said.

'It was good to see you.'

'Tell Steelie I said hi.'

Jayne smiled a bit sheepishly. 'Will do.'

She thought he was bending down to kiss her cheek, so she leaned toward him but he reached her first and pressed his lips to hers. It wasn't a bull's eye, landing partly on her mouth and partly on her cheek, fast but not fleeting. Then he left quickly, raising a hand in farewell as he disappeared around the corner at the top of the stairs.

She closed the door behind him and stood for a moment, shaking her head at the contradictions he seemed to show and feeling surprised at the slight moistness where his rather papery lips had touched hers. It was only then that she wondered how he was getting back to his hotel. She hadn't even called a taxi for him. She yanked open the door and clattered down the stairs, intending to catch him on the street but there was no sign of him. She realized she didn't even have his cell phone number. Then she heard the phone ringing in her apartment and she bounded back up, thinking it might be him.

She picked up the phone and answered breathlessly. But it was only Steelie, sounding shocked.

'Are you just getting in now?'

'No, we were here and then I just came back in again.'

'Wait. You had Gene come over to your place?'

'Yeah, why?'

'My God, Jayne. Do I need to remind you? The guy's an ignorant pig who—'

'He's mellowed since then.'

'People like him don't mellow.'

Jayne smiled, thinking about the number of times Gene had made her laugh that night. 'Well, he has.' Even she heard the smile in her tone.

'Have you forgotten that night at the Cadillac?'

'Yeah, he wondered if you were still holding that dance against him.'

'That would be a yes. But what's the deal? Are you seeing him again? And what was he doing in LA?'

'He was out here on business and all we did was a have a nice reminiscence session. Talked about life – post-mission life. It was good. I mean, he's still supercilious at times but he's fine. He did kiss me.'

'Ugh!'

Jayne laughed, knowing how abhorrent Steelie would find the idea. 'Yeah, it wasn't the best kiss ever. Kind of fourth-grade school yard, actually.'

'What, like, when no one knows what they're doing and a tongue goes up someone's left nostril?'

'God, no. There was no tongue, but there was something behind it ... I don't know. Something.'

Steelie was unmoved. 'Who cares what was behind it, so long as it wasn't a tongue?'

# DAY THREE

## Thursday

# NINE

Scott pulled into the curb in front of the next body shop on his list. Eric double-checked the sheet he was holding and suppressed a yawn. 'Sepulveda Body Shop.'

Scott caught his yawn. 'I shouldn't have skipped lunch.'

They got out of the car and walked into the gated concrete yard, which was packed with cars reflecting the light and heat of the summer afternoon, while all four bays in the building were occupied with vehicles up on raised pallets, mechanics working beneath them. Scott and Eric threaded their way past the parked cars and walked into the small office. An unattended desk whose trays were filled with files was shoe-horned into what appeared to be a closet but the room was dominated by a larger desk closer to the window-mounted air conditioner, which was spewing frigid air.

The young man behind this desk was wearing a blue shirt smeared with grease where he'd wiped his hands on it. The nametag read *Javier* and he was on the phone.

'If you bring it here before eight in the morning, I can get someone to have a look at it same day. But if it's rotors, it's gonna take a day to get 'em in.'

When he hung up the phone, the agents opened their badges, announced themselves and asked for Javier's surname.

'Ruiz.'

'What's your position here?' Eric asked.

'I'm the manager.'

'OK. Were you working Monday?'

Ruiz took on a wary look. 'Yes?'

'You get a van in here that needed body work to the rear doors?'

Ruiz glanced away briefly. 'Yeah.'

Eric restrained himself from looking at his partner. 'You note the license plate?'

'Well, I don't know if—' Something out the window caught his attention and he hurriedly got up from the desk, moving to the side just as an overweight man charged through the front door. He hardly glanced at Scott and Eric as he made his way around the desk. He only looked up after he'd sat down in the chair and put his head in line with the air conditioner.

'What do you need? Ruiz taking care of you?' He was rolling his neck around to expose all the folds to the air.

Before they could speak or take out their badges, Ruiz was saying, 'Mr Malbandian, these gentlemen have a government vehicle that needs looking at.' He shot a nervous glance at Eric.

'Well, help them, Ruiz. Help them. Out there.' He shooed them out with his hands.

Scott caught Eric's eye and they didn't pull out their badges. They followed Ruiz out into the hot forecourt. Ruiz went to a narrow area between two black SUVs liberally adorned with chrome accents and halted. It was like standing in a toaster oven.

'Look,' he said desperately. 'That guy's my boss. He doesn't know about this and he'd fire me in a second.'

'Because of something you did with this van?' Scott wasn't following.

'No, because I took some money that maybe should've gone to the shop.' Ruiz looked over Scott's shoulder.

'Take it from the top, Javier.' Eric encouraged.

'OK. This guy came in with a van. Looked like he'd been rear-ended. There was a lot of damage to the lower part of the back doors and it was stopping the handles from latching right. Nothing weird about it until he said he just wanted me to spray the van and do all the work from the outside. Under no circumstances could I touch the handles. I said, don't you want me to fix the lock, but he said that the padlock he'd put on was just fine. He had a chain through it too. He paid me six hundred dollars extra to do everything the way he said. And it wasn't easy, let me tell you. He was real particular.'

'Describe the van.' Scott had pulled out his pad.

Ruiz closed his eyes before recounting. 'Light blue Chevy, old. Maybe a pretty old Astro but it

105

didn't have its model on the outside. Um ... good tires, I noticed that.'

'And what color did you spray it?'

'Gold.'

'License plate?'

Ruiz looked embarrassed. 'That was part of what he paid me to not notice. But I know it was Georgia.'

The agents exchanged a look. 'Georgia?' Scott asked. 'You're sure?'

'Yes. But I didn't look closely at it.'

'You can't remember anything else about it?'

'No, honestly. I see a lot of plates and they don't mean that much to me anymore. Especially from out of state because they're a different layout to California plates.'

Eric cut across Scott's emerging exasperation. 'What about the man, Javier? What did he look like?'

'He was Anglo. Kinda tall. A light-colored beard. But he was wearing a baseball cap and sunglasses, so I didn't see much more.'

'What was his voice like?'

'I guess you could say it was soft. I mean, it was American and all. Just ... he didn't speak loud. You'd do better asking Margarita about him.'

'Margarita?'

'Yeah, she does the filing. She's not in today but I know she had some kind of problem with him.'

'They spoke to each other?'

'I don't know. She just came walking back into the yard here and said something, like, about the guy being weird.'

Scott was at the ready. 'Where can we find Margarita?'

'Um, I know where she lives. Over by Birmingham High School.' He gave Scott the address.

'Let's go back to the man,' said Eric. 'What time did he get here?'

'He was here when I arrived to open up at six thirty.'

'Just parked outside?'

'Yeah, like he was waiting.'

'Was anyone else with him?'

'Not that I saw.'

'And what'd he say to you?'

'Just said hi and that he needed some work done on his van, right away, and he was going to pay cash.' He shrugged. 'My boss wasn't coming in for two days, so I just decided to take on the job myself.'

'He say anything about where he'd come from or where he was going?'

Ruiz shook his head.

'Did he wait here while you finished the work?'

'No, the paint had to dry. He came back the next day, late in the afternoon.'

'But he just walked away when he dropped if off? Did he ask you for directions or anything?'

'No, he just walked. I figured he was going to the bus stop or something.'

'Is there anything else you can tell us about him?'

'I don't think so.'

'OK.' Eric pulled a business card from his shirt pocket. 'Here's my card. If you remember anything more, call me right away, any time, day or night. Got it?'

'So I'm not in trouble?'

'No but we may need to take a formal statement later.'

Ruiz put the card in the back pocket of his pants. 'And you're not going to tell my boss?'

'Nope.' Scott shook his head.

It wasn't until the agents were back in their vehicle, air-conditioner blowing, that Eric spoke. 'We're on to him, Houston. I can feel it.'

They drove directly to the address Ruiz had given them for Margarita, which was in a neighborhood of single-story ranch houses built in the 1940s and 1950s in the heart of the San Fernando Valley. The street they parked on was neat; dry lawns were cut short where only geranium and jade bushes held up against the heat. Margarita's house didn't have a car parked in the driveway but the swamp cooler on the roof suggested someone was home; its hum was audible to the agents as they walked up the front path.

The teenager who opened the door had a sullen expression. TV advertisements blared behind her.

'Yes?'

They identified themselves and explained why they needed to speak to her. She didn't invite them inside the house but was willing to describe the man who had brought the van to the garage.

'Javier dealt with him outside. It was just that I wanted to make a personal call and the owner is real strict about that, makes me use the pay phone on the sidewalk just outside the gate. So I go to use it but the guy with the van was already there and he gave me a look that really scared me. I went away but I was pissed because it was an important call I wanted to make.'

Scott asked, 'Did you hear him say anything?'

'Well, when I came over, he was speaking up so I heard him. It was like he was talking to one of those computer voices, y'know? Like an operator? He said, "Arizona" real loud.'

'Anything else?'

Margarita shook her head. 'No. Soon as he said that was when he realized I was there.'

'Can you describe him?' Eric asked.

'Just a skanky guy. White.'

'Hair color? Eye color?'

'He had a patchy beard that was kinda blond. I think his hair was blond but his hat hid most of it. I don't remember what color his eyes were. Maybe brown?'

'What was his voice like? Any accent?'

'No. I just heard him say that one word.'

Eric pulled out his card and repeated what he'd said to Ruiz earlier about calling if she remembered anything further. When they were back in the Suburban, Scott said, 'You might just get that gold star, Ramos.'

Eric started to reply but then Scott's cell phone rang. He picked up, listened, and said, 'We're on our way back now.'

He looked at Eric. 'Tony's got a name to go

109

with the surgical plate 31/1 found.'

Eric slapped the dashboard in excitement. 'Hot damn!'

'She's an Eleanor Patterson. Lance is checking her out right now to see if she was reported missing.'

'I told you. We're on to this guy.'

'We've got to track him down yet,' Scott cautioned as he started the car.

'Yeah, but if we're interpreting Margarita right, we know he's headed to Arizona. We know the color, the make, and the potential model of the van.'

'But no license plate and no name of the perp.'

'I'm not letting that stop me,' Eric asserted. 'We need to issue a BOLO to Arizona.'

Scott glanced at him as he drove to the canyon road that would take them back to their office. 'Let's do Be On the Lookouts for Arizona *and* California. He may not have made it to AZ yet.'

'OK,' Eric agreed. 'We'll ask LAPD to put it on their BOLO boards.' Now his cell phone rang and he answered. He muted the call as he listened and said, 'Lance is putting through a Detective Kragen from Carlisle PD, regarding the Patterson case.'

Scott nodded and went quiet.


When the caller identified himself as a coroner from Alaska, Carol put him through to Steelie in the lab. Steelie brought the phone to the computer so she could have the digitized X-ray of Thomas Cullen's head on her screen, then she took the call.

'Chuck Talbot,' the matter-of-fact voice said. 'Anchorage ME's Office.'

'Dr Talbot. Good to hear from you.'

'Chuck's fine. Look, this whole situation with the John Doe bullet has caused a bit of a stir up here.'

Steelie couldn't read his tone. 'Oh?'

'It's probably for the best, I don't know. But that's not your problem. I'm calling to inform you of a positive ID for this John Doe as Thomas Cullen. We'll be posting it on the ACB network this afternoon.'

Steelie jotted a note. 'This is great news. Can I ask how you got the match?'

'Dental. It turns out the teeth were where the breakdown was. Or maybe I just want to blame the odontologist.' He chuckled. 'We've been having a feud for years. But I can't actually blame him.' He paused. 'Are we confidential here?'

'Absolutely,' Steelie replied quickly. 'All communications between our agency and coroners are confidential.'

'Fine. So the odont gave us the dental chart on the Doe and we submitted it to the police misper unit for them to put it on NCIC. Like most coroners, I don't have direct access to NCIC. Been trying to get a terminal in my office for, what, seven years? Ten? Anyway, I gave the dental to Missings. Didn't go anywhere, I've now discovered.'

'Well, you definitely can't blame the odont for that.'

'No but I'm still tryin'. Seems that, on request,

111

my autopsy tech sawed out John Doe's max and mandible and couriered it to the odont for the dental report before starting the craniotomy. When I got round to doing the autopsy, I got the bullet no problem but I didn't have the mouth and I assumed the bullet was fresh. Figured the palate would show perimortem trauma, as the rest of the body didn't show signs of cause of death and the tissue was too decomposed for toxicology. So the main result of the post was that bullet. Case closed.'

'You've obviously got the mouth back now, though?'

'Oh, we've had the mouth back this whole time. It's been sitting in the fridge. Just no one looked at it when it came back from the odontologist to see if the trauma to the palate was peri or antemortem, or healed or what. And it *is* healed. That is definitely old trauma, old gunshot. So, we're all having to tighten our belts. My tech was hasty, I wasn't thorough, the odont only reported on the dentition itself and didn't bother to describe the palate, and our police unit didn't do the other half of its job.'

'Well,' Steelie said, wanting to ameliorate the impact of this sorry but not unusual laundry list. 'Even without you ageing the bullet correctly, NCIC would have made this ID if only your postmortem dental info had been uploaded into the system. So I don't think you have too much to beat yourself up about.'

'You think getting cause of death wrong is nothing to beat myself up about? Huh.'

'I meant, this was situational; it's not like you

need to go back to med school. But speaking of COD, do you have anything there?'

'Now that the bullet's ruled out? No. I mean, there wasn't much left of this guy for me to work with. No marks on the bones. It'll probably go down as undetermined, for both cause and manner.'

'And contact with the Cullen family?'

'I'm going to be calling them myself. I've got someone at a funeral home up here that can handle shipping the body back across state lines.'

Steelie looked down at the notes she'd been making. 'Well, Chuck, I guess I don't have any more questions.'

He cleared his throat. 'I've been asked to re-assure you that we are making some procedural changes up here so we'd prefer if you didn't go public with how this ID came about.'

Steelie's cheeks burned. 'We don't do that. We're just trying to facilitate identifications, and quietly.'

'Sure. But you never know what you might set off.'

'What do you mean?' Steelie asked warily.

'Ever picture what it would look like if every parent of a missing person found out that 13,000-odd coroners and MEs, between them, have tens of thousands of Jane and John Does sittin' on ice in this country? Just do the math. You've got a hundred thousand missing persons, at least. They've got one parent each, maybe two, and a couple of siblings. That makes for a heck of a march on Washington.'

Steelie had indeed pictured this but she wasn't prepared to admit it in this context. 'And that's a heck of an imagination you've got there, Chuck. But we're not a lobby group. We're not allowed—'

'But,' the coroner cut her off. 'What I'm also saying, Ms Lander, is that I'm not sure that would be a bad thing.'

He signed off and Steelie was left looking at the phone in her hand, wondering how many other coroners shared Dr Talbot's take on that kind of pressure from families. If she were still in graduate school, she'd do a survey. Maybe she could get someone else to do a survey. She walked to the front of the building, summoning Jayne from her office as she went.

Steelie stood at Carol's counter, knowing that their receptionist already had an idea of what she was about to say, since she'd put Chuck Talbot's call through and she could read Steelie's smile. But Jayne had no idea. She raised her eyebrows at Steelie, who announced, 'Thomas Cullen has been positively identified in Anchorage.'

Jayne just stood still, returning Steelie's grin, so it was Carol who started clapping first. A slow clap that skipped two beats in between, then gradually sped up to one beat in between. Jayne joined in, then Steelie, until they were clapping as fast as they could, like a team psyching itself up after a mid-season win.

Two men from A-1 Electrics delivered the generator to Agency 32/1 just after 4 p.m. As it turned out, they didn't need to spend much time

114

inside the building, as the generator was installed just behind the building, in its own security cage. Just before 5 p.m., Jayne heard Carol announce that Scott was holding on Line 1 for her. She located her copy of the examination report on the freeway body parts, expecting him to ask why there wasn't more to it. Leaving aside the surgical plate in the right arm, they'd only been able to conclude:

*Minimum Number of Individuals: 2. One female, one sex indeterminate*

*Left arm: Female, 40 years ± 15, possible Caucasian, healed fractures, possible ante-mortem defense wounds*

*Right arm: Female, 40 years ± 15, possible Caucasian, mid-shaft surgical plate conjoining proximal and distal humerus*

*Leg: Sex indeterminate, 20 years ± 5, possible Caucasian*

*Torso: Sex indeterminate, 18 years ±, possible Caucasian*

It hadn't looked like much because there was a limit to what a purely external examination could deliver. But then there was that surgical plate in the upper arm.

Scott sounded buoyant. 'I've got good news.'

Jayne sat up straighter in her chair. 'Let me have it.'

'We've got an ID on the arm. Or I should say, arms plural, though that'll have to be confirmed by DNA later.'

'Was it the plate?'

'Yes. That was a great find.'

'It was just sitting there waiting for us! The hard part was not reflecting back the flesh to expose the humerus right there and then.'

'You kind of scare me when you talk like that, Jayne.'

'Sorry. So is she one of your missing women from Georgia?'

'Unconnected. She's a Mrs Patterson from Carlisle, Oregon.'

'Carlisle?'

'Outside Portland.'

'Was she in NCIC?'

'That's the interesting part. She was but not listed as suspicious missing. And get this: she went missing two months ago. Eric's been trying to get details from Oregon. We'll be sending the arms to the coroner up there after we've got the results on whether the left arm goes with the right.'

Jayne looked at the report in front of her. 'And maybe you can run DNA on the torso? That's the other BP that could have been hers.'

'We're all over that.'

'I take it you won't be running DNA from the younger person's leg through CODIS, given that we couldn't even tell you what sex it was?' She was referring to the FBI Laboratory's Combined DNA Index System.

'Even if the Bureau would let me, it won't be

worth it – not enough information. And the leg's not one of your cases?'

'Not enough information.'

'Tell me about it.'

She recalled Scott's desire to get around the backlog at the coroner's office when he'd asked 32/1 to do the preliminary investigation. 'So you're OK with the leg and maybe the torso going to the LA coroner's office after all?'

'ID'ing Patterson makes up for a lot.'

'Yeah.' Jayne smiled. She had said almost those exact words to Gene when he was looking at the 32/1 filing cabinets. Gene had been negative but here was Scott, sharing her positive perspective. This was why she liked the man. 'How's the search for the van going, if you can say?'

'Actually, we've got a lead on that and ... I've ... gotta run.'

Jayne knew Carol had left while she was on the phone, so she went in search of Steelie and found her in the kitchen, washing up cups. She told Steelie about the identification of Patterson.

'*Mrs*? Sounds like he thinks she was married,' Steelie commented. 'I'll bet it was her husband who gave her all those fractures.'

'Or maybe she divorced him and married a new guy.'

Steelie looked at her. 'You live in a dream world.'

'You live in a lawyer's world,' Jayne retorted lightly.

'Oh, that reminds me. Did you remember the raffle ticket books?'

117

'Damn. I completely forgot.'

'It's OK. I did too, until someone from Legal Aid called to remind me that I'd volunteered.'

'You need them today?'

'Yeah. The raffle's tomorrow morning so I have to go straight there—but I don't have to stay. Can I swing by your place tonight and get them?'

'Yeah, I'll be in.'

'I'll call when I'm nearby. Should be around eleven.'

'That late?'

Steelie turned to go. 'I have that thing with those people. Don't ask.'

The pinky-white flower heads waved high above the gaura plants as Jayne carefully lifted them out of her truck. Next were the two geums: absolutely shameless doubles in a clear red, swooning in front of anyone who came near, and sure to meet with Marie's approval. Jayne nestled them in the two terracotta pots she'd bought to replace the ones by her door. She was still debating about whether the damage had been inflicted by possums or raccoons; either had the strength to tip over cacti pots. She made her way up the stairs to her apartment, reached the landing and then stopped.

Three metal washtubs filled with blooming white daisy bushes were arrayed next to her front door. The tubs were different yet complementary sizes, their shine artfully worn off in places. Jayne thought the arrangement was gorgeous, like something from a magazine, and it made her doorway look hip and inviting. She stood back, admiring first them and then her mother, who had to be responsible for this transformation. She'd have to remember to call her after she'd potted the other ridiculous flowers she'd bought, which could now live on the deck. She went inside.

# TEN

Jayne had fallen asleep on her sofa but the scraping noise woke her. She sat up, pushing the open book on her lap to the side, and turned to look at the front door. It was too early to be Steelie and it sounded too loud and definitive to be an animal poking around. It sounded like a person was out there and now ... were they gone? Without a window to look through, she only had a few choices. She could wait for the sound again and try to identify it, look through the peephole, or open the door. The peephole was out. She'd seen a film where someone was shot through the eye doing just that. And she had seen too many people lying dead on autopsy tables after having let their killers in the front door. So she waited to hear the sound again. She almost jumped out of her skin when her cell phone came to life, its vibrations creating a buzzing noise against the coffee table's glass surface.

'Hello?' she half whispered.

'It's Steelie ... are you OK?'

'I thought I heard a noise.'

'What kind of noise?'

'Hang on, I just heard it again. Something on the front landing.'

'Human or non-human?'

'Can't tell. There it is again.'

'Then keep your door locked. I'm less than a minute from your place.'

Jayne decided to sit on the floor, her back against the bedroom door. This gave her a clear view of the front door but kept her hidden from all the windows. She kept the phone cradled in her lap but didn't hear the noise again. When the phone vibrated with another incoming call, she didn't flinch but she still answered quietly.

Steelie sounded confident. 'It's me. I've looked around down here but don't see anything. I'm coming up.'

Jayne got up with relief and went to the front door. She opened it just as Steelie exclaimed, 'Whoa!' and there was a sound of footsteps thudding down the stairs.

'Steelie?!'

Her voice came from the bottom of the stairs. 'Make some noise up there, Jayne. You've got a mother possum on your stairs with her baby. And the baby's big enough to have a name. I'll wait in the driveway.'

Jayne started clapping her hands and whistling. Then she walked forward until she could see around the corner. The possums were about halfway down the stairs and the larger one was the size of a small dog. She was leading her cub in an unhurried manner down the stairs. When they reached the bottom, Steelie turned on the flashlight she was holding and mimicked airport ground staff guiding a plane into its berth, raking the light across the lawn and away from the driveway. The possums obediently headed off into the darkness.

Steelie trotted up the stairs. 'That's probably who you heard.' She looked down at the silver plant tubs by the front door. 'And you got off lightly with the mess. At my place, they get in the dirt, then put their paws in the water I leave out for the birds, wash their hands—'

She broke off and sank down into a crouch by the pots, flicking on her flashlight again. 'Look at this. There's something in the soil.'

'Where?'

'You're at the wrong angle. Come this side.'

Jayne walked over and they crouched down to look at one of the tubs. Something was glinting in the beam of light. It looked like the top of a metal plant marker.

'Has that always been there?' Steelie asked.

'I'm not sure.' She hadn't looked at the daisy bushes closely when she came home but thought she would have noticed the marker. She'd since forgotten to even call Marie to thank her.

'Mind if I pull it out?'

'No, go ahead. It's the sort of thing my mother would do. She's responsible for these things.' Jayne stood up and looked at the roofline of the duplex where a telephone wire seemed to be hanging loosely.

Steelie said, 'It's only got a series of dots, like Braille.'

Jayne looked sharply at the metal tag in Steelie's hand. It was a flat rectangle above a sharpened stake, now studded with soil. A series of dots were etched into the soft metal.

'You think your mother would have brought

122

this by without knocking on your door to say hi? No way, Jayne, not Marie.'

'She brought the plants without telling me.' They stood for a moment in silence. 'Why don't I call her?'

She stepped inside while Steelie began poking around in the other plant tubs. While Jayne waited for Marie to answer, she took the book of raffle tickets from the kitchen counter and waved them in front of Steelie, who pocketed them with a nod.

Marie answered after five rings.

'Well, hello darling! To what do I owe this pleasure?'

'I wanted to thank you for the daisies and the tubs. Sorry I didn't do it right away.'

'Daisies?'

'Yeah, the ones in the metal washtubs.'

'By your front door?'

'Yes.' Jayne was relieved that her mother remembered them.

'Well, I'm glad someone replaced those cacti, but it wasn't me, darling.'

'Wait. So you didn't leave a plant marker in them today?'

'No, but what a cute idea!'

'It's not cute if *you* didn't do it!'

'Jayne, what's going on? You sound ... frazzled.'

'Look, did you tell anyone about my cacti?'

'Why would I tell anyone?'

'You know, like one of your landscapers? Tell them to replace the cacti for me?'

'No. What *is* this? Jayne?'

She didn't answer because Steelie had come to stand in the doorway and was making a throat-slitting motion, which Jayne took to mean, *Get off the phone NOW.*

'I'll call you later, Mom. Bye.'

She looked at Steelie who now had a finger to her lips and was beckoning to her.

Steelie shined light into the plant tub closest to the house. She had excavated more soil than the possums had and the landing was a mess. The root ball of the daisy bush was exposed and nestled beneath it was a plastic box. Steelie gently tilted the tub to expose its underside. A coated wire snaked out of the central drainage hole and ran under the landing. Steelie used the light to trace the wire along the inner edge of the floorboards until it disappeared into a small hole just under the threshold to her apartment. The hair on the back of Jayne's neck stood up.

Steelie whispered, 'Get your purse and whatever else you want. You're coming to my place and we'll call for help from there.'

Jayne was filled with an overwhelming desire to get out of there and perhaps never come back. A few minutes later, she was driving behind Steelie, her overnight bag on the bench seat next to her, concentrating on the Wrangler's tail lights. She couldn't think; felt frightened out of all proportion and that fact bothered her as much as the situation itself.

Her cell phone rang and Jayne jumped again. She knew it would be half an hour or so before she settled down. It was Steelie on the phone, telling Jayne she was stopping for 'emergency ice cream' and confirming that Jayne had the spare key. Steelie pulled into the left turn lane for the Atwater Village Shopping Center, followed by the sedan behind Jayne, who herself indicated a right turn.

Jayne drove slowly through Atwater's rows of 1920's Spanish houses, each looking compact and picturesque under graceful towering trees. Few had fences, so the streets felt open and inviting. Narrow driveways separated most houses, enough of whose stucco finishes were painted in earthy tones to give away mild gentrification.

She parked in front of the *casita*, noticing that Steelie had left a light on inside but only sheer shades pulled over the front windows. That wasn't like Steelie but the effect was nice. The glow emphasized the arches of the tall living room windows while the up-lights among the aloes in the garden picked out the interlocking curves of the clay roof tiles. Jayne's shoes crunched on the gravel path to the front porch, reminding her of how Marie and Steelie had collaborated to make a water-conscious garden on a budget. She unlocked the door and stepped inside.

Steelie waited for the arrow, feeling a little worried. She was used to Jayne's fears, which almost bordered on paranoia, but she knew from where they originated. She'd learned it was better to address whatever had frightened Jayne rather than try to talk her out of it. PTSD didn't work like that.

But this was different. There was something man-made in the plant tubs outside Jayne's front door. Someone had put it there, and Steelie could not come up with a ready explanation. She made the turn into the shopping center parking lot. Almost immediately, she was blinded by light reflected in her rearview mirror. She put her hand up to cut the glare. The side mirror showed nothing but bright light. Then she heard the too-brief *wa-woop* of a siren behind her. It seemed to echo on the night air. Odd that she hadn't noticed a police cruiser before now and she didn't think she'd rolled through a red light anywhere.

There were plenty of parking spaces to choose from at this time of night and she navigated the Jeep into one. She locked the door, opened the window, and got out her identification, using her side mirror to see if the officer was approaching. She could barely see him because the spotlight on his vehicle had made a silhouette of his form but she noted his swagger and that he didn't make the usual stop to write down her license plate number.

When he reached her window, the bright light slanted across his oversized, tinted glasses. It was impossible to see his eyes.

'Ma'am.'

'Evening, Officer.' Steelie scanned his uniform for his badge. The way he was leaning hid most of his nametag – 'Marron' or 'Marion'.

'Do you know why I stopped you?'

'No. Is there a problem?' She was looking at his mouth since she couldn't see his eyes. A light-colored moustache all but hid his upper lip.

'One of your tail lights is out.'

'Really? Which one?'

'Step out of the vehicle, Ma'am.'

'Don't you want to check my license and registration?'

'Please step out of the vehicle, ma'am.' He took a step back and crossed his arms over his chest. 'I can help you determine if it's a fuse or a bulb. It's a lot cheaper to fix if it's a fuse.'

Warning bells were going off in Steelie's mind but she couldn't tell how much was Jayne's paranoia infecting her and how much was her ex-Legal Aid bias against police but she was going to follow Legal Aid's advice to its clients. 'Can I see your ID first, please?' She tried to smile. 'Never can be too sure these days.'

'No, ma'am, I guess you can't.' He came to the window and leaned his right arm on the door. He used his left hand to pull a vinyl badge envelope from his top pocket and flashed it quickly before replacing it.

Steelie barely made out a photo with some writing next to it. It had *looked* OK. She told herself to stop being paranoid and moved to unlock the door. Then she noticed his finger-nails. They were long. They seemed too long for a cop. Her pulse quickened.

'Sorry, could I see it closer, please?'

She wasn't ready when he tried to open the door, and then reached through the window. He seemed to know the lock was low and forward and his hand scrabbled for it, banging Steelie's knee. She screamed and grabbed for the ignition. She over-started the engine, which whined, then roared to life. Throwing the car into first gear, she slammed on the gas and popped the clutch. The car peeled out, the window frame slamming the cop's elbow.

'God dammit!' he shouted, leaping back.

One of the Jeep's wheels went directly over the concrete bumper at the front of the parking space and Steelie momentarily drove on the passenger-side wheels until the vehicle dropped back down. As soon as all four tires gained purchase, she was at the exit in an instant. Only the Jeep's high clearance saved it from scraping heavily across the deep gutter where the driveway met the road but her head almost hit the ceiling when the car bounced across the intersection. As she raced down the nearest residential street, her heart pounded. She barely watched the road ahead as she scanned her rearview mirror, looking for chasing headlights.

When she halted in her own driveway minutes later, she only calmed down when she realized she wouldn't be able to get her keys out of the ignition until she actually shut off the engine. A buzzer sounded as she opened her door and she whipped her head around to the street before recognizing the sound as her own car's warning that the lights were still on. She walked to the back of the car, expecting to see one of the tail lights darkened. Both lights were working. She squeezed her eyes closed for a second, then took a last look around the street before she turned off the lights, pulled a car cover over the Jeep, and ran to her front door.

\* \* \*

When Jayne saw the look on Steelie's face, she knew not to ask about the ice cream but when Steelie double-locked the front door and pulled closed the living room curtains, Jayne sat up on the sofa. Steelie kept moving fast toward the rear of the house. Jayne first heard the slap of venetian blinds as Steelie wrenched them closed at the kitchen window that overlooked the small back yard, then the sound of the fridge or freezer, followed by the microwave starting. When Jayne heard the bolt at the back door slide into place, she got up. She'd only known Steelie to throw that bolt when she was going out of town. She crossed to the kitchen as Steelie came in from the back hall and the microwave dinged.

Jayne asked nervously, 'What's going on?'

Steelie shook her head as she pulled a wax paper-wrapped parcel out of the microwave. She ate what Jayne recognized as a defrosted Krispy Kreme donut in three bites. Only then did she speak.

'I'm either about to be arrested for assaulting a cop or I've just escaped being kidnapped by a total nutcase. I know,' she looked at Jayne. 'You'd think I'd be able to tell the difference.'

Jayne wrapped her arms around herself. 'What happened?'

Steelie recounted the incident at the shopping center but she couldn't do it without pacing to the front window periodically and peering out at the street through a chink in the curtains. Finally, she said, 'At first I thought he was legit. But then there were those fingernails and I couldn't see anything! *And* he didn't want my ID! I mean,

129

that's so not like them. God, this sounds stupid now.'

Jayne sounded more confident than she felt. 'No, it doesn't. Cops are supposed to identify themselves properly, not wrench your car door open. It's not like he stopped you after a high-speed chase.'

'I should have known when he got out of the cruiser right away. Don't they usually sit there for a couple minutes while they run your license plate through NCIC?'

'I think so. But this was a tail light stop.'

'Except it wasn't.'

'Wait, what?'

'Sorry, I forgot that part.' Steelie glanced out the front window again. 'I checked. My tail lights are fine.'

'Oh my God.' Jayne came around to sit on the sofa. 'What the hell is this? Why would a cop tell you to get out of your car to look at a tail light you would immediately see was just fine?'

'Well, it would get me out of my car, wouldn't it? And once there, I'm just another vic he can overpower.'

Jayne was shaking her head. 'But if he assaults you, you could ID him later. It's risky as hell.'

Steelie sat down next to her, arms folded across her chest. 'Maybe it was a carjacking.'

'In Atwater Village?'

'Why not? Look at it. Late at night, deserted parking lot, some guy with a decommissioned police cruiser painted a dark color just waits for someone to pull in. Uses a fake uniform picked up at any Hollywood costume shop to get the person out of their vehicle on the fake pull. He hits 'em on the head or whatever once they're out, and he gets to go off in their – presumably nicer – vehicle. Parts will be sold to fifteen shops all over town by the time you can call the real cops.'

'Do you really believe that?'

Steelie was silent for a moment, thinking. 'No. It's an awful lot of trouble for your typical opportunist. So if he was a cop, he probably already has my license plate and he *will* come and get me...'

'I hear another "and" in there.'

'And ... I was thinking about your place. The wire. What if it's connected? Think about it, Jayne. We find some black box on your porch, in plant pots delivered by someone unknown. Wire is drilled into your house. We leave, you come here, I get pulled over by a fake cop who's followed me into the parking lot.'

Jayne grabbed her arm. 'I've just remembered! I saw that car pull in behind you. He had been behind me!'

'From where? How far back did you notice him?' Steelie looked at her intently.

'Um, let me think. He was there when we turn-ed on to Los Feliz.'

'By Griffith Park?'

'Yeah. I definitely remember him being there after we crossed the river, because I was looking behind me for anyone merging off the Five.'

'You're going forwards, Jayne. Did you see him *before* we turned on to Los Feliz?'

Jayne thought. 'No.' She exhaled. 'I don't

remember anything from before then.'

Steelie walked to the telephone hanging on the wall in the kitchen. 'I'm going to call Bud Reese. I'll bet his wife hasn't let him retire yet.'

'But doesn't he work out of Downtown?'

'He'll know who to call over here.'

Jayne listened as Steelie greeted Reese, one of the LAPD officers she had had a lot of interaction with while working at Legal Aid. She described what had happened to her that evening and then described the wire in the plant pots. Then she listened while making notes on a pad. She laughed once and said, 'Give me a little credit, Bud.' Eventually, she thanked him and hung up.

Steelie threw the pencil down on the pad. 'OK, so he says I have grounds to make a complaint because the guy probably was a cop – a bad one. He gave me the number to call. He doesn't think it was a carjacking, though they just picked up two guys for impersonating cops while shaking down undocumented immigrants who keep stalls in the Garment District. So it's not unheard of. But the wire in your pots is another story. He asked if we'd ruled out a self-watering system.'

'He thinks this is funny?'

'No, he thinks *he's* funny. The wire he takes seriously. He said wires going toward thresholds "scream" tapping to him.'

'Tapping? Like bugging?'

'Like that. He didn't want to touch it with a ten-foot pole. Said it was very unlikely whatever's going on will end up in LAPD's jurisdiction so he recommended we go direct to the

FBI.'

Jayne scrunched her hair. 'God, Steelie. I really, *really* don't want to call Scott.'

'Why not?'

'Because there's no way to tell him what happened without him finding out that I ... that I overreacted to some noise on my porch.'

'It wasn't an overreaction for someone with PTSD.'

'Argh! How many times do I have to tell you? I do not have PTSD!'

Steelie compressed her lips. 'Yeah, I got that memo. So, what you're actually telling me is that Scott doesn't know that you have symptoms of some *thing* that isn't Post-Traumatic Stress Disorder but, ya know, looks just like it?'

Jayne glared at her but then sighed and shook her head in the negative.

Steelie crossed her arms. 'Here I always thought you kept things going long-distance with Scott because you were holding out for when you two lived in the same city. Now I see you've just been hiding behind the telephone.'

Jayne only shrugged.

'God, Jayne, you have no reason to hide anything. You've nothing to be ashamed of! How many times do I have to tell *you*?'

Jayne's voice was small. 'I just know he'll see me as damaged goods and that'll be the end of it.'

Steelie crossed the room to put a hand on Jayne's shoulder. 'The problem isn't how he sees you, it's how you see yourself. Plus, he probably knows about trauma. He was in Kosovo when

133

the bombs were still dropping.'

'Exactly. And he's never mentioned repercussions.'

Steelie shrugged. 'That just makes him lucky, not superhuman.' She let go of Jayne and looked at her watch. 'I'm going to call him and Eric first thing tomorrow. In the meantime, you're staying here. Get up so I can make the sofa bed.'

Jayne went to the kitchen. 'I wasn't planning on leaving you here to get attacked by the rogue cop-carjacker who probably has your address.'

'He never even looked at my license!'

Jayne opened the fridge and leaned down to examine its shelves. 'You don't know what he looked at. You got anything to eat in here? What *is* all this stuff? Looks like pressed cardboard.'

Steelie came in from the hall with two pillows and some sheets in her arms. 'That's Tofurkey. Trader Joe's special.'

'Why did you give up meat only to eat false meat?'

'You want me to short-sheet your sofa bed? No? Then I suggest you shut up and be glad when I serve it up for breakfast tomorrow.'

Jayne straightened up and saw that Steelie's eyes were troubled despite her light tone. She closed the door of the fridge and leaned on it, overwhelmed with the desire to lie down and go to sleep.

# DAY FOUR

## Friday

# ELEVEN

Eric drove fast into the parking lot beneath the FBI building on Wilshire. He forced himself to slow down once in the dark, cramped space but he undid his seatbelt even before he'd turned off the ignition. Taking his briefcase from the back seat, he locked the car and headed for the elevator, which seemed to be running slower than usual this morning. Once inside the elevator, he hit four. Nothing happened. He hit the 'Door Close' button several times in quick succession. The doors crawled shut.

When they opened again, Eric turned sideways to get out shoulder first before the doors had finished their slow retraction. He unlocked the door to the hall that led to his office. Lance, the office administrator, wasn't in yet and neither was Scott. Eric unlocked their office and his eyes immediately went to the printer. Nothing. He sat down at the NCIC computer just in case something had come in from an Arizona police department or the California Highway Patrol

135

responding to the BOLO on the gold van. Nothing.

'Damn.'

His cell phone rang. When he answered, he could hear the road noise in the background and greeted his partner. 'Yeah, Scott.'

'Anything?'

'No.'

'OK, I think I have something. We know the perp's got body parts frozen in the back of the van, right? If he drove out to Arizona at this time of year, he might've done it at night because of the daytime heat. Now, unless he had a generator, he would have needed an electrical hook-up for the freezer if he stopped along the way. Following me?'

Eric was pulling a notepad toward him. 'Oh yeah.'

'We should check out campgrounds with hook-ups between here and Arizona, see if they had a visit from this guy during the week.'

'Going along I-10?'

'Let's start with that. It would make a long drive even longer if he was using blue highways and they're less likely to have places for hook-up. So, you on top of this?'

'Yes. What's your ETA?'

'Twenty minutes.'

They signed off and Eric started looking up campgrounds along Interstate 10. The phone on his desk rang and he glanced at the caller identification. It was a Los Angeles area code but he didn't recognize the number. He picked up and identified himself.

'Hey, Eric, it's Steelie Lander.'

Eric relaxed and his eyes went back to the computer screen. 'Hey, Steelie. Where are you calling from?'

'My house. Why, you can you see the number?'

'Yeah. How you doing?'

'Not bad but I wondered, would you and Scott have some time for us today? We'd like to run something by you.'

Eric was scrolling down the list of campgrounds on the screen.

Steelie added, 'In your professional capacity.'

'That shouldn't be a problem. It might be late in the day. Can I ask what it's about?' He clicked on a web link.

'Bugging, speaking generally.'

Eric's eyes fixed on the information that had just come up on the screen. 'Well, that sounds mysterious enough. I'll call you as soon as I can.'

Eric barely registered Steelie's thanks before he signed off with her and began dialing an outside line.

Sitting next to Steelie in the lab, Jayne felt groggy from lack of sleep and the after-effects of stress. Steelie's sofa bed was not the most comfortable and she had been awake too long thinking about the wire in the plant tubs. She tried to re-focus on the conference call she and Steelie had just accepted from Thomas Cullen's parents.

Donald and Patricia were each talking over the other. Patricia's sniffles were audible.

Donald was saying, 'We've heard from a coroner in Alaska – here dear, take the whole box. And they said that—' He was interrupted by Patricia, who seemed to have regained her composure.

'They said that information you gave them about Tom was what made the difference and—'

Her husband leapfrogged again. 'We'd like to thank you, very much.'

'And we wondered if the doctor told you how Tom died?' Patricia sounded hesitant and hopeful.

'Wasn't he able to tell you anything?' Steelie had to tread carefully, unsure of how Chuck Talbot would have worded things or if there was any mention of the earlier gunshot wound that left the bullet in their son's head.

'Well,' Donald began, 'he said they couldn't tell how he died. Now, we didn't think that was possible, but we get most of our information from TV. Is it possible to just not know?'

Jayne answered, 'Yes, sometimes it can be difficult to tell how someone died, if the body hasn't retained enough traces. If you're concerned, you can have an investigation done by a private pathologist, although they're expensive and may still not give you any answers.'

'Yes, well, I don't know if we'll go to those lengths,' he said hurriedly. 'But we thought that before the funeral, we'd make a decision about any more ... investigation.'

'Right now, we're just glad to know where he is and to have him back. Thank you – both of you. We never expected answers so quickly.'

Patricia sounded on the verge of tears again.

Jayne sat silently watching Steelie as she hung up the phone and wrote a note about the call to add to the Cullen file. Feeling like a sleepwalker, she followed Steelie to the front of the building where Carol was gathering her things for her usual early departure on Fridays.

Steelie asked, 'Did you speak with the Cullens before you put their call through?'

'Yes,' Carol paused in her actions.

'Thanks. They seemed to be in a good place, despite the fact they've just learned their son's been dead for years.'

'Well, we talked about moving past things we can't change, whether it's related to anger at the police for not finding him sooner or anger at themselves for not being able to prevent what happened.'

Jayne turned from where she was staring absently out the front window. 'Did you get a sense of how they're going to cope with not knowing exactly how Thomas died?'

'I think Patricia is finding it difficult. She told me that she's a statistician and is used to mining information for as long as it takes to turn it into meaningful data but...' Carol waggled her hand from side to side. 'She can't really apply that to this situation. I think it's shaking her entire foundation for life, work, everything.'

As Carol left, Steelie handed all her notes related to the Cullen case to Jayne. Jayne stood at the window a minute longer, listening to Steelie walk away, and then she turned into her office. She filed the notes in the folder labeled

139

'CULLEN, Thomas, (Tom)' and then took the whole folder to the cabinet that held closed cases. Opening the drawer reminded her of Gene's visit to the office and how unimpressed he'd been by the Agency's completion numbers.

So far, every missing person who'd been found using an Agency 32/1 profile had been found dead. There was no way of telling how many of the missing people were alive or whose bodies had been hidden by killers in the hope they would never be found. She wondered if the killers realized that they harmed countless others by this practice? That it was a further injury?

As she slotted Thomas Cullen's folder in the drawer, she found herself thinking about the bodies she'd helped to exhume from the mass graves near Srebrenica, the steep slopes of Kigali. She thought about the attempts made by the killers to hide the identities of the dead. How it stunted survivors' attempts to grieve, to move on through the healing rites of washing the deceased's body, a funeral followed by cremation or burial, the therapeutic ritual of visiting their relative's grave for the rest of their lives.

The lack of those rituals tortured survivors; individuals who perhaps never came into contact with their torturers. It was in this way that the killers planted seeds of disruption that would germinate well into the future. And in the meantime, bodies lay in the ground, mingled with friends and strangers, teachers, lovers, the person standing next to them when they were pulled off the bus and shot, the person they fell on to when they were hit across the forehead. Jayne saw them all in her mind's eye, the bodies they'd been unable to identify. She'd never known whether subsequent teams had identified them. Yes, it was torture to not know.

She knew where these thoughts could take her but she was still surprised to hear the sob escape. It came from so low down that she clutched her abdomen, thinking she could stop the next one. But it erupted, always stronger than her will, and caught her breath, forcing tears. She wiped them away impatiently and looked at the open drawer of closed cases. The dark recess of the empty section felt like a reproach. She slammed the drawer closed.

'Pull yourself together,' she muttered. Then, louder, 'And stop talking to yourself.'

'Hey, that's my line.'

Jayne whirled. Steelie was in the doorway. 'Did you have to creep up on me like that?'

Steelie walked into the room. 'Oh, please! Most of LA heard that file drawer slam shut. I was just the one who pulled the short straw to go investigate.'

Jayne wiped her face and went to sit at her desk.

Steelie looked down at her. 'Look ... we just helped get one person home. Right? Focus on the positive.' Her cell phone rang and she looked at the readout.

Jayne listened to Steelie say, 'Eric! How ya doin'?' and then decided to follow Steelie's advice. She tapped out a short email to Gene, almost boasting that the Agency had closed another case. She pressed *Send* and looked up to see her friend checking her watch.

'Yeah. Can we make it Café Tropical on Sunset? Do you know it? 'Kay, see you there.' Steelie hung up and turned off Jayne's desk lamp. 'Come on, let's get some food in you.'

# TWELVE

Driving along Hyperion towards Sunset Boulevard, Jayne kept checking her rearview mirror. 'Another dark Chevy or maybe a Lincoln Town car.'

'You've got to look for a spotlight on the driver's side,' said Steelie, turning around to look out the window behind the truck's bench seat. 'I think whatever you just saw turned into the parking lot at a bank.'

Jayne glanced at Steelie. 'You say you're not scared by what happened last night and yet you didn't want to put your car on the road today.' She looked in her rearview mirror before glancing over again. 'I think maybe you are a little scared.'

Steelie jerked a thumb out her window. 'You just missed the shortcut to Sunset.'

'Oh, damn.'

Forty minutes later, they were finished with a dinner consumed under an umbrella on the sidewalk outside Tropical. Inside, the Cuban café was busy, diners crowding around varnished pine tables after moving potted spider plants to windowsills to make more space.

Steelie had just gone inside to order coffee when Jayne saw Scott and Eric drive past,

143

looking for a parking space on the adjacent residential street. She ducked inside the door and told Steelie to increase the coffee order.

The Suburban parked at the end of the block. When Scott and Eric came up the street, Jayne noticed that they were still wearing their office clothes: dark pants and white shirts, the latter now open at the neck. They'd removed their jackets and ties but still didn't quite fit in with the Friday evening crowd at the café with its mix of sandal-wearing academics, kids wearing Che Guevara t-shirts, and people who were either too cool or too broke to go to the Westside for entertainment. As she watched the agents advancing, she realized they'd probably never fit in to a café culture because they were too watchful; they took in rooflines and locations of cars, their posture looked more alert than most, and they walked in step with each other without looking like they meant to do it.

Steelie came out as they arrived. They shook hands. 'How you guys doing?'

'Glad it's Friday,' Eric replied, taking a chair.

'I'll second that,' said Scott, putting his hand out towards Jayne.

She took his hand but was afraid he would be able to tell she'd been crying less than an hour earlier, so she addressed Eric. 'Long week?'

'Oh yeah. But next week's going to be a doozy.'

'Why's that?' asked Steelie.

'Well, we're going to Arizona and if it wasn't bad enough to lose a day driving there, we're on stake-out for a couple of days.'

'And nights,' said Scott, waving his finger. 'Can't forget the nights.'

'What's in Arizona?' Jayne asked, stealing a look at him over the top of her mug.

'Ironically, it's where the Georgia license plate takes us.' He settled in his seat and told them about tracking down the van through body shops near the freeway.

Steelie said, 'OK, so you've got this description of a guy and his van and you know he tried to call someone in Arizona. What does that add up to?'

'Well, we initiated a search of campgrounds between LA and Tucson, figuring that if he headed out there he had to rest at some point.'

'And,' interjected Eric, 'given he's got a freezer in the back, he'd need to stop at a place where he could hook up power or recharge a battery.'

'We got a hit at a KOA campground nine miles west of Phoenix. The old guy who runs the ground doesn't hold much stock in keeping records of license plates but told us that a van matching our description hooked up there last night for just a couple of hours. Seems this old guy had a nice chat with the driver of the van who mentioned he was heading over to Mesa.'

'Old guy reckons he can learn more about people from talking to 'em, not taking down their ID,' Eric added.

'Turns out he might be right,' said Scott. 'We put out a request for Phoenix PD to look out for the vehicle in Mesa and it seems they've found it parked in a suburban side street. The van's the right make and model, the right color, and has a padlock on the back door handles.'

Steelie and Jayne looked at each other.

'That sounds like the one, right?' said Jayne, turning to Scott.

'Maybe,' replied Scott. 'But it's not wearing a Georgia plate. That may or may not be significant because it's easy to flip a plate. But there's enough to warrant checking it out.'

'I hope it's the right one,' Jayne said, then had to avert her eyes when she had a sudden vision of the body parts by the freeway. A leg, a midriff, Mrs Patterson's arms. Jayne pictured the van in Arizona leading to the rest of Mrs Patterson.

Steelie pushed her chair back. 'Anyone for more coffee?'

'I'll get it,' Eric said, joining her as she turned into the café's side door.

Jayne hoped that by looking upwards, the tears welling up in her eyes would just slide back to where they came from. Music from the café's outdoor speakers was suddenly more audible, a live recording of Ruben Blades' *America*.

'Hey,' Scott said gently.

Jayne chanced a look at him. The tiny movement gave a waiting teardrop its big break and it scudded down her cheek before she could brush it away. But something in his expression made her feel like she might be able to leave the wet trail, that when it was dry, it would be as though it had never happened.

'Hey, yourself,' she replied. It was their traditional phone greeting and the fact that he'd used it now comforted her.

'Thinking about Mrs Patterson?'

Her lips parted in surprise. 'How did you know?'

'I was thinking about her myself. Or I should say, talking about this case with you and Steelie always makes me think about the victims, not the perps.'

He put his elbows on the table as he looked toward the traffic stopped at the light on Sunset. 'Y'know, when I was sent to Kosovo, I was just thinking about killers – people who burned their victims alive after locking them in a house – what their psychology was. But once I'd been in one of those houses, trying to work out if my eyes were tricking me or if the ash on the floor was actually a person reduced to a ... to a fucking shadow...'

Jayne felt her arms come out in goose bumps as she watched him.

He looked back to her. 'Well, I came out just thinking about bodies. And I'd guess that's how it is for you all the time.'

Jayne was stunned into silence. Any time they'd talked about Kosovo before, he'd never described this; just as she'd never described seeing Benni blown to pieces by a mine when on their way to a gravesite ... that day in northern Kosovo, that day of blood, and sweat, but no tears. Those came later, when she was home, jumpy and demoralized, not sleeping well, the type of person for whom an empty filing cabinet could now produce an outpouring of pent-up grief; mingled grief about victims and killers, graves and booby traps, life and loss. These were her reasons for omission with Scott, and other people. And now she knew he'd omitted things too.

She examined his face, his features softened in the glow of lights threaded along the café's umbrellas, looking for physical traces that he was like her. But he didn't look like damaged goods. He looked rested, excited, and engaged, his fingers twirling the salt shaker on the table between them. She sensed his anticipation to get to Arizona and now understood this fundamental difference between them, why he seemed so balanced. The same phenomena might demoralize them both but where she got stuck or felt overwhelmed, he pushed through, powered on, and closed the case. Maybe he could be future-oriented because it was his job to catch perpetrators who were still out there, not stop at digging up evidence of their past deeds, as she had done, as she had had to do with the UN.

She noticed he had stilled the salt shaker. She wanted to pull his hands to her lips and thank him for caring about people reduced to shadows. Especially when he needn't because that wasn't his job; when he needn't look back, only forward.

Steelie's voice came from behind her. 'Here you go. Long line but worth the wait.'

Eric put a mug down in front of Jayne. 'Steelie tells me you've got some kind of situation at your place.'

Scott looked from Jayne to his partner. 'What's this?'

'Looks like maybe someone planted a bugging

device outside Jayne's apartment.'

Scott's eyebrows lifted. *'This* is what you wanted to talk to us about? When Eric said bugging, I figured you meant legals or clearances. If you'd have said something, we could have brought sweeping equipment.'

Eric said, 'We did bring sweeping equipment.' He responded to Scott's look of surprise. 'That's why they pay me the big bucks. Now, tell us what you know, Jayne.'

'Look, I don't really *know* anything,' Jayne said, feeling frustrated with Steelie for no good reason. 'There's a wire coming out of a box inside the soil of a plant pot—'

Steelie interrupted. 'That was left on Jayne's porch anonymously.'

Jayne countered, 'But my situation, as you're calling it, is probably nothing compared to Steelie's.' She enjoyed watching Eric turn on Steelie.

'You didn't mention anything.' Eric sounded almost accusatory.

Jayne continued. 'She didn't say she was pulled over on a fake tail light stop by a cop who maybe wasn't a cop and tried to drag her out of the car?'

He looked concerned. 'Give me that again.'

Jayne gestured at Steelie, who described the events from the Atwater Village Shopping Center the night before.

Scott had the first question. 'You drove off while his arm was in the car and he didn't follow you?'

'Yeah. Stupid, right?'

He smirked. 'More like gutsy. You report it?'

149

Steelie shook her head. 'I just called an old friend at Parker Center. He said I had grounds for a complaint, which I can file even if I don't know whether he was an officer or just pretending to be one. I guess the Ombudsman – or whoever – will work that part out. But let me ask you, do you think a cop would act that way?'

'Well,' Scott replied, 'some aspects don't sound right. The fact that he was riding solo, him not letting you get a good look at his badge, grabbing the lock on your door. And, of course, not following you. Most cops would track you down, if only to save themselves from being a laughing stock back at the House.'

Eric said, 'If he was a cop, you'll be getting a summons in the mail any day. If he wasn't ... you maybe got a lucky break in getting away from a real piece of work. And you should watch your back.'

Steelie frowned. 'What do you mean?'

'You live in your own house, right?'

She nodded.

'Alone?'

Steelie jutted her chin upwards slightly. 'At the moment.'

'Got a dog?' Eric asked.

'No.'

'Got a gun?'

'Hell, no!'

'Well, ma'am,' Eric had assumed a southern drawl. 'What *do* you have?'

'Don't listen to him,' said Scott. 'You don't have to get a gun. Just stay alert. And maybe curb your late-night ice cream runs.'

Eric added: 'And you should call us – either of us – if something like that happens again. I'm in Hollywood and Scott's in Downtown. Only a few minutes from either of you.' He saw Steelie's expression. 'Guess you didn't know we lived so close, huh?'

She recovered, 'No, I just didn't realize government agents *had* homes. What do you guys do there, anyway? I'd find that interesting from an anthropological perspective.'

Looking at Jayne, Scott said, 'It wouldn't be more interesting than finding suspicious boxes hidden on your porch,' said Scott. 'Where're you parked? We'll follow you over.'

Jayne tried not to leave the Suburban behind at any traffic lights on the way to her apartment, so she was driving slower than usual. It made the drive hypnotic as the narrow road wound gently uphill from Sunset.

Steelie said, 'The reservoir looks calm tonight.'

Jayne looked across the water, catching glimpses between trees. 'In a dark way.'

'Maybe I should get a dog.'

'Maybe I should, too.'

They lapsed into silence. Jayne pulled in front of her duplex and waved her arm out the window for Scott to park in the driveway. Then she drove further along Silver Lake Boulevard until she found a parking space. They walked back.

Eric was holding a case. 'Lead the way.'

Jayne went up the stairs first. What she saw as she rounded the corner of the landing surprised her so much that she came to a dead halt. Scott collided into her back and put a hand on her waist. Behind him, Eric exclaimed but was able to stop in time and put out a warning hand to Steelie, who called up to Jayne.

'What is it?'

Jayne looked past the others to Steelie, her eyes wide, the porch light casting a hazy glow across her face. She spoke through clenched teeth.

'They're not here.'

The landing was clean. No pots, no soil, no wire.

# THIRTEEN

Scott could feel Jayne start to tremble and knew she wouldn't be aware that she was trying to back down the stairs even though he was right behind her. As nice as it was to have her moving against him, he would enjoy it more if she intended to do it. He could only see the back of her head, but with his hand firmly on her waist he knew he was reading her right. She was experiencing a fear made more intense because it was brought on by the absence of something.

He slid a hand over hers and moved it to the railing, forcing her fingers to curl around it by using pressure from his own. Then he twisted around to Eric and gestured upwards with his head. Eric nodded and squeezed past them to reach the landing.

Scott then looked at Steelie and saw that her usual wry-tough expression was gone, replaced with something taut and far away, like she was speed-thinking through a million topics. He knew he had to get her to lock down on something. 'Steelie.' He watched her focus on him. 'Keep an eye on her, OK?'

When she spoke, her voice had its usual clip. 'No intention of doing otherwise.' She came up the stairs as he let go of Jayne's hand. Then he stepped on to the landing.

Eric was crouched in front of the door with a flashlight. He ran a gloved finger across the wood siding on the wall just above the floor of the landing and then stopped. Holding his finger in place, he passed the flashlight to Scott who kept it steady on his partner's hand while Eric selected a tiny metal tool with a curved end from the open toolkit beside him. He dug at the wall gently and a plug of material softer than wood but well camouflaged against the siding came away on the tool and left a small hole.

He glanced up at Scott, who returned the flashlight and turned to Jayne, who was still gripping the handrail. She was looking at the doorway, brows knitted and chewing her bottom lip. Scott wanted to make her stop and kissing her would have been his preferred method.

'When were you last here?'

Steelie spoke when Jayne didn't respond. 'Yesterday. She stayed at my place last night.'

'Can we open your door?' He was still directing the questions to Jayne.

She was watching Eric thread a wire into the hole he'd exposed. She nodded.

'Just need your keys,' said Scott.

She spoke without taking her eyes off of Eric. 'Don't know where they are.'

'I think they're in your hand.'

She looked at him then and he saw confusion and fatigue in her eyes. Steelie was the one who took the keys from her and passed them over. Scott unlocked the front door. He opened it but didn't go in. Instead, he waited for Eric to continue threading his wire through the hole on the outside. When Eric depressed a switch at the other end of the wire, light glowed weakly from under the metal bar over the threshold. After a bit more threading, the wire and its bright headlamp came out through a hole where one of the screws on the threshold plate should have been, but wasn't.

Eric spoke softly to Scott. 'No doubt there was something here. Probably audio, though it's the right size for a fiberscope video package. Whoever set it up has done a nice clean-up job.'

He began pulling out the wire. 'I don't think we'll find anything in here but let's sweep the place.'

Eric looked back at Steelie and Jayne. 'We're going to check the place for bugs and then you should come in and see if anything's missing or out of place.'

When they entered the apartment, Scott was acutely aware that this was a step beyond the peculiar closeness he and Jayne had maintained over the years. Turning on the lights revealed a large room that seemed like two rooms due to the placement of the living room furniture; two yellow sofas made an L under a beam bisecting the ceiling. Narrow tables backed both sides of the L and were laden with large lamps and neat stacks of *Architectural Digest.*

When he turned from checking the lock on the sliding glass door to the deck, he pictured Jayne sitting on the sofa, her feet on the glass coffee table, looking at the corner fireplace. Then he realized with a start that the image had turned into one of him lying intertwined with her on that sofa. He tried to get back to the task at hand. Eric was continuing methodically with the bug detection unit, now passing it behind bookshelves and a pine TV cabinet. So far, the unit wasn't raising any red flags.

Scott crossed the full length of the room, past the glass dining table and the front door where Jayne and Steelie were hovering, and stepped into the kitchen. He checked all the locks on the windows. Nothing had been forced or tampered with so he moved on to the bedroom, knowing Eric would follow him with the detection unit.

Scott was surprised by the femininity of the bedroom compared to the rest of the place. A blanket was draped at the foot of a large bed and numerous pillows of different shapes were ranged at the head under a sizeable window. He went directly to the window to check its lock and had to navigate a complicated set of semi-transparent curtains running on different tracks. Leaning in, he jogged the bedside table and looked down to make sure he hadn't knocked anything to the floor. Along with a small stereo unit, three books-on-tape, and a slim silver pen, there was a pad of paper whose top sheet looked like a list.

He registered a few words and then stooped to take a closer look.

*Kigali. Blocked road.*
*Genocide starting. Ripping shoulder joints.*
*Driving but no rides. Child with fever.*
*Embassy. Knowledge of ignorance.*

He started to re-read it, hoping it wasn't what

156

he thought it was and then he heard someone step into the room, their tread soft on the carpet. He turned quickly to see Jayne in the doorway, looking more like herself, if somewhat pale.

'I was just...' He couldn't explain why he was reading her private notes.

She walked toward him and looked down at the paper. 'It was just a dream.' She flipped the pad over so its cardboard back was uppermost.

He was looking at the top of her down-turned head. 'You're dreaming about road blocks in Kigali.' He couldn't make it a question.

'Yep.' She met his eyes and he was surprised to see a defiant look. He was even more surprised when she jabbed an index finger toward his chest and hissed, 'And don't you dare judge me.' She turned and began walking away.

He couldn't believe she thought he didn't know what this dream was about. 'Jayne, wait.'

She stopped by the door but didn't turn around.

He continued, 'I know what the books-on-tape are for.'

She turned toward him but spoke warily. 'They're entertainment.'

'No, they're not.' His tone was harsher than he'd meant it to be but he was trying to hold her there with his voice, desperate to stop her from putting up more defenses. He could practically see her throwing up the scaffolding, so he talked, fast. 'You have them so that when you wake up from a nightmare so real you think you're there, you can hit "Play" and know that you're here. Here; *not there*. And maybe you feel guilty about that.'

He tried to read her expression. He couldn't be using the right words. She looked stricken. He closed his eyes, mustering all his energy to say the most important thing, the thing he should have said first. 'You know what, Jayne Hall? You're not the only one who sometimes needs a reality check to get through the night.'

Saying that out loud made him feel like he'd eaten something bitter and he swallowed before opening his eyes, hoping to see understanding on her face this time. But she wasn't there and he didn't know when she'd left. He felt rooted to the spot.

Eric stepped through the doorway. 'I just told Jayne we're clear in the other rooms, including the bathroom. So I'll check this one, then we'll do the outside.' He frowned at Scott. 'Everything all right, man? You weren't shouting at her, were you?'

'No.'

'OK, maybe not shouting, but that thing you do that sounds like shouting to everyone else.' Eric started to sweep the bug detection unit around the walls and closets but he kept an eye on Scott, who sat down on the edge of the bed.

'OK, maybe my voice was raised.'

Eric stopped in mid-sweep and looked him over.

Now Scott felt defensive. 'I just don't want to be misunderstood on any of the stuff that matters.'

Eric turned back to the sweeping. 'Houston, I have never known you to care what other people think about you.'

'Yeah. Well, I care what Jayne thinks about me.'

Eric came to the end of his circuit around the room and rested a hand on his shoulder. 'My friend, you will be lucky if that woman thinks about you, at all. Ever.'

Scott knew exactly what Eric was doing and it had worked: he wanted to punch him. His blood was flowing again, the bitter taste gone.

He exchanged an amused look with his partner and said, 'Get your hand off my shoulder.'

Steelie stood next to Jayne in the front doorway, watching Scott and Eric's flashlight beams moving around the garden as they checked the exterior of Jayne's apartment. They came closer to the building and then went under the stairs that led to the front door. Jayne turned back inside and dropped on to the sofa. Then she kicked off her shoes and turned to lie down.

Steelie came to perch on the arm of the sofa. She tried to see Jayne's expression but her hair was obscuring her face. Steelie pushed it back from her forehead and noticed Jayne's freckles were standing out. Usually they were almost invisible against her skin but she was decidedly pale this evening. Steelie pulled up her shirt-sleeve and pressed the inside of her wrist to her friend's forehead. 'You're warm. How do you feel?'

'Kind of cold.'

'Hm. I think you need a hot shower and a hot drink.'

'My shower's probably bugged.'

159

'They said the place is clean.'

'Feels dirty.'

Steelie recognized the stubborn tone and got up. She went to the kitchen, put on the electric kettle, and started rummaging in the cupboard that held tea and coffee. She pulled a few things out and straightened up just as Scott and Eric walked in through the front door. Eric was using a surgical glove to hold a small box. He came over to the kitchen while Scott walked to the living room and sat on the sofa next to Jayne.

Eric put the item on the counter, resting it on another glove.

'What is that?' Steelie was curious.

'A radio frequency transmitter. It's a type of wiretap.' He was keeping his voice low.

'Where was it? I mean, is it something to do with Jayne?'

He nodded. 'It was on the exterior part of her phone line.'

'Jesus. But who...'

He shrugged and looked over to the living room. Steelie followed his gaze and saw that Jayne had sat up. She was shaking her head, as though responding in the negative to something Scott was saying.

Eric said, 'He'll be asking her some questions about her phone before we say anything about the tap. Listen, you said she stayed with you last night? Can you keep her over there for a couple more days?'

The kettle's on/off switch popped up and Steelie turned to pick it up. 'Yeah, I can, but she's already complaining about the sofa bed.'

160

She emptied packets of powder into four mugs, then poured water over them. She pulled out a drawer to find a small whisk, which she used to vigorously stir the drinks.

She pushed a mug toward him and indicated the wiretap. 'How serious is this?'

'I don't know but we're in "better safe than sorry" territory.' He took a sip of the steaming, frothy drink. 'What the hell is this?'

'Matcha au lait.'

He just raised his eyebrows, apparently expecting further explanation.

'Instant green tea with milk. Chinese,' Steelie said.

'Got anything stronger?'

'Jayne doesn't drink so, no, we don't got anything stronger.'

She took a sip from her own mug and made exaggerated noises of satisfaction. 'Think Scott'll dig it?'

'I think you'll be lucky if he put the safety back on his gun. That'll buy you some time to get away.'

They carried the drinks to the living room, leaving the transmitter on the counter. Jayne looked like she'd been in a wind tunnel, hair pushed this way and that, her eyes watery. One of Scott's sleeves was rolled up, the other down, and he looked like he'd come in contact with some dust. *Same wind tunnel*, Steelie thought.

'So, what's your professional opinion?' Steelie asked.

Eric put his mug down. 'We clearly found a place where a wire could have been inserted into the floor of the apartment. That's not to say a wire *was* inserted there, but I gotta say that the location makes it likely. It's common practice to install a listening or video device in a threshold segment because it can be easy to access without entering the premises.'

Jayne covered her face with both hands.

Scott compressed his lips and shook his head at Eric, who got the message and rushed on. 'As I said, this is only an indication. There may never have been any device. But the reason I mentioned video is that we found a tap on the phone line—'

Jayne splayed her fingers so she could see Eric with one eye.

He spread his hands. 'All I'm saying is that whoever put on the tap could already hear you. No need for another audio bug in the threshold, which just leaves video.'

'Sounds like Big Brother to me,' Steelie said, crossing her arms. 'How do we know it's not some other arm of your office that put this in?'

Scott sounded impatient. 'Why, because that racketeering thing Jayne's been developing has finally taken off?' He shook his head. 'Look, this stuff wasn't Government and it wasn't sophisticated. The person who did it had some knowledge but no experience.' He turned to Jayne. 'Do you use your landline for work-related calls?'

She dropped her hands but looked unhappy. 'No. I mean, occasionally Steelie and I might mention something while on the phone.'

'How many people have the number? Are you

listed?'

'I'm listed. Last name, first initial.' She paused. 'What are you getting at?'

'Well, one interpretation of what we've found is that the person who planted this stuff may know you but not well enough to get invited in. Doesn't stop him from wanting to get closer to you and maybe he doesn't mean any harm. You'd probably never even notice the guy. And he'd have to be nearby to pick up the low signal this transmitter would've given out. Who lives downstairs?'

Jayne answered. 'Alex, but you're not seriously suggesting—'

'How well do you know him?'

'Like, Hi/Bye.'

'What does he do? Do you know?'

Jayne stood up and went to look out the sliding door. 'Something to do with computers...'

Scott and Eric exchanged a glance.

Steelie noticed it. 'This is crazy!'

Eric put his hands out in a calming gesture. 'You won't know what it is until you get more information. And until you do, Jayne, you might want to stay somewhere else.' He twisted to look at her. 'Your place is fine; we've checked everything and disabled the tap outside but that could also draw him back, to see why his transmitter's not transmitting. And you should have what we found tonight evaluated by professionals.'

He faced Steelie again. 'Get the Agency premises checked, including your phones, in case this isn't just a Peeping Tom.' He pulled his Black-Berry from a shirt pocket. 'I'll give you some names of people. Reputable sweeping companies, ex-Bureau guys. Tell 'em we told you to call.'

Steelie eyed him. 'What, so they'll charge us double?'

Jayne opened the sliding door and stepped on to the deck. Her table looked bereft without its white cloth. The tea light holders' glassy surfaces were dulled by dried wax drips. She walked to the railing and looked down into the driveway. Her neighbor's car wasn't parked in its spot. She was trying to recall what kind of car he drove – a white Subaru, she thought – when she realized that Scott had joined her.

He said, 'Steelie thinks you should go to your mother's until you know what's going on.'

She looked at him in exasperation. 'But why can't I just go to Steelie's?'

'Because she'll be at your mother's.'

She saw his mouth twitch and she smiled reflexively. The movement broke the surface tension that had kept her face taut since she'd hissed at him in the bedroom.

And then he was walking away from her, moving on, pushing through, going forward.

# DAYS FIVE AND SIX

## Saturday and Sunday

# FOURTEEN

Scott caught the mayonnaise just in time as it squirted out the bottom of the sandwich. He looked to see how his partner was doing. Eric had the Suburban's steering wheel in one hand and his sandwich in the other. On his first bite, barbeque sauce dripped out in a fat droplet. Part landed on his pant leg and part on the fabric seat, but, to his credit, the vehicle's speed remained steady as it hurtled east along Interstate 10 towards Arizona.

'Shit,' Eric mumbled while he chewed, then noticed Scott. 'What's so funny? Turner's not going to be laughing when you bring his vehicle back looking like a minivan after a trip to Disneyland.'

'I got the impression from Turner that he couldn't care less if we brought it back at all, so long as we secured a suspect.'

He leaned across and balanced a paper napkin on Eric's thigh. 'I'm not wiping it up, even if you ask me nice.' But he forgot to keep an eye on his own food and mayo got on his shirt. 'Dammit.'

Eric looked pleased. 'Did Turner get a call from Franks?'

'He didn't say as much.'

'But he was concerned we were on a wild-goose chase?'

Scott nodded as he chewed.

'Did he actually use those words?'

'No, but you know Craig Turner. He can be a diplomat. A nice quality in a boss.'

'For a change. Man, when I think about how Franks held us back on this case in Atlanta! Who knows how many leads we missed.'

'It's not like we stopped following leads.'

'Yeah, but we didn't have the resources to do proper surveillance to generate the high quality leads. You know we were slowed down by only getting the leads the streetwalkers could *remember* to give us. We had a short list of suspects—'

'Hey, you don't have to remind me.'

'And thanks to SSA Franks, we couldn't do what was needed to rule 'em in or out. And now we're tracking the same perp out here. He's probably killed again, too.'

Scott balled up his napkin, put it in a paper bag, then balled that up and threw it in the footwell. 'We don't know that it's the same guy. Our perp's stomping grounds are in Atlanta. Right now, we're in...' He looked out the window just as they passed the sign for the Arizona State Line. 'We're fifteen miles west of Quartz-

166

site. What's our perp doing in Arizona?'

'I don't know,' Eric admitted. 'But it's the same guy. Maybe he wanted to take a road trip. He took the northern route, killed Patterson in Oregon on the way down south, got rear-ended in LA—'

'The van was going north when it was hit, Eric.'

'So he was lost. He gets back on the road and goes to Arizona to get some sun. Or, wait ... he could be from Arizona originally and it was time to come home. Things getting too hot in Georgia the past few months. I mean, you were on the news and in the paper, what, every couple of weeks for a while? Appealing to the public, "We're looking for a van that might be driven by a man abducting women in Atlanta." *I'd* get out of town if I had you on my tail.' Eric put the last of the sandwich in his mouth and held out the trash to Scott. 'You still think it's the same guy, right?'

'Yeah. But I'll tell you what I didn't tell Turner. I think it's the same guy because I want it to be him. It's not based solely on the evidence because the evidence isn't strong enough to say it is our guy. It's just a perp with a Georgia license plate hauling female body parts around.'

'What *did* you tell Turner?'

'I just told him there was no need to hand off to Phoenix, wasting time bringing them up to speed. At the very least, we'll get forensics that relate to the LA body parts and we'll get the van's owner, who's either the perp or someone who's helping him. We can tie up the LA end of

167

the case no matter what.'

'And Turner doesn't care about what happened with us in Georgia?'

'I barely mentioned Georgia. I mean, if Franks *has* called him from Atlanta, then Turner already knows that when it comes to that case, I'm ... what did Angie say Franks called me?'

'An ego-driven maverick who can't see the forest for the trees.'

'Right.' Scott looked at the instrument panel. 'Watch your speed, Ramos.'

Eric immediately glanced at the speedometer and eased up on the accelerator pedal. 'It's thinking about Franks that does that to me.'

'Remember, he's our *old* boss.' Scott reclined his seat and closed his eyes.

'Not if he's calling Turner with bedtime stories,' Eric replied, an edge to his voice.

'Turner's too smart for that kind of game. And if you're going to be thinking about Franks while I'm getting some shut-eye, put it on cruise control.'

Eric focused on the road. It was still another couple of hours to Mesa, so he turned the radio on with the volume low. He'd just missed the news.

An hour later, Scott woke suddenly and then oriented himself. He brought his seatback up and cleared his throat. 'How far out are we?'

'Thirty miles.'

'You need to switch?'

'No, I'll take us to the location and get in some rest when we change vehicles.'

Scott drank from a bottle of water, then pulled

a file folder from the seat behind them. 'You get a chance to look at this stuff from Phoenix PD before we left?'

Eric shook his head. 'Not in any detail. The D who I spoke with, Czuzak, is up to her neck on a drug bust so she sent a couple of rookies to babysit the van.'

'She sure the van's associated with that address?' Scott was pulling papers out of the file and putting them in some kind of order.

'Well, it's parked in front of that address. The rookies have seen one man emerge from the van and go into that address but not by the front door. He went down the side. Could be a side entrance, could be nothing. Could be a shortcut to a neighbor's.'

'Right. Says here that the house at that address is owned by a couple in their seventies by the name of Spicer. Been there since '99. Previous address is Burbank, California. No arrests, no convictions. No problems with property taxes or mortgage payments. No van registered in their name or associated with the house.' Scott paused.

'They could know the perp. Let him park at their place.'

'I see you're presuming Mr Spicer isn't our perp.'

Eric gave him a look. 'He's too old for the description we have. Plus, how many seventy-year-old *active* serial killers you heard of? What about the people who live on either side of that address?'

'Uh, let's see.' Scott flipped through some

169

pages until he found the right one. 'To the west we have a Mr Knox, the owner since '98, unknown to police but resident with him is one Alice Elizabeth Smith whose priors include possession, dealing, and acquiring goods through deception.'

Eric raised his eyebrows. 'Possession of what?'

'Ah ... pot. Same for the dealing.'

'Interesting.'

'Maybe.'

'She could be someone who crossed paths with the perp.'

'Possibly.'

'And on the other side?'

'Neighbors on the other side are tenants.' Scott yawned. 'Phoenix hasn't run down the info on them yet but the owner lives outside the US and that's confirmed. Let's give the rookies a punch list of backgrounds we need when we get to the station.'

'Make sure they know it's a punch list and not a wish list. It's Saturday night, so a list isn't going to make them happy.'

Scott yawned again. 'They've been on stake-out. What makes you think they won't be happy?' He twisted to look at the back seat. 'We got anything else to eat in here?'

Steelie watched Marie snip the thin branches of the mint bush and held the willow basket out for her. Then she hurried to keep up as Marie moved on to a rose bush whose flowers grew in bunches, some buds yet to open, others just past their glory.

'I think we'll have some of these, too.' Marie started cutting off little bouquets.

'You're putting roses in the mint tea?'

'No, dear, these are for the table.' Then she peered at Steelie over the top of her vintage sunglasses. 'You're teasing me, aren't you?'

'Hey, I found rosemary in my scone this morning so I had to check.'

'I would have thought that you experimented with all kinds of herbs and spices, Steelie.'

'Why, 'cause I'm a vegetarian? As someone pointed out, we don't just go and eat a fistful of the nearest bush. Like you don't pick up the nearest squirrel and throw it on the grill just 'cause you eat meat.'

Marie threw her head back and laughed throatily. 'It is always such a treat to have you around, my dear. Come on, we've got enough of everything now.'

They walked up the sloping lawn of creeping thyme to the Cape Cod-style house shaded by two ancient oaks. The white siding contrasted with a particular shade of blue on the window shutters to give the effect of country retreat rather than beach house. The rear porch was screened in and the wooden door slammed gently behind Steelie as she followed in Marie's perfume contrail. The lunch table was set with tulips but Marie picked the vase up as she swept into the house.

They passed through the dining room, its long table flanked by ten chairs, and into the bright white kitchen with its woodblock counters and island.

'Right, give me the mint and I'll leave you the roses. Here's a vase.' She handed Steelie a pot-bellied ceramic jug and the pruning scissors and pointed her over to a section of counter by a small sink. She hummed as she pulled iced tea from the refrigerator and prepared to submerge the mint in it.

After a few minutes, Steelie turned around with the jug. 'How's that?'

Marie looked at the rose arrangement, head tilted. 'There's hope for you yet.'

Steelie hoisted herself on the counter to watch Marie make salad dressing. Her gaze traveled over the room and came to rest, as usual, on the large framed watercolor that dominated the far wall, a bookcase on either side, each jammed with cookbooks sprouting bits of note paper, their colourful spines a contrast to the ephemeral quality of the watercolor. It was a portrait of Marie and Jayne when she was four years old, painted by her father, Elliott.

'Tell me about the painting again.'

Marie looked up. 'Again? But you know the story.'

'Again!'

She shrugged elegantly. 'We were in our back garden in Caracas. Nothing like this.' She glanced out the kitchen windows. 'Much smaller but *wonderful* soil. I was planting seeds I'd been experimenting with. Jayne had watched me harvest them and then decided to help me plant. I taught her how to hold the trowel and she was very good. No seeds too deep, nothing tamped down

172

too hard.' She smiled at the memory. 'The plants began to grow. Everything was fine. Then one day, I went to check on their progress and discovered that she had excavated their roots. Not dug them up; no, no. She just wanted to see what was going on underground so she had simply *exposed* them, poor things. It was quite clinical. They never recovered.'

Steelie smiled. 'Just think, you were the one who taught her to use a trowel. Little did you know.'

'That's what Elliott says.' Marie turned back to the salad and began tossing in the dressing. 'Little did we know our girl was going to grow up to be a forensic anthropologist. We'd never heard of such a thing.'

Steelie jumped down and came over to rescue a piece of cucumber that had fallen from the salad bowl on to the counter. She popped it into her mouth and crunched. 'How is Mr Hall? It's been, what, a couple of months since he was here last?'

'Oh, he's fast approaching emeritus level and there's only so long the university will allow an old painter to hang on. So he's asking himself if he can stop being an expatriate and come back to the States. It's difficult, as being an expatriate rather suits Elliott. Has done since 1967.'

'You wouldn't go back to Venezuela?'

'My home is here. I am a true *emigrante*.' She handed the salad bowl to Steelie and directed her toward the front porch. 'Besides, how would the listeners of *Weekends with Prentis* manage without me?'

'As your lawyer,' Steelie called back, 'I'd have to advise you to take the title with you at the very least.'

Marie joined her on the porch and put the roses on the table. 'Now, do you think Jayne will be here soon or shall we begin without her?'

Steelie glanced at her watch. 'I'm actually surprised she's not back yet. Did you see her this morning?'

'No, but she'd left a note in the kitchen that she was going to Carol's.'

'Yeah.' Steelie pulled out her cell phone and dialled Jayne's number. 'Either her phone's off or she's out of range.' She started to dial Carol's home number and said to Marie, 'Let's go ahead; I'm sure she'll be here soon.'

Jayne walked out to the back porch to find Steelie and Marie at the table with the remains of lunch. Half the quiche was just crumbs and the salad looked picked over. She sat down at the place setting that had been left for her and reached for the salad.

'How'd she take it?' Steelie's tone was eager.

'You know Carol – with equanimity. I tell her my apartment's been bugged and we need her to call some TSCMs—'

'TSCMs?' Marie cut in.

Jayne spoke while examining the salad. 'Technical Surveillance Counter-Measures. I can tell Steelie's been here because there's no avocado left and yet I can see smears of avocado stuck in the crenulations of the lettuce.'

'They do say it's trace evidence that gets you

174

every time.' Steelie didn't sound remorseful.

Marie ignored their asides. 'Couldn't you have just called Carol?'

Steelie answered because Jayne had too much salad in her mouth. 'Well, Eric said that it wasn't always recommended to do what they did at Jayne's apartment last night; I mean, to dismantle the bug. In a business setting, it's sometimes recommended to leave it in, plant disinformation in it, and then see where that comes out to find the source of the spying. So in case this is all to do with the Agency and not just someone spying on Jayne, we're not using any phones to discuss this or make the appointments with the TSCMs. If there are wiretaps at the office, we don't want whoever planted them to take them away before a professional finds them.'

'It all sounds rather sinister. I can see why you converged on me for the weekend.' She stood. 'And you're welcome to stay for longer.' She went inside.

Jayne looked after her, then cut a generous slice of quiche for herself. She regarded Steelie. 'You're having fun, aren't you?'

Steelie threw her arms wide. 'Why wouldn't I? Great company, a comfy room, delicious food. *My* mom's idea of lunch is tuna and potato chips on white. Followed by Jell-O on a bed of Cool Whip. And if you ask her what flavour the Jell-O is—'

'I know; red.'

'Yeah. I mean, that's not a flavor!'

'She's just speaking a different language.'

'How come I never hear you say that about

175

your mom when she's talking to you about, oh, your choice in clothing?'

'That's not just another language. It's another planet.'

'She loves you.'

'You know she wishes I was a bit more ... vah-voom.'

'You're wrong about that.'

Jayne polished off the last of her quiche and looked at Steelie. 'This is why I don't like leaving you two alone together. What part of my life was discussed?'

Marie arrived holding a tray with a cake on a stand and a coffee pot. 'Your childhood, darling. And I don't need to seek permission to do that seeing as I was there for it, too.'

She began cutting the cake, which was iced white with a coating of coconut shavings. She put a slice in front of Jayne.

'What's that?' Jayne was poking at a dark line between the two layers of yellow sponge. 'Looks like blood.'

'Raspberry jam, as you well know.'

Steelie sniffed her own slice appreciatively.

'Now, this particular cake,' Marie said, 'is ideal for a garden party. Say, when you want to introduce a special someone to your parents.'

'But you already know Steelie.' Jayne almost kept a straight face.

'Layered, this cake could even work for a garden wedding,' Marie continued.

'Good God,' Jayne muttered.

Steelie chimed in, 'You'll have to ask Scott if he minds your maid of honor wearing pants on the big day.'

Jayne glared at her. 'Traitor.'

By Sunday morning, Scott and Eric had traded the Suburban for a surveillance vehicle. Scott turned on to Prickly Pear Close and saw the gold van parked three-quarters of the way down on the right. The street itself barely lived up to its name. A single prickly pear did exist against all odds at the corner where the street came off the main road in a T-junction but the cactus did more to catch tumbleweed than it did to establish the suburban vista envisioned by fast-talking developers in the 1980s.

Most of the houses on the street had given up all pretense of a garden, even a desert garden, as front yards had been turned into off-street parking for extended family who had moved in during economic hard times. Five of the thirteen houses on the dead-end street had some sort of camper parked in their driveways, chocked up on bricks, curtains closed against the heat. People were living in them full-time. So Scott and Eric knew it wouldn't surprise anyone to see one more RV arrive on the street, nor would it be unusual if its sunshades permanently obscured all of its windows from the searing Arizona sun.

From the outside, the surveillance vehicle looked like a motor home on its last legs, its many badges from past trips appearing to do as much to hold the fiberglass skin together as the rivets themselves. The badges also suggested that the owners were happy albeit tired seniors, many of whose road trips belonged to another millennium: 'W.B. Caravan Club–Wichita Meet 1991'; 'We Bridged the Great Divide–1994'. It was plausible that the owners were 'snowbirds' – Northerners or Easterners who used to travel annually to southern Arizona for its warm winters but this year never left, their camper coming to rest in this dry subdivision while looking for a final parking place.

Inside the RV, the agents adjusted the antennae and activated a live video feed of the gold van. Eric prepared the receiver to pick up the audio from the listening device they would plant after dark. Scott called the rookies who were still on surveillance up the street and received confirmation that there hadn't been any movement in or around the van during the night. He then informed them that they were relieved of duties. The agents heard the engine of the unmarked police car start, then fade as it drove away.

# DAY SEVEN

## Monday

# FIFTEEN

Prickly Pear Close, Phoenix: High Noon. The beeping of a digital watch alarm woke Scott and he quickly pressed a button to silence it. He swung his legs over the side of the fully-made bed at the rear of the camper. His ankle-high boots were already on and he was dressed in combat pants and a t-shirt, so there wasn't much more to do besides a few stretches, preferably avoiding banging his hands against the curved ceiling. He walked the two paces to the foot of the bed and pulled back the plastic accordion door that separated the bedroom from the main room.

Eric momentarily turned his head from monitoring a television screen. 'Morning.'

'Anything happening?'

'Nope. All quiet on the western front.'

'Got my breakfast?'

'Your latte's right here.' Eric waved a packet of instant Maxwell House coffee.

Scott turned into the bathroom. It was too

179

small for an adult to close the door and still be comfortable, so he left it open; he and his partner had been on enough long stakeouts to get over privacy issues. But the toilet's holding pan had been filling inexorably, as the surveillance had only been broken by bathroom breaks or naps.

'Would ya close the lid on that nuclear power plant, already?' Eric called out.

Scott flushed the toilet and popped his head out of the bathroom doorway, already lathering his face with shaving cream. 'Worried it's going to curl your hair, darlin'?'

'It's interfering with the reception on this show I'm watching. Seems to have frozen the image for the past three minutes. Wait, make that six hours.'

Scott finished washing up. He emerged feeling like he'd woken up properly but nonetheless decided to make coffee to go with some energy bars.

He sat down next to Eric at the monitoring station. 'Nothing on the audio either?'

Planting the listening device had been a quick operation that hadn't afforded any examination of the van itself because some joyriding teen-agers had chosen that moment to park in Prickly Pear Close to smoke marijuana, car windows open, listening to music in the dark. The teen-agers had stayed until 4.30 a.m., by which time Scott had deemed it too close to daylight for them to try for an undetected examination of the van without knowing the sleep patterns of the street's inhabitants. They would try again that night.

'Just that same hum,' replied Eric. He turned a dial on the audio receiver next to the video screen. A medium pitch, uninterrupted hum became more audible.

'No fluctuation whatsoever?'

Eric shook his head and turned the volume dial down to its previous position.

'And no sign of anyone? Not even the home-owners?' Scott moved on to a second energy bar.

'No, but it's summer in Phoenix. If they didn't get out before eight in the morning, they know better than to come out now.'

Eric pushed himself up from his seat in front of the monitoring station and made a note in the log they were keeping of their hours in the hot seat. Scott moved into the chair, downing the last of the coffee, his eyes already glued to the screen.

Eric walked to the bedroom but halted before closing the accordion door. 'You made the bed for me. I'm so touched.'

Scott held up his middle finger in Eric's direction without looking at him.

'OK, I'm set for nineteen hundred hours unless a party starts,' Eric said.

Scott settled into the chair, preparing for the challenge of maintaining a high energy level. He was always surprised that it was hard to sustain energy on a stakeout even though in terms of physical activity, it wasn't all that different to his usual job behind a desk; sit at a screen of some sort all day, get up every now and then. There were fewer phone calls on a stakeout. Maybe that was it. He contemplated calling Jayne. He told himself it would just be to ascertain if she'd

181

arranged to have the Agency checked for bugs.

He knew he wouldn't call. It was one thing to think while watching the surveillance screen but it was something else to talk with an outsider while on stakeout. Especially with this case. They didn't even have confirmation this was the right van so they were still hunting those body parts. This just got him thinking about Jayne again.

He smiled to himself, remembering when they'd first met at Quantico. Her confident belief that inefficient processes could actually be improved had struck him as naïve yet liberating, coming as it did on the heels of his months of study of how a bureaucracy fights crime. Her face and body had displayed the last traces of youthful roundedness, as though her figure represented a tightrope between gullibility and mistrust and she was still working out on which side she would dismount.

Now, she looked like she'd tried both sides and found each problematic, deciding that perhaps it was easier to negotiate the tightrope, arms out to the side, inadvertently keeping people away as she waved and balanced. Scott knew his interpretation was self-serving since he felt on a tightrope himself and he hadn't met anyone else along it, besides Jayne. He'd known for a long time that he wanted to take hold of her but he hadn't known if that was for the sake of her balance or his. That uncertainty had been at the heart of why he'd never tried to move things to what other people called the 'next level'.

His previous girlfriends – the 'lightweights' as

Eric had referred to them – had been easy to pick up so they'd be easy to let go, with the idea of Jayne always in the background and never put to the test. Now that he was around her again, he was even more aware of the reality of his attraction to her. He had no intention of leaving things to his imagination forever. Ever since she'd backed into him on her stairs Friday night, he'd been thinking about the inward curve of her waist and the outward curves above and below ... he knew he'd have to save that train of thought for after the stakeout. There was no way he could watch the screen, listen to the audio feed, and think those particular thoughts of Jayne all at the same time.

When Jayne heard Carol come in the Agency's front door, she intercepted her and indicated that they should have a word outside. Out in the parking lot, she asked, 'Did you find a pay phone that actually worked?'

Carol replied, 'Third time lucky. The city still comes through on phones even if it can't keep up the phone books. Someone from Jeppsen, Inc. will be here shortly.'

'Was that the first one on Eric's list?'

'No, the second. The technicians at the first place were busy all week.'

Jayne shook her head. 'I can't believe there's this much call for people who do private bug detection.'

'Well, I spoke to one of the principals at Jeppsen. He seemed nice enough.'

Jayne heard the phone ring inside and darted in

183

ahead of Carol. She listened to the deep, Mid-western-accented voice rumble down the phone line. 'This is Bill Ledbetter from Wisconsin. I'm Amy's father. You wrote my wife and me an email about Amy around a week ago.'

Jayne placed Amy. She'd gone missing while on her way home from the Dairy Queen several years earlier. 'Hello, Mr Ledbetter. Nice to have a voice to go with an email. What can I do for you?'

'Well, we've been thinking over what you said about Amy being alive but maybe not knowing who she is. I gotta admit, that hadn't occurred to us. We know she's alive. Plus, the cops up here already used Amy's hairbrush to see if she had ... passed away and they didn't get any matches.'

'You mean, they tried to do a DNA match?'

'They sure did. Right at the beginning.'

'I see.' Jayne knew that whenever DNA was involved, many people tended to see things in black-and-white, even though DNA doesn't always lead to a match even when it should. Often, a failure to find a DNA match only proves that DNA isn't in any system at the point a search is run. Jayne knew it would have been difficult for a detective to look the Ledbetters in the eye, explain that, and then watch hope borne of certainty yield to fear borne of uncertainty.

Mr Ledbetter said, 'When we got your email, we thought we'd like to go ahead and do a profile at your organization, just for the hospitals.'

'Well, Mr Ledbetter, when we make up a forensic profile of a missing person, the police

184

will automatically compare it to all unidentified persons. The FBI keeps one big file for everyone, alive or not.'

'Really?'

'Sure. And it makes sense, since how we identify people doesn't really change that much either way.'

Jayne heard two female voices shouting in the background on Bill Ledbetter's end.

His voice became somewhat muffled as he covered the phone's mouthpiece. 'Melissa! Becca! Please keep it down. I'm talking long distance.'

Then a young girl's voice. 'But, *Da-ad!* She took my hair band.'

'OK. I'll be off the phone in a minute.' Then he was back with Jayne. 'Sorry about that. Well, let me talk to my wife, and then I guess the main thing we were wondering was if we had to come out there to do the profile?'

'Not at all. We can talk to you about Amy over the phone and we can tell you what kind of other documents we'd need. You can send these to us in the mail and when we're done, we'll send the originals back.'

When they hung up, Jayne pictured Bill Ledbetter's world. He was still being a parent while dealing with something that no parent could expect and prepare for. *It's always the same*, she thought. *We're all the same.* She heard Carol greeting someone and went forward to Reception, where Carol said the two men from Jeppsen, Inc. were waiting on the front steps. Jayne summoned Steelie and they all went

185

outside.

Lex Jeppsen was a big man who introduced himself to Agency 32/1 as the 'brains', while his partner, Michael Eagen, was the 'hands' of their bug sweeping operation. They had been in business for three years, since leaving the FBI in search of better pay and more flexibility. They asked how the Agency found them and Jayne mentioned Scott Houston and Eric Ramos. Lex and Michael laughed and asked how 'those two sonsabitches' were doing. Then they asked Jayne, Carol, and Steelie to stay in Reception while they worked.

They all trooped inside. Lex first used a machine, holding it a few inches out over the walls, while Michael took apart the telephone on Carol's desk. Eventually, Lex asked if they had a key to the cage surrounding the generator outside. Jayne gave him the key and listened to him whistle as he went out the back door again.

When they returned, Michael was smiling and holding an object. Jayne and Steelie exchanged a worried glance and they all stood.

Lex began. 'First question: you have three phone lines here?'

'Yes,' replied Jayne.

'You get any wrong numbers or hang ups in the past couple of months?'

She shook her head.

'How long you been in this building?'

'About a year.'

Lex looked at his colleague, who shook his head and said, 'Hasn't been there that long.'

Steelie interrupted. 'Can I just ask if that's a

listening device or what?'

'Indeed it is,' replied Michael. 'RF transmitter, just like what was found at the apartment.'

'Where was it?'

'On the one phone line outside but within the cage for the generator.'

Jayne said, 'Well, we just got the generator.'

Lex answered. 'It could predate it but we'll check it out. When we find this type of wiretap at a business, it's usually at corporate headquarters or an office were corporate secrets are discussed.' Lex paused to look around the modest room, taking in the aloe plant in the corner. 'You're running a charity here?'

Carol nodded.

Lex continued: 'You got a competitor? Or have any proprietary methodology – something not patented?'

Steelie said, 'Competition's a bit thin on the ground in our line of work.'

He looked around the room again. 'What is it you do here?'

'Forensic profiles of missing persons.'

Michael raised his eyebrows. 'You do anything to piss off the cops?'

Jayne refrained from offering up the possibility that Steelie drove over a policeman's foot on Friday night. 'What we do complements law enforcement. And we have contacts with LAPD. If they want anything, they just ask.'

Michael shrugged and started to pack up his gear. 'Might not be LAPD. Could be any cops anywhere, if I'm correct in assuming your profiles go national.'

'Or if you're dealing with data on missing persons,' resumed Lex. 'It could be someone who wants to get stuff for identity theft while the owner's AWOL. Whatever it turns out to be, we know your outside line was tapped and whoever did it didn't need to gain entry to put it on. They'll know you've disabled it. We want to come back and sweep in a month's time.'

He had been filling out some boxes on a clipboard. 'Here's the invoice for this location. Payment address at the bottom.' He ripped off a carbon copy and gave Jayne the top sheet. 'Now, about the apartment location. Carol here said that the tap in the Ziploc bag was found on the outside phone line under the stairs?'

Jayne nodded.

'But you had it swept?'

'Eric and Scott said there wasn't anything inside the apartment.'

'Good.' Lex turned the Ziploc around in his hands and passed it to Michael. 'Listen, this tap from your place is identical to the one we found here so our opinion is that whatever you're dealing with is related to your work somehow as it's unlikely a Peeping Tom wants to hear your work calls. And it's someone nearby or a person who can get near to you. This little sucker isn't going to be useful for anyone at a great distance. You could consider getting more security for your property.'

Michael added, 'Alarming the building isn't enough when people don't need access to plant a device.'

Steelie's voice was flat. 'I think we're getting

188

that picture.'

Michael gathered up his briefcases and held up the bag with the tap in it. 'You guys want these or you want me to take 'em?'

'You can have them,' answered Jayne.

As soon as the two men had left the building, Steelie said, 'We're going to have to tell Scott and Eric.'

'That we inadvertently gave their case some exposure? Absolutely,' agreed Jayne.

'You couldn't have known,' said Carol.

Steelie was matter of fact. 'That doesn't matter. Those two agents are in the middle of a homicide investigation and they passed an ID over what turns out was an open line.'

Jayne pulled out her cell. When she got Scott's voicemail, she left a message simply asking him to call, without referring to the bugging, intending to explain more fully when they spoke.

At eight minutes past seven on Monday night, Eric had again taken his position in front of the surveillance screen in the camper. Scott was in the bathroom when Eric said, 'Someone's coming to the party.'

Scott emerged from the bathroom quickly, tucking in his shirt. He saw Eric turn up the volume on the audio feed and press *Record* on both the video and audio screens. On the video screen, a tall man dressed in sweat pants was doing something at the back of the van. The audio relayed the sound of a key being inserted into a lock.

'Which house did he come from?' Scott asked

189

quietly.

'Garage of 1501.'

On the screen, the man pulled a thick metal chain from between the rear door handles, opened the doors, and jumped in. The doors closed before they could see the interior of the van and then they heard the sound of a padlock being closed.

Eric put on a headset to focus on the audio while Scott tried to monitor both stations. The video screen remained static. The sound of someone moving around. Another lock being turned, then a hydraulic sound. A voice came through, somewhat muffled. Scott glanced sharply at his partner, brow furrowed. Eric shook his head. He hadn't understood the words either.

The audio feed hummed, then the sound of locks again. The man emerged from the rear of the van and suddenly bent down by the corner of the rear bumper. Scott couldn't see what the man was doing until he twisted to look under the van. Something narrow and dark was dangling down from the van to the ground. It hadn't been visible on the surveillance screen before because the bumper camouflaged it.

'What the hell is that?' asked Scott, pointing at the screen.

'He's not saying anything,' Eric said, his voice slightly raised.

Scott leaned in closer to the screen but that didn't help. The man replaced the chain through the van's door handles, locked the padlock, and walked back to the garage. His gait was unhurried and he didn't look around. As soon as he was out of the frame, Scott said, 'What did he say when he was inside?'

'It sounded like "Good for my pincers".' Eric looked at him.

'Go over that again until you can confirm it.' Scott sounded edgy. He noticed Eric's expression and lightened his tone. 'And make it make sense.'

Eric smiled grimly and rewound the audio.

Scott sat at the monitoring station and used another screen to run the video back. He enhanced the image until it was just pixels and then zoomed it back out again, considering and rejecting conclusions as he did so. Suddenly, he pushed away from the counter, swiveled in his seat to a cabinet behind him and pulled out a file. Inside were eight sheets of smooth fax paper stapled together. He flipped the pages over one by one, quickly scanning the top of each sheet. When he got to the final sheet, he swore.

Eric had turned around to look at him and now pulled off the headset. 'What?'

'This fax from Phoenix PD?' Scott waved the sheets in the air. 'It's got pages one through eight of a nine page document.'

Eric groaned. 'That fucking fax machine.'

Scott was up and trying to pace in the tiny camper.

Eric asked, 'What do you think was on page nine?'

'How about, "Yeah, we've got your gold van out here and guess what? It's got an electrical extension cord running out its back end and into

191

1501"?' He threw the papers on to the monitoring station, pulled his chair up next to Eric, and sat down again. Eric stared at the screen. 'You're probably right about that being an extension cord. Who lives in 1501?' He picked up the papers. 'The Spicers. Sally and Frank.' He put them back on the counter. 'About the fax. I should have checked it when I grabbed it on Friday.'

Scott slapped him on the shoulder. 'Doesn't matter. Page nine might have just said, "Drive safe, boys." Whatever it said, we'll confirm the extension cord tonight.'

Eric nodded. He rewound the tape and pushed *Pause*. 'I'm going with "Gold for my princess" on the audio.'

He pushed *Play*. The man's voice came through more clearly this time. Now it sounded loving and triumphant: 'Gold for my princess.'

# SIXTEEN

A bathrobe-clad Frank Spicer first turned on his porch light and then opened his front door at 1501 Prickly Pear Close to find four people on his doorstep. They had been pounding on it for the entire minute it had taken him to get to the front of the house. Two were men holding Federal Bureau of Investigation badges open towards him. The other two were wearing Phoenix Police Department uniforms. One of the FBI people handed him some papers. The front page had *WARRANT* typed across it in letters big enough for Frank to read without his glasses. He did need glasses for the rest of it, so he invited the authorities into the house. After all, he had nothing to hide.

As it turned out, the law enforcement officers did not want to search his house. It had all been a mistake, as Frank was sure it would be. They wanted to search that old van parked in front of their house, a vehicle they had nothing to do with. Frank told them that and his wife, Sally, seconded him, now that she had joined them in the front room, wearing a pink terrycloth muumuu.

'That's right, the van isn't ours. We have a Saturn. It's in the driveway.'

'Ma'am,' the blond FBI agent said. 'The van has an extension cord running into your garage.'

She reared back. 'I beg your pardon?' She crossed to the window, pulling her husband with her. 'Frank, had you noticed that?' She looked at him in wonder.

Frank felt tired. 'No, I sure didn't.'

She appealed to the four people standing like statues in her living room. 'We've been out of town for a few weeks. Maybe someone was trying to steal our electricity while we were gone?' She broke off and looked at Frank again, who shrugged. 'We thought the van belonged to someone visiting a neighbor. I never noticed the extension cord.'

Scott regarded Frank and Sally Spicer. Neither fit the image of the person he'd seen going into the van the previous evening. 'Mr and Mrs Spicer, does anyone else live here with you?'

'Our son, Wayne, lives with us.' Sally sounded puzzled.

'We'll need to speak with him to determine if he's the owner of the van. Where can we find him?'

'It's not his—' Sally began.

'Let me get him,' said Frank. 'It'll be easier that way. He doesn't like to be disturbed,' he said over his shoulder as he began to leave the room. One of the police officers followed him.

Scott stood across the room from Sally Spicer. She didn't look concerned about the unfolding events, only as befuddled as would someone who had been woken up abruptly after having

194

gone to bed for the night. She tried to fluff her short grey hair, then smiled self-consciously at him. He maintained a polite expression.

The person who followed Frank into the room was a very good match for the tall man seen by Scott and Eric on the surveillance video. He was still wearing dark sweatpants but now had on a white vest. His body hair was long and pale and stuck to his skin in rivulets of sweat, as though he had come from a room without air conditioning.

Scott turned to the newcomer as the two police officers quietly moved to block the doorway.

'Are you Wayne Spicer?'

'Yes.' The man seemed surprised that anyone knew his name.

'Do you own the van sitting in front of this property?'

'Yes. It's mine.'

Scott noticed Sally grip Frank's arm.

'We have a warrant to search your van, sir.'

Eric came to stand next to Scott, holding a second copy of the warrant papers they had had issued.

Wayne's eyes darted between Scott and the window.

'Why? It's not parked illegally. I didn't do anything wrong.' Wayne's voice took on a higher pitch with every phrase.

'Take a seat there, sir.' Scott indicated the flowered sofa. 'Here's your copy of the warrant.'

Eric handed the papers to Wayne. Scott expected the large man to resist in some way but he looked like he no longer heard or saw them.

Sally pleaded, 'Wayne?'

He didn't respond.

One police officer remained in the living room with the Spicer family while Scott, Eric, and Officer Perez walked outside.

Perez went to her cruiser, which was parked across the Spicer's driveway, and put her spotlight full beam on the back of the van. Eric brought a camera out of an equipment bag he carried with him. Using the flash, he photographed the entire van and then took several shots of the padlock securing the rear doors. Perez arrived with a bolt cutter she had retrieved from the trunk of the cruiser and Eric photographed her actions as she cut through the padlock and removed the chain from between the door handles. She then carefully opened both doors to their widest position while Eric photographed. Scott flicked on a flashlight and surveyed the scene before him.

The extension cord traveled up from under the bumper and into the van's floor via a rusty hole partially ringed with short pieces of black electrical tape. Scott's eyes followed the cord. It met another, this one white and protruding from the back of a white, mid-sized chest freezer. A grey rubber strap ran like a belt around the front of the freezer and was bolted to the wall with shiny screws that looked new. There was barely space for a path between the freezer on the right and an army cot on the left. At the far end of the van, a tarp hung from the ceiling and obscured the front seats.

Eric photographed the van's interior. Perez

climbed in to cut through the padlock securing the freezer's lid and then Eric traded places with her. Scott lifted the lid so Eric could photograph the inside. Scott couldn't see in from his position, so watched Eric's face. But Eric lowered the camera without taking a photograph.

'What is it?' Scott asked.

'You gotta see this.' Eric took three flash photographs in quick succession and jumped down.

Scott climbed into the van and shined light into the freezer. There was a dead woman tucked inside it. She was resting on her back, held in a crouch with her head against the left wall and chin tucked down. Dark hair curled about the young face and across shoulders pushed slightly inwards by the front and back walls. Her arms were extended and crossed over her body, which was clothed in a bra and underpants. Her hands lay palms-down over her abdomen. Her appearance was innocent and peaceful, preserved intact by the cold.

Scott locked eyes with Eric. 'We got him. We finally got the bastard. Perez, get us hooked up with a flatbed. We're impounding this vehicle.'

Wayne Spicer remained silent throughout his arrest. He nodded to indicate that he understood his Miranda rights and looked dully at his parents before being led out of the house in handcuffs. Scott glanced at Frank and Sally Spicer as he left their living room. They looked as though they had fallen into the sofa and weren't getting up any time soon. He closed the front door quietly behind him.

Eric stayed with the van. He would maintain continuity of evidence for the transport crew from the Medical Examiner's Office after they arrived to formally confirm death and he would wait for the police tow truck unit who would take the van away on a flatbed.

Wayne sat in the back of the police cruiser as Officer Perez drove out of Prickly Pear Close and through the quiet streets of Mesa. He looked out of the window, taking shallow breaths and sweating. Sitting next to him, Scott was trying to keep his own breathing under control as he thought about how they would be able to use the body in the freezer against the suspect during interview. He couldn't imagine this guy didn't know he was going down. They would make him cough up the locations of the other women he'd killed and then he and Eric would finally close the cases in Atlanta.

# DAY EIGHT

## Tuesday

# SEVENTEEN

Scott and Eric left their hotel in downtown Phoenix, having decided to get the coroner's preliminary report on the girl in the freezer before starting the interview with Wayne Spicer. Scott was aware he hadn't yet returned Jayne's call from the previous day and vowed to do it that afternoon. He checked the paper in his lap. Dr Bodell was the forensic pathologist on duty at the Maricopa County Medical Examiner's Office.

At the ME's office, the agents were able to stay in their street clothes by standing in the viewing room whose window overlooked the large suite where Dr Bodell was working at an autopsy table. The window took up most of the dividing wall and Scott felt as though he was in the room with the pathologist. He was startled when her voice came through a wall-mounted speaker as a tinny amplification of the rich British timbre he'd heard when they'd met in her office earlier.

'Can you hear me all right?' A Tyvek-suited Dr Bodell was directing her chin upwards to a microphone hanging from the ceiling as she looked at them through the window. The young autopsy assistant pulled the microphone slightly closer to the pathologist.

The agents nodded even though they'd been shown how to operate the wall-mounted microphone so the pathologist could hear them.

'I understand you found the body in a freezer,' she stated. 'Any idea how long it had been there?'

When the agents shook their heads, Dr Bodell continued.

'Well, I'll be able to give you more information when the body's thawed some more and we do a full post, but for now I can tell you that your Jane Doe is Caucasian, in her twenties, five-feet-six-inches tall, with a slim build, and X-ray shows a COD of broken neck.'

Dr Bodell paused to give Eric time to take notes. She watched him, then continued. 'I thought you'd like to know that we've got good material for an ID. Take a look at your screen.'

They looked down at a video screen mounted in a console in front of them. The screen was black at first, then an image took up the whole screen, blurry and full of motion. Scott glanced at Dr Bodell, who was manipulating a pen-sized tube around the body's mouth. The autopsy assistant moved to the nearside of the table and immediately but unwittingly blocked Scott's view. He looked back to the screen and saw teeth as the camera moved around the mouth.

Dr Bodell's voice came through the speakers again. 'There. You see the filling in the canine?'

They replied simultaneously, 'No.' Then Scott remembered to press the microphone button so the pathologist could hear them. He pressed it and repeated, 'No.'

The pathologist chuckled and her assistant passed her an implement.

'Look at your screen again.'

They watched as a dental pick came into view and traced an oval on the outside surface of the canine.

'See how it's slightly whiter there on the labial surface?'

They could barely discern it and said as much. Dr Bodell seemed to be enjoying herself.

'A very expensive dentist somewhere would love the answers you two are giving.' Her assistant laughed and the pathologist continued.

'This is a high quality synthetic filling. Plus, there's some bonding between the canine and the lateral incisor.' She looked up at the two visitors. 'That kind of work isn't the norm for most of the Jane and John Does we get through here, so if she is in the system, the haystack just got smaller, gentlemen.'

She looked back down at the body. 'I can see why such good work was done on a mouth like this. Look at the teeth, the smile.'

She was now running the camera slowly across the front teeth. Scott mentally agreed that the teeth seemed unusually uniform in size and color.

Dr Bodell said, 'If you've got the money to

preserve a smile like that, you spend it.'

Scott looked from the screen to the pathologist. At that moment, the autopsy assistant stepped to the side, affording him a view of the body again. Scott's eyes automatically went to its mouth where metal clips now held back the corners of the upper lips. The dead woman appeared to be smiling.

Jayne came down the stairs and followed the voices to her mother's kitchen. Marie was wrapping sandwiches in wax paper while Steelie sat on the counter.

Steelie looked up at her and said, 'Your mom wants to help "cleanse" your apartment.'

'Thank you.' Jayne gave a slight shudder. 'I'd love to paint it, actually. Just totally lose all trace that a prowler was there.'

'Understood,' Marie said as she put the wax parcels into a paper bag. She handed this to Jayne. 'For the Agency lunch today. The vegetarian's for Steelie of course and I want you to ask Carol how she likes my wasabi mayonnaise.'

Jayne gave her a hug that lasted so long, Marie looked over her shoulder at Steelie and raised her eyebrows. Then she kissed her daughter. 'Does this mean you'll stay here a few more days?'

Jayne smiled but only said, 'Come on, Steelie. Carol's going to beat us to the office at this rate.'

As they walked to Jayne's truck, Steelie asked, 'Did you try to call Scott again?'

'Yes, and it went to voicemail again but this

time I left a detailed message.' She gave a shrug as she rolled down her window and started down Marie's winding driveway. 'Who knows what's going on out there? For all we know, the stakeout turned into a shootout.'

Steelie glanced at her. 'It may be Arizona but it's not the Wild West.' But she gauged Jayne's mood and added: 'Look, bad news travels fast, so if you haven't heard anything, he's fine.'

Eric and Scott had been questioning Wayne Spicer for two hours in an interview room at the Phoenix police station. Wayne had waived his right to a lawyer, so Scott had started by asking about the body in the freezer, her rigid smile coming into his mind as he looked at Wayne across the table. The suspect hadn't spoken except to ask for a soda, which he was still nursing, wiping spills from his chin with the inside edge of the shirt he'd been given to wear when the police took his clothes as evidence.

'She was a nice looking woman, Spicer.' Scott leaned on his elbows and tilted his head at the man, whose eyes closed against his voice. 'Where'd you meet her?' He leaned back in his chair. 'Were you watching her for a long time?'

Wayne's eyelids flew open but he didn't speak.

'What'd you do with the rest of her clothes? You keep those? Hmm, Spicer? You wear 'em?'

Wayne cupped his large hand around the soda can, swigged quickly, and wiped his chin.

'Not really your size, her clothes. She was just a tiny thing.' Scott leaned back across the table. 'What'd you do? Trick her to come with you?'

There was a flicker of a response in Wayne's face but he still did not speak.

When Eric took over questioning ten minutes later, he began by repeating questions he'd asked earlier in a different form. 'That really is a nice van you got, Wayne, with the cot in the back. Like going on road trips?'

No response.

'You like going north? Need to get a taste of rain every now and then, eh?' Eric chuckled and put his hands behind his head in a relaxed manner.

'You like Portland? You've been up there, right, Wayne? How about Georgia? Savannah's the real thing, isn't it?'

Scott watched from the wall. There wasn't even a flicker in Wayne's eyes as he looked directly at Eric.

Scott spoke without lifting his head from the wall. 'When were you going to cut her up?'

Wayne jumped up, sending his chair backwards to the floor. Eric got to his feet, preparing to fend off the big man but Wayne was stumbling backwards, toward the wall behind him and pointing his finger at Scott, who was standing at the ready across the room.

'I would *never* do that to her!' Wayne's voice cracked. 'She ... I...' He faltered, his face suffusing with blood. 'I would never do that.' After a moment, he righted the metal chair and sat back down, wrapping his hands around the soda can.

Eric glanced back at Scott, who nodded. Eric asked, 'Want another soda?'

Wayne contemplated this for a moment and

204

then nodded mutely.

'OK, we'll get you a soda.'

The agents left the room together and asked the police officer standing outside to wait with the suspect. Once Scott closed the door, he stopped in the hallway, ran his hands through his hair, and then smoothed it all down again. Eric crossed his arms and leaned against the wall. Phoenix police officers and administrative staff passed but took no notice of them.

'Well, at least you got a reaction,' Eric began.

Scott puffed out his cheeks. 'He doesn't like talking about the dismemberment.'

'Let's push him on it, then.'

Scott nodded. 'This guy has been under the radar according to NCIC. No criminal record, no voting record, no parking tickets. Where's he been putting the bodies? And why go back and forth between Georgia and Arizona?'

'I'll get the soda.' Eric went down the hallway and returned a few minutes later with a can. They re-entered the interview room and the police officer left.

This time, Scott sat at the table. He waited for Wayne to start the next soda before speaking.

'Let's talk about the cutting.'

Wayne's eyes flashed but he didn't speak.

Scott continued. 'We know you like to cut them up.'

Wayne frowned but remained silent.

'After all, that's what you did with Eleanor Patterson. And the others.'

Wayne gripped the edge of the table.

'Yep, we found your stuff on the side of the

205

freeway. Thought you could hide Mrs Patterson by cutting her into pieces, didn't ya?'

Wayne started breathing heavily and looked first at Scott, then at Eric, who was standing by the door, and then back at Scott.

'Well, she's getting her own back. Her finger's pointing at you, Spicer. The others will too.'

Wayne wiped sweat from his upper lip.

'Where's the rest of Mrs Patterson, huh, Spicer? I'm sure her family would like to know. Where'd you put the rest of them, the other girls?'

Wayne looked panicked for a moment, then used the hem of his shirt to wipe his face all over. 'Uh ... I need a break.'

Scott rolled his eyes toward the ceiling.

'I need a break,' repeated Wayne. 'I need to go to the bathroom.' He tried to smile. 'Can I get something to eat, too?'

'OK,' replied Eric.

Wayne looked up at him gratefully.

'Someone will bring you lunch and take you to use the head.'

The agents left the room and ushered in the police officer through the doorway.

'You rattled him,' said Eric.

'Let's get on to the ME; see if she's got a hit off of those teeth yet. If the woman in his freezer is from Georgia, this case will have a bow on it.'

But Scott's call to Dr Bodell was re-routed as soon as he identified himself. She had directed the receptionist to put the agent through to Cliff Lockwood, one of three medical investigators in the Medical Examiner's Office. Scott already knew that two of them were former detectives and one was a forensic anthropologist turned investigator. They went to scenes of all unattended deaths, tracked down identifying material on every Jane and John Doe in Maricopa County, and notified next-of-kin for any body processed where the family was not already aware of death.

Cliff Lockwood was one of the former detectives and had been at the ME's Office since – according to Dr Bodell – the year dot. When he came on the line, his voice was as gravelly as that of a life-long smoker.

'Yeah, we got an ID on your girl already.' Lockwood broke off to cough and brought up a loogie that Scott could hear being spat out somewhere.

'I'm ready,' he replied impatiently, raising his voice over Lockwood's hacking.

'You've got a Katherine Ruth Alston. That's Alpha, Lima, Sierra, Tango, Oscar, November.' He cleared his throat. 'Date of birth: one niner of '79. Caucasian. Five-six, one-twenty-five. Brown and brown. Missing from Los Angeles, California on five-twelve of '99.'

Scott immediately started calculating. Her disappearance pre-dated the cases of the missing prostitutes in Atlanta. Had she been Spicer's first kill and he had kept her body as a prize? 'NCIC number?'

'Mike-one-niner-seven-seven-three-one-niner-five-three.'

'What were her circs?'

'Suspicious missing – abduction. She was an

adult, car found on a freeway, no sign of a struggle. A student reported missing by her parents. I'll be making contact today.'

'Which freeway?'

'Says the 101. One more thing, Houston. We ID'd her through dental records on NCIC and there's a note on the file that they didn't come direct from a doc. Some shop out your way was involved. An Agency 32/1. You know it?'

'You could say that.'

'What the hell do they do?'

'Forensic profiles of mispers.'

Lockwood let out a low whistle and said, 'Leave it to you Californians to find a niche market. They been around long?'

'No, but you'll see their stuff on NCIC, usually related to cold cases. I'll bet your ME's have heard of them.'

As soon as Scott was off the call, he picked up another voicemail message from Jayne. He first relayed the Alston identification details to Eric and then Jayne's description of the results of Jeppsen's search of the Agency 32/1 offices.

'Do they have any idea what the bug's about?' Eric asked.

'I don't know. But it's gotta be one of their own cases.'

'Didn't you give Jayne the Patterson ID on the Agency's landline?'

'Yeah but I'm not concerned about someone overhearing that. It wouldn't mean anything to an outsider.'

'We can take a minute for you to call her now.'

'No.' Scott looked at his partner. 'What I want

208

is to get in there with our new ammunition against Spicer.'

'Fine. Let's wrap him up.'

# EIGHTEEN

Eric had resumed his position near the door inside the interrogation room. Scott sat across the table from Wayne, who appeared to have perked up after eating. His hands were clasped loosely on the table as though he was about to close a business deal and he was smiling childishly, like he had a secret.

Scott opened the thin manila folder he had brought into the room. It held a single typed sheet of paper, the font small and all in capitals, difficult to read upside down. From Wayne's position, it could look like a printout of a police document. From Scott's side of the table, it looked like a printout of turn-by-turn driving directions from the Mission Hotel to the Maricopa County Medical Examiner's Office. Scott looked down at the sheet of paper and spoke.

'We know where you picked her up, Spicer. The girl in your freezer.'

Wayne's smile faltered.

Scott looked at him. 'The 101 a favorite of yours?'

Wayne jerked his arms off the table, putting his hands out of sight.

Scott looked at the sheet of directions again, then stared at Wayne. 'She must have been

210

different from the other ones.' He watched a bead of sweat develop on Wayne's upper lip. 'We figured she was different because you didn't cut her up.'

Wayne suddenly bared clenched teeth and pounded his fist on the table. 'Stop saying that word!'

'But once you had her in the van—'

'It wasn't a van!' Wayne almost yelled. Then he spoke more softly. 'It was a car.'

Scott remained silent.

Eric spoke quietly from his position by the door. 'Your car, Wayne? You have a car as well as a van?'

Wayne smiled at Eric's gentle tone, and directed his reply to him, ignoring Scott who was now leaning back in his chair. 'No, I *had* a car. The van's mine but it wasn't always mine.'

'When did you get the van?'

'A little while ago.' Wayne's eyes looked beyond Eric, towards the door. A smile played on his lips. 'I was going to go away in it. With Katie.'

'Who sold you the van?'

'I don't know his name.'

'What'd you pay for it?'

'It was a trade. I traded him my car for his van.'

'That's pretty unusual, Wayne. Most people like cash. Sounds like you're making this up. It's always been your van.'

'No, I told you, it was a trade. That nosy hag across the street will tell you. She saw the whole thing.'

Scott tensed. If Wayne had a witness, then this was a different ballgame. He waited impatiently for Eric's next question.

'When?'

'Like I said, a little while ago.'

The answer was vague but Scott's mind was already running with the implications of this. If Wayne Spicer was telling the truth, he was linked to the death of Katherine Alston but wasn't responsible for the body parts they had found on the freeway, so likely had nothing to do with the crimes in Georgia. Scott's mind raced. The Vehicle Identification Numbers on the dash and door of the van had been mutilated, which meant finding the registered owner would take time because the Crime Lab would have to dismantle the vehicle to locate the confidential VIN on the van's frame. So *if* Wayne was telling the truth, they needed a description of his car and they needed a description of the man now driving it because that person was the real owner of the van. Scott glanced at Eric, who nodded and spoke.

'When exactly, Wayne?'

Wayne's focus came back to Eric but now he looked more petulant. 'A couple of days. He swore it was clean.'

'His name, Wayne. What's his name?'

'He doesn't have a name.'

'What do you mean, he doesn't have a name?'

Wayne smiled. 'I know his screen name.'

Eric had begun pacing around the room. Scott assumed his partner shared his impatience. If this man with no name really existed, he had eluded them again and they were spinning their wheels on the Freeway Case by interrogating Spicer for so long.

'What are you talking about, Wayne?' Eric sounded tense.

'I met him on off-the-grid-dot-net.'

'A website?'

'*The* website. I've been getting tips there for when I go off ... with Katie. No one will be able to find us. We'll just be on a road trip all the time. Lots of people are doing it.'

'OK. What's his screen name?'

'Tripper.' Wayne sounded like he was boasting. 'You won't find him. He's a Level Three. You never find those guys. They find you.'

'So Tripper's driving your car now, Wayne?'

He nodded.

'Describe the car.'

Wayne put his hands back on the table and looked back at Scott for the first time. He became serious.

'Only if you leave me and Katie alone.'

Scott looked at him. He tapped his pen on the tabletop as if he was considering opening negotiations but he was actually thinking about the fact that a serial killer was still on the highways. They needed to post a nationwide All Points Bulletin for 'Tripper' and the car without delay. He didn't convey this through body language, only shrugging and looking towards Eric to draw Wayne's eyes back there. Eric crossed to the table, looking at Wayne curiously.

'Are you trying to bargain, Wayne?'

'Well, yeah. I mean, you need me.' He laughed

uncertainly, seeming confused by the new edge in the agent's voice.

Eric rested his palms on the table and brought his face down to Wayne's ear. The angle was sharp and Wayne couldn't turn his head to keep eye contact.

'That's where you're wrong,' Eric all but whispered. 'If you don't tell us, we're going to track it down in the California DMV archives and your old registration is going to be right there, which will lead us straight to your car. Give it up, Wayne. There is no bargaining.'

Wayne looked back at Scott and then closed his eyes. He started to rock side to side in his seat like a schoolchild who needs to go to the bathroom.

'Look at me, Wayne.' Eric's voice was firm as he stepped away.

Wayne looked but his lips were moving, forming silent words.

'You're not getting out of this.'

Wayne kept rocking and looked at the door. He was smiling and rocking. 'Katie. Katie.'

As Scott watched him, he realized he believed Wayne. Tripper existed and Katie had been Wayne's most cherished possession. He knew how to break him down. Scott leaned back in his chair and spoke.

'They've cut her up, Spicer.'

Wayne stopped murmuring and rocking and squinted hard at Scott, who continued.

He smiled at Wayne. 'You knew that, right?' He pulled his chair up to the desk and looked at the file folder before speaking again, keeping his

214

voice mild.

'She's not your Katie anymore, Spicer. She's Katherine and they've cut her down her middle.'

'You're lying!' Wayne spat out the words, saliva landing on the table in tiny, bursting bubbles.

Scott shook his head. 'We saw her. Right before we came over here this morning.'

Wayne shook his head, faster and faster.

'You know why they had to cut her up, right?'

Wayne looked at him, his mouth open in wonder.

'Because of you.' Scott shrugged. 'If you had not abducted and killed her, that never would have happened.'

Wayne shut his eyes tight and sucked in his lips.

'How do you think they worked out who she was? They had to cut her up, check her out. Had to look at her bones – all that pretty flesh was no use. Didja know that, Spicer?' Scott's voice rose as he continued. 'She's not your Katie. She's just a girl whose teeth are more important than everything else about her now.' He was shouting now. 'They took her teeth right out, Spicer. Cut 'em right out of her head.'

'NO!' Wayne shouted and pounded the table. 'No!'

Scott stood up and leaned on the table, staring at Wayne's face, which was screwed up tight, tears and sweat mingling on his quivering cheeks. He opened his eyes as though the room was too bright.

Scott caught his gaze and held it, speaking

215

rapidly. 'Her parents are going to pick her up. Ever think about her parents, Spicer? Huh? They're taking her back home. By tomorrow, you won't even be in the same state as her. Tell us about your car, Spicer. It's just you now. Katie's gone.'

Wayne looked panicked but couldn't tear his eyes away from Scott, who decided that Wayne looked hungry for information and redemption.

'Give us Tripper, Mr Spicer. Give us Tripper and you're out of here for today. That means you can sit in the holding cell, which is right next to the morgue. Did you know that? You can spend one more night next to Katie. She'll be next door. All wrapped up for her big trip tomorrow.'

Wayne wiped his face with his shirt. He struggled to form one word through his chattering teeth. 'Please.' Once he'd uttered it, he couldn't stop. 'Please. Please. Please.'

By the time Scott and Eric were back in the hallway outside the interview room, Scott was holding notes of Wayne Spicer's description of Tripper, the alleged original owner of the van with the Georgia license plates. It didn't differ significantly from the descriptions given by the witnesses in LA. Now, they just needed his real name.

They'd also obtained a description of Wayne's car and dispatched Phoenix Police Department uniformed officers to Prickly Pear Close to conduct interviews that could confirm or refute Wayne's story about his trade with Tripper. Their next job was to interview Wayne Spicer to get the details of how he had abducted Katherine

216

Alston from the Hollywood Freeway in 1999.

They started down the hall to their temporary office, swerving around local officers making their way between ends of the building. Two male officers, one with a short afro and the other redheaded, both appearing almost too young to be in employment, stopped them. Neither officer addressed the agents with any deference and the redhead was chewing gum that was visible when he spoke.

'We're just finishing the report on the search of the Spicer garage. Do you want a verbal?'

'Yeah,' Scott replied. 'What'd you find?'

'Nothing,' replied the one with the afro.

'What do you mean by "nothing"?'

'The guy's a computer freak. He doesn't own anything besides a huge chest freezer – totally clean – a fast computer, and some clothes. And, oh yeah, we *deduced* that he's still into Halloween.'

The rookies laughed.

Scott looked at them and shifted on his feet. 'What are you talking about?'

The redhead took over. 'He's got this closet, right? Everything's all neatly folded, yeah? Sweat suits, pants, shirts. Except for this one Halloween costume hanging up. What a joke.'

Scott's tone was flat. He was tired of having to extract each piece of information with a question. 'What kind of costume?'

'Police uniform.' He snapped his gum loudly and looked down at his own uniformed front. 'Pretty shitty imitation of an LAPD kit.'

Scott went cold.

Eric grabbed the redhead's upper arms. 'Listen to me, was there a badge?'

The young officer's gum fell out of his mouth in his surprise at being manhandled. He turned his head away as Eric's face came frighteningly close to his.

*'Was there a badge?'*

Scott pulled down on Eric's arms. He dropped them to his sides but kept glaring. The rookie looked like he wanted to get away from both agents. He directed his response to Eric.

'No, man. No badge.'

Steelie answered her cell phone and was surprised to hear Eric launching into questions without so much as a greeting, and they weren't questions about the wiretap at the Agency.

'I need to know if you ever got a summons after driving away from that cop.'

'No.'

'What did he look like?'

'I mostly remember his swagger—'

'Could you tell his ethnicity?'

'I'm pretty sure he was white. Light-colored moustache. Couldn't really see his face because of his glasses and the hat.'

'What about build?'

'Regular. Maybe slim.'

She heard him speaking to someone else. 'He wasn't overweight. No way it's him.'

'What's going on, Eric?'

His voice came back to her. 'Look, a fake LAPD uniform was found with the perp we've pulled in out here. It made us think of what

218

happened to you because this guy might have used the uniform to get the vic into his car.'

'Shit.'

'But our guy doesn't match your description so it's either a coincidence or there's another guy out there doing the same thing. And listen, Steelie, we caught a 32/1 case out here. I can't give you any details but we want you all to have a head's up.'

Steelie hung up but sat trying to recall the cop – she'd convinced herself it had been a cop – who'd stopped her, when Carol's voice came through the desk telephone to say that she had Ben Alston holding on Line 1 for either Steelie or Jayne. Line 1's blinking red light went solid before Steelie could get to her desk, so she trotted up to Jayne's office.

Jayne was clearly being told a string of facts because she was only murmuring 'I understand,' or 'OK.' Steelie read Jayne's notes from upside down.

*Call fr MI in Maricopa. Kate ID'd. COD broken neck. No sexual assault. Liaise tomor-row—*

Then Jayne said, 'All right. Did the medical investigator tell you which medical examiner you'd be dealing with? Bodell? You'd be fine with her, she has a very comfortable manner ... No – of course, if you would like us to liaise, we will ... All right, Ben, thank you, that's very generous. We'll hear from you shortly then.' She stood as she finished the call and Carol came into the room.

Carol asked, 'Has something happened? I

219

could hear it in his voice when I answered the phone.'

Jayne shook her head in consternation. 'He's completely worked up. Kate's been found dead but even though he's been told she died quickly and wasn't assaulted, he can't understand why he got a phone call from a medical investigator at the ME's Office in Phoenix. The police told the Alstons in '99 that there were no signs of a struggle in or around her car when it was found on the Hollywood Freeway, so they're trying to figure out why she would have willingly gotten out of her car and gone with someone to Arizona.'

Steelie raked her hair back from her forehead. 'I think I know why.' She thought for a second then let her bangs flip back. 'OK, I just had a call from Eric, asking me about my tail light stop last Thursday. He said they've picked up a suspect in Arizona who's a civilian with a fake LAPD uniform. And he also said that they've come across one of our cases out there. There's a chance it could be Kate Alston and the uniform is related.'

Jayne sat back on the edge of her desk. 'Well, the Alstons are hell-bent on finding out what happened. They're flying to Phoenix in the morning and I agreed for us to liaise when they go to the ME's office. They're picking up our flights too.'

Steelie said, 'Well, if Scott and Eric's case does involve Kate, then someone may be able to tell her parents what happened.'

Jayne looked at Carol. 'You're the expert on

this.'

Carol spoke without hesitation. 'The family needs to know. Give them the hard stuff and they *will* handle it.'

'But the detail about the uniform will be sub judice, so ... we can't tell them but we can urge Scott and Eric to divulge it, to help the Alstons deal with this.' She looked at Steelie. 'Call Scott. Tell him we don't need confirmation on whose body they've found but if it's Kate and if the suspect has actually stated that he used a uniform to get her out of her car, then they should give the parents as much consideration as they can. This has to come from them.'

'You got it,' Steelie replied, going back to her office.

As soon as Scott and Eric issued the All Points Bulletin for Wayne Spicer's car, they went down to the holding cells of the Phoenix Police Department.

When they identified themselves to the duty sergeant, he buzzed them into the small room beyond his station. The room had four cells coming off it like satellites and they could see Wayne through the bars of his cell to their left. He was stroking the yellow-painted wall in the direction he believed the morgue lay, with Katie's body within.

The agents had already agreed to take a tender approach with Wayne, going down his Memory Lane while trying to get him to separate fantasy from reality. Scott set a tape to record and re-cautioned Wayne, then Eric began with an

221

admiring comment on the verisimilitude of the police uniform found in Wayne's closet. Wayne took the bait and was off, his words like a current of water rushing along a country brook.

He said he had come up with the idea of getting a false police uniform after several people mistook his car, a black Crown Victoria, for a police cruiser and had pulled over to let him overtake when traffic was badly backed up on the busy Los Angeles freeways. After his parents moved to Arizona, Wayne had stayed in LA and bought the patrolman's uniform from a costume shop. When he wore it, some people waved at him; people who would normally never give him the time of day.

Then he purchased a swirling red light that he rigged up into his car's electrical system with wire and a control switch, using rudimentary electronics skills he'd gained while working at Radio Shack. But he had never used the red light, or even tried to stop and talk to anyone, until he saw the brown Datsun ahead of him on the 101 Freeway early in December 1999, its hazard lights flashing a distress signal.

He was wearing the police uniform that evening. He had the false badge on the seat next to him. At the last minute, he had decided to pull over and see if someone would actually talk to him. He didn't care if it was a man or a woman, as long as it wasn't more than one person. He had thought that more than one person could be dangerous because 'you never know what sort of people there are out there.' He had pulled on to the shoulder, cutting off other cars whose drivers he saw glare at him through his rearview mirror, their faces softening when he turned on the swirling red light.

The young woman in the Datsun was beautiful. She smiled and rolled down her window. She barely glanced at his badge and so he had put it in his pocket. He'd asked her, 'What's the problem, ma'am?' just like he'd seen police do on television. She had explained that the car had broken down and she had been hoping a tow truck or a police officer would come along because she didn't have a car phone or a cell phone. She didn't give him the pitying expression he was used to seeing at his job or when he tried to talk to people waiting in line at the supermarket.

He had wanted to talk with her more. He asked her to 'step into' his vehicle, on the passenger side, so that she'd be safe from the traffic hurtling past. But once she was inside, she looked uncertain. He forgot the 'cop routine' and she began to look panicked. She had tried to get out of his car but the door handle on the passenger side had been broken since he bought it. She didn't know that so she had started screaming and kicking her legs and trying to get the attention of passing cars. He wanted to let her out. When he leaned across her, it was only to roll down the window so he could open the door from the outside handle. But she didn't know that either. She tried to climb past him, into the backseat.

She had managed to put her thumbs into his eyes and, well, he couldn't see then, could he?

He had fallen against her and the weight of his body had pulled them both down on to the front bench seat, his feet slipping on the loose floor mats and her small body half under him. He couldn't get any purchase with his hands so had wrenched his elbow up and it connected with some part of her. She was instantly still and quiet.

He didn't even know what had happened to her. He had tapped her cheek; her head lolled loosely. He tried to make her speak; she would not talk anymore. The police badge was digging into his thigh and he pushed himself up off the girl. He turned off the red swirling light. Looking at her, he knew he couldn't leave her there on the freeway by herself. He opened her handbag and found her driver's license. Next to the photo it said her name was Katherine. He looked over at her, the dark hair, her smooth skin. He knew she was a Katie. A car honked as it passed, its headlights catching his peripheral vision. She would be his Katie, but they would have to leave California. 'She's been the only one. She'll always be the only one.'

At that point, Wayne had looked in the direction of the morgue and refused to say more. The agents left Wayne Spicer in his cell, his big body pressed against the wall in a flat embrace.

As they emerged from the police station, Scott checked his cell phone and saw he had two voicemail messages. He listened to them as he followed Eric over to the Suburban. The first one was from Steelie and didn't require a return call. The second was from Cliff Lockwood, the Mari-

224

copa County medical investigator. He had asked Scott to return his call as a matter of urgency, even if it was after-hours, and had left a cell phone number.

Lockwood sounded somewhat less gravelly now that it was evening. Scott suspected a liqueur had lubricated his throat.

'I've got the parents of your girl flying out here from California ASAP tomorrow. They got a lot of questions I can't answer yet. But I figured maybe you could. Can you make it over here at eleven hundred hours?'

Scott thought for a moment and looked over at Eric, who was driving them to the Mission Hotel where they would stay the night, due to get on the road for Los Angeles at 7 o'clock the next morning. If he stayed to meet the Alstons, his partner would need to go ahead of him to coordinate the search for Tripper, an endeavor that would be headquartered in their office in LA.

Scott stalled for time by asking a question he already knew the answer to, thanks to Steelie's message. 'What kind of questions are we talking about?'

Lockwood sighed. 'Seems they want to know how their daughter ended up out here in AZ in the hands of some perp. I'll be telling them about the freezer before they view the body but that's about the extent of my knowledge.'

Scott briefly considered just instructing Lockwood to tell the Alstons about the LAPD uniform costume. He could hear a television sitcom and canned laughter in the background on Lockwood's end of the phone. Scott realized he wasn't even sure about the MI's bedside manner. It was his duty, not Lockwood's.

'I'll be there.' He hung up and relayed the details to Eric, then told him about Steelie's message, which recommended someone inform the Alstons about the circumstances of their daughter's abduction.

Eric nodded as he pulled the car into the parking space at the hotel. 'By the way, have you called Jayne since we were at her place and you basically shouted at her?'

Scott opened his door, paused, and then got out. 'No.'

Eric exhaled as he cut the engine. 'Don't let the other guy get her, Scott.'

Scott frowned at him. 'What other guy?'

'I don't know, but there will be another guy eventually. You shouldn't give up unless you're ready to see that ... *and* go to their wedding.'

'Who said I was giving up?' Scott said as he closed the door.

# DAY NINE

## Wednesday

# NINETEEN

Southwest Airlines Flight 597 from Phoenix to Los Angeles had arrived on time and Eric was walking into his office on Wilshire Boulevard by mid-morning. The first call he made was to the Information Technology investigators on the third floor to get an update on the request they'd phoned in from Phoenix to have the ITI monitor www.offthegrid.net for activity by the screen name 'Tripper'. They reported no activity yet, but they were pulling caches of old posts by that screen name. So, no leads yet on Tripper's identity.

Eric glanced behind him at the computer that was dedicated to NCIC traffic. He was waiting for a beep on it that would indicate a hit. There was no guarantee it would be a hit on their All Points Bulletin for Wayne's car because the system would beep for any report filed by the Los Angeles office on any case since the database had been in use. But he was still waiting for that beep.

227

The phone rang and he picked up. It was the Phoenix Crime Laboratory. They had a preliminary report on the examination of Wayne Spicer's/Tripper's van: numerous particles of biological trace evidence had been located inside the vehicle. Although the van's interior appeared to have been cleaned thoroughly, the criminalists had collected traces of blood, saliva, and epithelial from its faults, joins, and other surfaces. It was too early for the lab to tell if all the biological material came from a single source or from multiple sources, or whether any of it could ultimately link Tripper to the vehicle. They told Eric they would need reference material from people known to be in the van; for example, the man behind the screen name.

Eric looked back at the computer. Nothing.

Scott's first thought when Cliff Lockwood opened his office door was that he could have been Kris Kristofferson's stunt double. His barrel-like chest blocked the doorway for a moment before he invited Scott in, indicating a seat to the left that was turned to face two people who were rising from their chairs.

The room wasn't large and with everyone standing up, Scott felt like he had walked into a closet that was already too full. But it opened up the moment Lockwood sat down behind his desk. He introduced Ben and Linda Alston, describing Scott as the law enforcement officer who had found their daughter.

Linda Alston had brown hair caught in a loose bun. Her eyes were a clear blue and she was looking at Scott with undisguised relief. Ben Alston had a close-cropped brown beard. He extended his hand to Scott, then folded his other hand over the handshake. Neither man spoke. Linda smiled at Scott but didn't shake his hand. She was holding a sizeable piece of cardboard to her chest.

'Please take a seat, Mr and Mrs Alston,' Lockwood began. 'Agent Houston is here to answer any questions for you that he can. As I mentioned before, he may be limited by the needs of the ongoing investigation into your daughter's case but those limits will be lifted as soon as possible.'

Ben and Linda nodded.

Linda turned to Scott, still holding the cardboard tight. 'We wanted, first of all, to thank you for finding Kate.'

Scott nodded gravely.

She continued with more difficulty. 'We've seen her now and—' She broke off, her mouth twisting, and her husband put his long arms about her shoulders. She drew herself up. 'And we wanted you to know what a beautiful girl she really was.'

She turned the piece of cardboard around and Scott was looking at a large portrait of a smiling version of the woman he'd found in Wayne Spicer's freezer. He felt as though the color ink had flowed through her like blood, bringing her to life. And then he took in her smile. He would recognize those teeth anywhere.

Ben was saying, 'Kate was very bright. A bright, beautiful ... good girl.'

229

Lockwood said, 'All of that is very clear to us, Mr Alston. I hope you understand that.'

Linda had more to say. 'Mr Houston, how did she end up out here?'

Scott knew from Steelie's phone message that if he said nothing else to the Alstons, he had to answer this question. He had been going over it with Eric the night before at the hotel, each trying to put the known facts into more palatable terms, and failing. Eric had finally said, 'It won't be the words you use, it'll be the way you say them.'

Scott glanced at Lockwood, who was looking back at him while reclined in his chair, his mouth obscured by his fingers, which were interlocked in a steeple. As Scott turned to the Alstons he played in his mind the visit to Spicer in the holding cell the evening before.

The words that Scott would use to tell the Alstons this story were censored by his law enforcement training, which protected the future prosecution of Wayne Spicer and were informed by his sense of what the Alstons' image should be of their daughter's last moments. He tried to soften the edge of every word.

'Mrs Alston, the person who abducted your daughter was wearing a replica of a police officer's uniform when he approached her sitting in her broken-down car on the shoulder of the Hollywood Freeway. It was by showing her what looked like a real police badge that he was able to get her to leave her own vehicle. He's kept her body with him since that time.'

Scott suddenly realized that although Ben

230

Alston had remained motionless, tears were streaming down his face. He did not wipe them away but kept one hand gripped around his wife's shoulder and the other on her arm.

Linda Alston smiled, her eyes bright and fixed somewhere behind Scott. 'Kate always minded people in authority.' She patted Ben's knee as she wiped her eyes quickly with a tissue she pulled from under her watchstrap. 'She did what I would have done.' Her voice caught on the last word and her hand flew to her mouth, the tissue only half covering the pain hidden behind it. A muffled 'Oh, God' escaped and she collapsed against her husband, who tilted his face down into her hair. The photo of Kate smiled back at them from where it lay in Linda's lap.

Scott felt as though the Alstons were radiating a sorrow so raw that it was palpable. He found himself swallowing several times and looked back at Lockwood, who nodded at him slowly. Scott realized he'd just passed some kind of test and knew he'd underestimated Cliff Lockwood. He needed to leave. He returned Lockwood's nod and walked out, not stopping until he was beyond the front doors of the Medical Examiner's Office. Immediately, he was assaulted by midday heat and a blare of nearby ambulance sirens. The morgue was next to the hospital, not the police station and its yellow holding cells. He had lied to Wayne Spicer on that point.

Dr Bodell interrupted the story she was telling Jayne and Steelie to introduce two colleagues who were emerging from the autopsy suite. One of the men said, 'I understand you had a role in this freezer case?' He nodded back to the suite, where a technician was rolling Kate Alston's bagged body on a trolley back to the refrigerated storage room, now that her parents had finished their viewing.

'It looks like the full dental profile we managed to get added to the misper file helped with the ID,' Jayne said.

Steelie gestured at Bodell. 'If it wasn't for the dental worksheet Liz made for us last year, we wouldn't have even known how to code half the synthetic restorations for NCIC.'

Dr Bodell turned to her colleague. 'They're too modest.'

He smiled faintly, assessing Steelie. 'Well, it's good to meet you.' He looked at Dr Bodell. 'Lunch, Elizabeth?'

She nodded and said, 'I'll catch up with you, Hal.' She motioned for Steelie and Jayne to head for the rear exit doors.

When the three of them reached the bay where two body recovery vans were parked, Steelie leaned into Dr Bodell and whispered, 'Is there something we should know, *Elizabeth*?'

Dr Bodell smiled but ushered her on. 'Go on around front. Your clients will be needing you. Jayne, come back to visit again soon. You needn't bring Steelie and her innuendos.'

As Jayne and Steelie rounded the building, Steelie said, 'That makes me sound like I'm part of a band. Steelie and The Innuendos. But what would we play?'

'Something heavy-handed,' Jayne said as they

took up a position under the mesquite trees casting dappled shade at the front of the building. Only their reflection was visible in the tinted double doors that led into this side of the structure, where relatives of the dead came and went. The reflection showed someone emerging from a car behind them and then a voice called out their names. They turned around to see Scott next to a Suburban one row back in the parking lot.

Going toward him, Jayne said, 'Scott? What are you doing here?'

His mouth was a grim line. 'The Alston case.' He looked at Steelie. 'I got your message. They're in there with the MI now.'

'Thanks for arranging that,' Steelie replied.

'I didn't do anything.' His tone was sharp. He wiped a hand over his face. 'Sorry. Are you escorting them?'

Jayne nodded.

'Good. Well, I've got to get on the road. Eric's already in LA.' He gave a lopsided smile. 'It's nice to see you guys.'

As he turned away, Steelie nudged Jayne while calling after Scott. 'Um, Scott? Do you mind taking Jayne with you?'

He turned back and looked at Jayne. 'No. Why?'

'Because I...' Jayne looked questioningly at Steelie.

'Because of the turbulence,' Steelie said. 'It was a bad flight out and you said you'd prefer to drive back if you could.' She turned to Scott. 'She was ready to get a rental car, so this would be perfect.'

Scott appeared to accept the explanation and went to move something from the passenger seat of his vehicle.

Steelie murmured to Jayne, 'He needs back-up, Jayne, if only to keep awake. I'll stay with Ben and Linda.'

Jayne nodded and Steelie gave her a quick hug in parting.

It took seven and a half hours of driving for the essence of the meeting with the Alstons to percolate through Scott's consciousness and then it hit him hard.

It happened in stages. The first stage made him feel like he couldn't breathe. As he gulped air, he hyperventilated. That was the second stage. The third stage made him think he was having a heart attack. His hands tingled where they gripped the steering wheel and his chest was tight. He felt there was a direct electrical current between his heart and his hands.

He veered wildly from the right lane on to the shoulder, spraying loose gravel before steering into the upcoming exit lane, and that's when he became aware of Jayne calling out his name. He automatically read the exit sign as he passed under it: *Calimesa*. Scott had never heard of it and he didn't care. His eyes were watering and he needed to stop the car.

On the exit ramp, he pulled sharply on to the shoulder and put the transmission into park. He didn't turn off the engine because he felt like his breathing was getting easier, even though it was made up of deep breaths he couldn't control. Jayne was gripping the dash and he sensed she was staring at him but he was calming slightly, sure now that he wasn't having a heart attack. He closed his eyes in relief and that's when he saw her: Kate Alston. Preserved in the cold stillness of the freezer. Smiling at him from the autopsy table. Living in her parents' photograph. Her parents. Their devastation.

The sob was dry but shocked him into opening his eyes. He slammed the palms of his hands against the steering wheel and then gripped it tightly. He squeezed his eyes shut and, immediately, the same physical sensations tore through him, followed by an image of Kate Alston's teeth, disembodied, ruthlessly exposed. He didn't realize Jayne had opened a door until hot desert air filled the cabin with the musky scent of creosote. He opened his eyes again and saw the back of Jayne's head, her familiar wavy hair just in front of him as she reached under his arms to turn off the engine. He couldn't speak.

'Come on,' she said. 'You need to get out of there.'

He felt like her voice was coming from a great distance away. She reached around him and undid his seatbelt, then pulled his hands from their hold on the steering wheel.

'It's all right, Scott. Come on.'

Tripper cruised the streets in one of his favorite Atlanta neighborhoods, savoring the familiarity of both the dark stretches and the residential blocks where elderly owners lived in the back at night, the volume on their televisions cranked up because Medicare still didn't cover hearing aids. He'd taken risks in Los Angeles – especially with the surveillance gear – even though it had provided the answers he needed and thereby allowed him to move freely again. But it had still involved risks. He'd mitigated them by retrieving the repeater from outside the brunette's apartment, which ensured that, if anyone ever found the wiretaps, they'd assume a Peeping Tom, not someone at a distance, put them there.

Tripper considered the white hatchback he'd been following, looked at the street they were on, and decided it was time to get started; he did need new dump material. He turned on the red light on his dashboard and the hatchback dutifully pulled over ahead of him.

The only building on the street was an office complex under construction. Its windowless bulk was dark, the workers long since home for the night. As Tripper walked up to the car, he missed his van and the old method. But the van had to go and this new method had potential. He leaned into the driver's open window.

'License and registration, ma'am.'

The driver handed the two items to him without speaking.

Tripper stood up and perused them. Her name was Pamela Winton. He leaned back down.

'You sure were in a hurry back there, Mrs Winton.'

'It's *Ms* Winton.'

'Step out of the vehicle, ma'am. I require you to complete a sobriety test.'

236

She sighed and got out of the car. Tripper smiled to himself. The new method had passed its test. *Ms* Winton, on the other hand, has just failed hers. He watched her move to the sidewalk, which was disappearing under sand and gravel seeping out from the construction site, unhindered by the tall chain-link boundary fence.

He directed her in a friendly tone: 'Put your hands out to either side of your body at shoulder height and walk towards me, one foot in front of the other, with your eyes shut.'

As soon as the woman closed her eyes, Tripper moved behind her, clamping an arm around her body and a hand over her mouth. She raised both hands and tried to pull his hand off her face. He wrenched her to the side so forcefully that her feet left the ground for a moment. But when she came down again, she stamped hard on his right instep. He inhaled sharply, inadvertently relaxing his grip enough for her to get the purchase she needed to pull one of his hands down and she bit the soft skin between his thumb and first finger.

Now he only had one hand firmly on her and she repeatedly jabbed her left elbow behind her in gawky, unplanned movements. He was aware that while the method he'd used had got the mark out of her car, it didn't get her *into* his car. It was always easier, and safer, when they got in themselves instead of him fighting them first. He moved in to control her but this allowed a jab that ordinarily would've only bruised him to hit his solar plexus and he keeled forward, struggling to breathe. The woman seized him by the hair and pulled downwards. As Tripper's face thudded against her right knee he was reminded of how little fat covers a patella once the knee is bent.

Pamela Winton whimpered as she stared down at the police officer. He was lying on the sandy pavement, face down and silent. Then he groaned and she leapt away, crying out. As she stood in the beam of his patrol car's headlights, she could see him slowly pull himself to lie on his side, and then he collapsed on to his back. Blood flowed freely from his nose and across his face, only pausing at his earlobes to pool before the overflow dripped on to the gritty pavement.

Pamela Winton clutched her shirt about herself and trembled. She knew no one would believe that a policeman had attacked her unless she had some proof of her own. She looked up and down the street. It was deserted; not a single car or person visible in the glow of the streetlights. She peered at the policeman. He was breathing but his eyes were closed. His badge reflected the swirling light from the dashboard of his vehicle. Pamela Winton took a deep breath and then lunged at him, screaming in fear as she ripped his badge off along with most of the shirt pocket. She continued to scream even as she sped away in her hatchback. Her distress trailed out her open window only to be trapped by the car's slipstream and stay with her.

# TWENTY

If Atlanta security guard Troy Purcell had
rounded the corner a minute earlier, he might
have heard Pamela Winton's tires leaving a
rubber deposit as she cornered at the end of the
street. But his scheduled perimeter check of the
construction site was all out of whack that night,
on account of someone throwing eggs at his car
while he was inside the security trailer. He knew
from experience that egg had to be washed off
immediately, preferably with a clear soda. So
he'd had to find his boss's stash of Diet Slice,
clean the car, and then make a careful note to
replace the soda as soon as his shift ended at
6 a.m.

When he saw the prone body by Gate 5, he
knew someone was having a worse night than he
was. But he was filled with dread when he saw
the swirling light making patterns on the dirty
rear window of what had to be a police cruiser
parked ahead with its headlights on. Troy Purcell
pulled into the curb and looked to see if anyone
else was around. No one. He got out and locked
his own car, noticing the transfer on its door:
*Premium Security Corp.* His pride at seeing that
renewed his determination and he walked over
to the body.

The man was bloodied but breathing. He was wearing a dark uniform with a hole in his left chest pocket; a wounded police officer.

The security guard made two calls on his phone. The first was to the ambulance service and the other was to the local police station, Chesterton.

Before either unit arrived, the officer lying on the ground regained enough consciousness to murmur something and attempt to sit up. But Troy Purcell was not going to have that on his head. He held the officer down, his palms on the wounded man's chest, while he reassured him that the ambulance and his brother officers were on their way. When the sirens were audible, the officer stopped trying to get up and Troy Purcell believed he'd lost consciousness.

Eric was frustrated. The evening was closing in and he hadn't had a single call about Wayne Spicer's vehicle. He had been hoping some fresh patrol officer somewhere would be enthusiastically monitoring APB's and then miraculously catch Tripper on a routine traffic stop. Eric was just getting up from his desk to get a cup of coffee when his supervisor, Craig Turner, walked into the room, holding a single sheet of paper.

Eric had only been working under Turner for a few weeks but they had met a number of times at Quantico where the Bureau veteran regularly ran seminars or flew in to do special trainings. So Eric knew that it was normal for the wrinkles on Turner's forehead to be reaching up into his receding hairline. What wasn't normal was the resigned way Turner indicated that Eric sit back down.

'Where's your partner, Eric?'

'En route from Phoenix, sir.'

Turner perched his lean body on the edge of the desk and fixed him with the unblinking stare that had earned him the nickname of 'Ice' among Quantico newbies – a devolution from 'IC', which was the acronym for Turner's original nickname, 'Iron Curtain'.

'OK. Bring me up to speed on the freeway body parts case. In fact, take it from the top.'

Eric leaned back, marshaled his thoughts, and then recounted the essentials of the investigation up to the eventual discovery of the frozen body of a woman inside the suspect van.

Turner consulted his paper. 'This is Katherine Alston, missing from California.'

'Yes, sir. On interview, the suspect confessed to the manslaughter of Alston in nineteen ninety-nine, stated that he has kept her body in a freezer on his premises, first in California and then Arizona. He was in preparation to go mobile with her body in the van, which he had recently acquired from another individual. That individual is who we suspect dropped the body parts on the freeway.'

'Do you have a name for that suspect?'

'We only have an alias: Tripper.'

'What else do you have?'

'We've got a physical description of the suspect: White, blond and blue, approximately six-four, clean-shaven—'

'Has that description supported or refuted your

theory that this Tripper was driving the van when it was hit on the freeway here?'

Eric paused. Turner's use of the word 'theory' was setting off alarm bells. 'It backs up the description given by two witnesses who had contact with the driver of the van after it was hit.'

'No variation?'

'Yes, but only in the areas that can be easily disguised.'

'Hair color, eye color?'

'We've got a match on hair color. It's the facial hair that varies.'

'So you're good on race, height, and eye color.'

'We don't have corroboration on eye color because he's sometimes been seen only in sunglasses.'

Turned nodded and consulted his sheet again. 'In your last memo you indicated that there was a hold-up on ID'ing the previous owner of the van you located in Arizona because the VIN was mutilated?'

'That's correct, sir.'

'And what'd the Crime Lab out there tell you on estimated time to get to the frame VIN?'

Eric spread his hands out. 'I'm just waiting for the phone to ring.'

Turner fixed him with the stare again. 'So, in sum, you have no leads on this suspect's name.'

'Not yet, but I've got the IT guys working on getting the name of whoever registered the alias Tripper on the Internet.'

'OK, so tell me this: if you have no sense of who this guy is, why have you activated a BOLO to all the local PD's in the state of Georgia, stating the make, model, and VIN of the vehicle you believe he just *might* be driving?'

Eric opened his mouth and then shut it quickly. He felt like he was on Day One at Quantico, sitting in the front of the class, and Turner had asked him a question that not only was he unable to answer but he'd also clearly missed the summer reading.

Eric tried to make sense of this. He hadn't issued a BOLO to Georgia law enforcement and, as far as he knew, Scott hadn't either. And if Scott *had* issued a BOLO but *not* told Eric, that would raise Turner's eyebrows. More to the point, if there was a special BOLO for Georgia police, how had Turner heard about it over here in LA?

Eric decided to hedge his bets. 'No matter who's driving that vehicle, we need to locate it ASAP. It's part of an ongoing criminal investigation into the death of Katherine Alston.'

He could tell that Turner knew he'd side-stepped the question and was deeply relieved when his supervisor just responded with a slow nod. But then Turner loosened his tie, his bony fingers working themselves into the knot, and Eric knew he wasn't off the hook yet.

'I had a feeling you were going to say something like that because I just got off the horn with SSA Franks. He wasn't happy.'

Eric wanted to say, 'I was posted under Franks for three years and the man was never happy,' but he held his tongue.

'And now I'm not happy because this is the

second call I've had to field from him since you and Houston got posted out here.'

'Sir—'

'Are you familiar with these allegations, Eric?' Turner snapped his sheet of paper straight and cleared his throat. 'An anonymous complaint was lodged direct with Franks regarding the conduct of SA Houston during the investigation into missing prostitutes in Atlanta. The complainant alleged that Houston was 'friendly' with prostitutes who were part of the investigation, during Bureau hours and in a Bureau vehicle.'

'This is just Franks—'

Turner cut him off with a look. 'No. Franks protected Houston by not referring this to the OPR.'

Eric inwardly winced at the reference to the FBI's Office of Professional Responsibility. The image of those internal affairs agents competed with his thoughts on who the complainant could have been.

Turner continued. 'Franks took an interest in Houston's activities and gained evidence of him giving prostitutes rides in his Bureau vehicle, which, as you know, is in itself against regulations. He purchased food and drink for them. He fraternized with them alone and after hours. Franks pointed out that, for all the attention SA Houston was giving these streetwalkers, it was ironic that two of them later went missing.'

Eric shook his head in disbelief but had learned not to interrupt his supervisor.

'Now, in Franks' estimation, the reason you two never cleared that case was because you

244

developed the erroneous theory that there was a lone abductor who was the lone serial killer. At the time you were transferred out here, he described you both as 'obsessed'. I told him it was my practice to give experienced agents their reins. But as soon as your BOLO on this vehicle came across his radar, he called me to find out what you're working on. I only gave him an outline but it was enough for him to inform me in no uncertain terms that you and Houston are pursuing a dead-end theory that will now leave my office with a case that can't be cleared, taking valuable resources and man-hours. He advised me to take control of this case ASAP.'

Turner rubbed his fingers hard over the faint stubble on his chin, jutting his lower jaw out as if to stretch it. 'Now, I'm capable of drawing my own conclusions about you and Houston but I do have one more item that needs clearing up.'

Eric braced himself.

'What in Sam Hell did you think you were doing when you allowed two civilians into the crime scene at the freeway?'

Jayne recognized the symptoms. While she had fallen asleep like a baby in the passenger seat, Scott had not done the same at the wheel; nor was he ill. He was experiencing a flashback of some kind. She didn't know if it was about the Alston case or if the case had simply triggered something else, but she knew she had to get Scott out of the car. Long drives conducted alone, or, in this case, in silence, had a way of breeding meltdowns. Steelie had once referred to this as Jayne's Law. Steelie had probably seen this coming when they were still in the parking lot in Phoenix, where Jayne had thought Scott was suffering more from fatigue than anything else. She had to get him out.

She said his name again and he turned his face toward her but his eyes were still staring forward, out the front windshield. She was shocked by the vulnerability of his expression, the red rims of his eyes contrasting with a paleness around his lips. She took his hands and pulled on them, urging him out of the car and now he slipped down from the driver's seat. When his feet hit the ground, he pulled away from her, muttering 'Christ' as he strode quickly away, walking along the edge of the tarmac, disturbing a ribbon of blown desert sand. Jayne let him go. He eventually stopped and she watched his back, seeing him apparently loosen his tie, then clasp his hands behind his head as he looked up at the dusky sky. After a minute, she walked over to him, purposely stopping slightly behind him but close enough so he'd know she was there.

He turned his head, putting her in his peripheral vision. 'How do you guys do it?' His voice sounded choked, tired.

'Do what?'

He turned his head away, his hair catching under his fingers. 'I've gotta tell ya, it about killed me to meet the Alstons.' He paused. 'I kept picturing their daughter in the freezer, at the morgue. Those teeth. I've never seen such perfect teeth. She was dead but there they were, just like life. For *Christ's* sake!' He brought his arms

246

down and crossed them tightly against his chest.

Jayne was reaching to touch him when his voice came out in a whisper.

'I feel inadequate.'

Shocked, she drew her hand back and looked at the back of his head. Could he really have said those words? Did he feel what she felt? She knew what he meant. The dead were still dead, despite everything you'd done – despite all the Good, all the Investigation, the Uncovering, the Recovery, the Holding Accountable, the dead were still dead and you couldn't bring them back. She *knew*. He was talking again.

'I've never felt so glad to clear a case and then felt so ... terrible.' Scott's head dropped down as his shoulders started to shake.

Jayne reached for him then, turning him and pulling his head to her chest, feeling his exhalations, hot and damp, on her shirtfront. She automatically began rubbing his back and her words came out despite her defences. 'I know, I know.' She said them over and over until she was murmuring them into his hair, which muffled the words into noises only for them to resurface as kisses that landed on his ear, his brow, damp cheek, and then his arms were around her, tightening when his mouth found hers.

# TWENTY-ONE

A single glance was all it took for Chesterton Police Officers Cobb and Hayden to know that the man on the stretcher was not 'one of theirs', as the security guard had announced when he had called the station minutes earlier frantically shouting, 'Officer down! Officer down!' But he could have been from another substation. The paramedics would not let them speak to the barely conscious man so Cobb had let the ambulance leave for the hospital after they had searched the man's pockets and not found any proof of identity.

While Hayden took a statement from the security guard, who was sitting on the curb, Cobb searched the dark blue sedan for the officer's identification. There wasn't a single item in the body of the vehicle. He opened the trunk and looked in the dark interior. It was lined with several layers of heavy duty clear plastic. This struck Cobb as unusual but not outside the range of possibilities for an undercover unit. The only step he could take to determine who owned the vehicle was to run the license plate number through the NCIC hook-up in his cruiser.

NCIC listed the owner of the Georgia license plate but the plates were registered to a different car than the one illuminated in Cobb's spotlight. Plates can be moved from vehicle to vehicle but Vehicle Identification Numbers pose more of a problem, so Cobb walked back to the dark sedan and leaned in to read the VIN from where it was screwed into the dashboard on a metal plate. He transcribed the 17-digit number on to his pad, double-checked it, and returned to his cruiser.

When Cobb saw that there was an All Points Bulletin out on that VIN, it triggered a distant memory of a BOLO that had gone out earlier that night. But it was the APB information that caused his blood pressure to spike. The driver could be armed and dangerous and must be detained. His immediate thought was to race after the ambulance but he couldn't leave his partner on the side of the road with the witness. He radioed the station and hurriedly told the duty desk to dispatch a unit to Chesterton General to intercept the ambulance on the way to or at the entrance of the emergency room. Then he radioed a colleague on another floor of the station and asked him to enter an NCIC response report that the wanted vehicle had been recovered, along with an unconscious man who may or may not have been the driver.

Tripper had been careful to respond to the paramedics with enough vital signs to get them to relax about his condition but not so many that they were going to start asking him questions about his identity. They correctly deduced that he'd suffered a mild concussion, which he was coming out of, but they had no concerns about a cracked skull or fractured ribs that could cause major complications. They were driving with lights but not siren and not at great speed. He could hear the two of them at the front of the ambulance, joking about the construction site security guard and discussing where they would eat on their break: fast food or an all-night place called Rick's.

Tripper lifted his head. His eyesight was blurred but the blood that had been flowing from his nose was drying. He could feel clots deep inside his nostrils and the symptoms of a massive headache. Squinting down his body, he could see the seatbelt-like straps crisscrossing the ruined police costume and keeping him attached to the stretcher as the ambulance moved. It was easy to undo the straps but leave them looking as though still clipped into place. What he did next would depend on where the paramedics pulled in at the hospital: the emergency room or a main entrance. He waited, fighting the desire to close his eyes against the headache and fall into delicious sleep.

The ambulance coming to a stop jolted him into full consciousness. He stayed prone until he heard both paramedics jump down from the front of the ambulance and walk to the rear. He knew they had arrived at the main entrance; otherwise emergency room staff would already have opened the ambulance doors. In one swift movement, Tripper sat up on the stretcher and the searing pain in his head flared up, accompanied by flashes of white light in his peripheral vision. He pushed the straps clear of his body and swung his legs on to either side of the stretcher.

When the paramedics, still chewing the fat, opened the rear doors, he catapulted himself out on to the ground and ran toward the darkest part of the street he could see. He heard their startled 'Hey!' but knew he had the advantage of surprise and as he ran, he felt every sense in his body sharpen while his legs and arms began to pump in perfect time, the blood clots in his nose clearing as he breathed deeply, the pain in his head masked by the adrenalin released by his body for this very purpose.

Eric didn't immediately respond to his supervisor's query about 'civilians'. Turner had to be referring to Jayne and Steelie, but who had told Turner that the women had even been at the freeway site? The Highway Patrol officers wouldn't have gone over Scott's head and the Critters had no reason to talk to Turner. And what did this have to do with Franks over in Atlanta? How could he have known about Jayne and Steelie? It just didn't add up.

Turner looked up from his sheet when Eric didn't respond. 'I've looked into this. They were not only at the crime scene but here in the building. You authorized SA Weiss to log two scientists from an outfit called Agency 32/1 into the building as visitors yet he took them up to the tenth floor. That's reading like a potential violation of chain of custody protocols. Clarify it.'

'Sir, those scientists assisted us with gaining leads on this case.'

251

'Dammit, Eric, those body parts were supposed to be en route to the LA Coroner's Office, not being pawed over by every Tom, Dick, and Harry while in our custody.'

'At no time did the scientists come into physical contact with the remains, sir.'

Turner looked at him with interest. 'Can anyone back you up on that? *Besides* your partner?'

'Absolutely. Tony Lee.'

'OK. Get him in here.'

Eric went to reach for the phone but, at that moment, the computer behind him emitted a beep. He whipped around in his chair, scanned through the green binary code on the old monitor, and quickly interpreted it. There had been a hit on the APB for Wayne Spicer's car. The responding agency was Chesterton Police Station in Atlanta, Georgia.

'I need to make a call to a PD,' Eric said, reaching for the desk telephone.

'Put it on speaker-phone, SA Ramos.'

Eric paused momentarily but he did it and they heard the southern accent of the man who answered.

'Officer Lake, Chesterton PD.'

'Officer, this is FBI Special Agent Eric Ramos. I'm the originator of the APB you just responded to. Can you give me further details, please?'

'OK, Agent Ramos but I gotta tell ya, it ain't such good news.'

'Just give it to me.'

'Well, we've got your vehicle all right, but the unidentified man who was driving it is AWOL.'

'Wait. Your response says the driver was taken

252

to hospital unconscious.'

'Apparently, the boys on the scene thought he was unconscious or as good as. Maybe he just regained consciousness. Either way, by the time our units caught up with the ambulance at Chesterton General, the man had absconded from the stretcher and they'll be damned if they can work out where he went. He *was* wounded.'

'And no one got an ID?'

'No, but the vehicle was wearing plates registered to a male, name of King, DOB 1960. I'm faxing you the sheet now.'

Eric almost got goose bumps. He spoke rapidly. 'I need you to put out a BOLO on that individual with whatever descriptions you have and I need it to maintain that he is armed and dangerous.'

'You got it, Agent Ramos. I already had a BOLO underway. We sure are sorry about this but we're on top of it.'

Eric disconnected the call by lifting and replacing the handset but he kept his hand on the phone as he said to his Supervisor, 'I need to call Scott.'

Turner shook his head. 'First, Tony establishes for me that you two are not conducting this case like a bunch of cowboys. Call him now.'

What Eric really wanted to do was smash the telephone against the wall while picturing his old boss Franks' smug face but he steadied his hand and dialed Tony Lee.

When the Critter arrived and saw their supervisor was there as well, now sitting in Scott's chair across the room, he looked at Eric. 'What

253

do you need?'

'Tony, SSA Turner needs your chain of custody protocols for when Weiss brought Steelie Lander and Jayne Hall up to Critter Central.'

Tony cleared his throat. 'Agent Ramos gave the scientists from Agency 32/1access to the main room of the lab. I then escorted them into the cool room once they were fully suited up in protective gear. I was present the entire time they observed the body parts they had been asked to review. I handled the body bags, body parts, and all the equipment.'

Turner's tone was brusque. 'Photographs?'

'I took images but retained those images at the lab. Later use of the images for the purposes of analysis was conducted by the scientists at our laboratory and in my presence.'

'So, you're saying that neither scientist even touched the body parts?'

'They barely breathed on them.' Tony crossed his arms.

The telephone on Eric's desk rang and he looked at the digital read-out. It identified the call as coming from the colleague who took over his desk in Atlanta, Georgia. He pressed the speaker-phone button before Turner could order him to do it.

'Ramos here.'

'Eric, it's Nicks. You got me on speaker or something?'

'Yeah, Angie. You're broadcasting to SSA Turner and Tony Lee. Go.'

She resumed, speaking fast. 'OK, Wilson and I got a PIN-to-PIN from Houston this afternoon.'

Eric hoped that, in light of SSA Franks' witch-hunt, Turner didn't find it suspicious that Scott had used his government-issued BlackBerry to send the type of instant message that was more difficult to track than a text or voice message.

Angie was still talking. 'He asked us to check the shortlist of suspects you guys drew up on the missing women before you got transferred out. He suggested that we use the APB you guys just put out on that vehicle, on the thinking that the driver might be our Georgia perp.'

'Tell me something good, Angie,' he said, trying to make it sound like he'd been aware of his partner's request all along while simultaneously trying to place when Scott had leapfrogged to a Georgia focus instead of sticking to the idea that they would find Tripper somewhere on the road between Arizona and Georgia.

'We've got a lead,' Angie said. 'We've been checking through the shortlist since we got the search warrants and all your suspects were home in the time period you're looking at for this guy being in California and Arizona except for one. We're not clear if he wasn't at home then, but he's not at home now, then we saw the BOLO go out on him from Chesterton PD.'

'King?'

'Yep. He hasn't been seen for weeks but as soon as we saw that BOLO, we got a search warrant that would allow us to enter the property in his absence. House seems clean but his backyard reeks of decomp.'

'Yesss!' Eric sounded triumphant.

'Hang on, Eric,' Angie warned. 'The reason

I'm calling is that we've just had the ME down there to take a look. The yard is apparently full of bones buried pretty shallow and the doc says he can't handle it. Can't tell which ones are human or animal and he thinks there's some of each. Says he's got some university students – volunteers – who'd probably be glad to go through all of it but it could take them weeks and they don't have a lot of experience. So we're in a holding pattern here. What do you want to do? It's yours and Houston's case.'

Eric looked over at his supervisor, who was leaning forward in the chair, elbows on knees. He liked what he saw in Craig Turner's eyes and liked the man even more when he stood up while crumpling the sheet of paper he'd been carrying with the notes from SSA Franks' phone calls.

Turner spoke, his tone authoritative. 'Call in Agency 32/1.'

He turned to leave the office, then turned back. 'And clear it with Houston first.'

Eric smiled at Tony Lee and then said toward the phone, 'Got all that, Ange?'

'Ten-four.'

'I'll call you back ASAP.' Eric's tone was jubilant.

Scott slid his hands up Jayne's back until they were on her neck, in her hair, pulling her to him. He wanted her even closer but they couldn't get any closer. Their kisses were turning into something else altogether and Scott could feel his pulse speeding up. But the roar in his ears wasn't related. There was a vehicle exiting the freeway and rolling too slowly toward them. He and Jayne surfaced simultaneously but he held her to him as they watched the pick-up truck pass, then turn right at the bottom of the exit ramp. Scott became aware of other noises now ... cars on the freeway, a fly buzzing past, Jayne's fast breathing, her chest rising and falling in syncopation with his. And something else ... his cell phone. He looked to the Suburban where the driver's door was wide open.

He started for the car and drew Jayne with him by taking her hand with a familiarity he didn't want to lose. She let him pull her into the confined space between the door and the seat, let him keep contact between them even as he reached for his phone in the center console. In the first seconds of hearing Eric's voice, Scott was still in the moment with Jayne, whose gaze was fixed on his mouth, causing him to look at hers, wanting to kiss. Then the import of what Eric was saying broke through. Scott tensed.

Jayne looked up at him with a questioning expression but it was faster to simply hold the phone out to her. 'I need you to listen to Eric.' He activated the phone's speaker.

'Jayne?' Eric's voice sounded thin but audible. 'We've got a situation where we need the Agency's help. We may have a multiple or mass grave in a backyard and the ME's out of his depth. We don't need you to exhume it but 32/1 could assist us to get a lead if you could do a day's assessment and some training of the volunteers they've corralled to help the ME. This is urgent but it does involve traveling to

257

Georgia, to the premises of a suspect who is still at large. I'm not going to pretend there's no danger quotient but you and Steelie would be under Federal protection. Can you do it?'

Scott thought he read excitement, concern, and then duty on Jayne's face before she said, 'I'll need to confirm with Steelie but, yes.'

'Good,' Eric replied. 'Because Steelie's already on her way over here with your overnight bag. Scott, see you at LAX as soon as you two can get there. We're all booked on the red-eye.'

# DAY TEN

## Thursday

# TWENTY-TWO

FBI office, Atlanta. 9.45 a.m. Scott rolled his shirtsleeves above his elbows and leaned on the briefing room's long conference table. The lights were dimmed to allow a screen at the end of the room to take center stage.

Eric contemplated the blurry portrait of a man projected on the screen, while Agents Mark Wilson and Angela Nicks looked at Scott from the other side of the table. Scott looked at his watch. 'OK, Jayne Hall and Steelie Lander will be here in fifteen and I want to make sure we're all on the same page before they arrive.'

He pointed to the portrait on the screen. 'Starting with descriptors on our suspect, King: white male, forty-five years old, six-foot-four, blond and blue. Holds the title to 1320 Mead Street and witness statements sug-gest he is also resident there. Eric and I put him on our list of suspects for the prostitute abductions about a year ago because he was alleged to have associated with some of the missing women. We

259

never had any hard evidence on him, thanks in part to a lack of surveillance. So we never got a search warrant for his property.'

Eric pointed at the screen. 'This image is the most recent photograph we have of him. It's the one on file at his work. The facilities contractor at Atlanta Airport employs him part-time, primarily cleaning floors and he alternates between employee areas and the arrivals transport section. Right now, they have him down as on vacation. He's had the job for a year and a half. No previous employment record.'

Scott used the remote to bring up the next image.

'This is the photo of King on file at the Department of Motor Vehicles. It's five years old.'

The man in the portrait hadn't smiled for the shot. His narrow face was pale in a manner that made him appear older than his age.

Scott continued. 'His appearance is a good fit for the man local police had contact with last night and it was his Georgia plate on the car we were tracking from Arizona. The address for the license plate is the Mead Street one. What's the latest from your house-to-house?' He directed the question to Angie.

She was pulling her thin braids into a ponytail, exposing a neck that was slender despite a well-known penchant for daily workouts. 'Usual story from the neighbors,' she replied. 'He's quiet, don't see him that much, puts his trash out on time. Can't track down any friends or social set and no one at his work has socialized with him or been to his house.'

Mark added, 'He doesn't own a cell phone – in his name, at least – so we can't track him that way.'

Eric nodded. 'He has used the Internet, however. We've been following info we had from this website, off-the-grid-dot-net, where we believe King was operating under the screen name Tripper. And if he is Tripper, he successfully masked his identity while online. The IT guys are monitoring the site but there's been no recent activity under that screen name. There are no leads there right now. Catch is, if King *is* Tripper and he's gone to ground, he probably knows how to stay there.' Eric looked to his partner.

Scott forwarded the image on the screen and a map came up. He used a laser pointer to point out a street on the map. 'Here's where police recovered the vehicle that was wearing King's license plate. The man driving the vehicle matches King's description on the basic levels and we are working on the assumption that the man, who was wounded and wearing a police uniform or replica, was indeed King.'

He pointed to another location on the map on the screen. 'Here's Chesterton General, where King escaped on foot. And here –' he pointed at another location two miles away – 'is King's residence. At about the time he was escaping from the ambulance at the hospital...' Scott paused to consult his notes.

Mark finished his sentence. 'We were breaking down his front door on the search warrant. If he's tried to come home, then he knows we're crawling all over it.'

Angie's cell phone rang but she addressed the room as she pulled it from her pocket. 'We've got surveillance at both ends of the street in case he does turn up. Nicks.' This last was said into her phone. 'Thanks.' She stood up. 'The scientists are here. I'll escort them.'

Jayne and Steelie still had damp hair from the quick wake-up showers they'd taken at the motel after the overnight flight from Los Angeles. But hot water could do only so much and they'd maintained a fatigue-induced silence during the ride in a government vehicle to FBI Headquarters. The woman who met them in Reception introduced herself as Agent Angela Nicks and they hurried to follow her to the security station. Her swift pace befitted her short but compact stature and she led the way as soon as they had their Visitor badges.

She glanced back at them as she walked. 'Motel OK? You need anything?'

Steelie pulled her glasses from the pocket of her shirt and began cleaning them. 'Weirdly, I think I'm ready for breakfast.'

'We've got stuff in the briefing room. Muffins, bagels, coffee. Sound OK?'

'Sounds like I should come 'round here more often.'

They were passing offices that came off both sides of the hall and open doors revealed agents at work. Jayne half expected to find their way barred by the infamous Supervisory Special Agent Franks about whom Eric had told infuriating stories last night at the airport. She was still smarting over the fact that SSA Franks had acted on an anonymous tip about impropriety between Scott and Agency 32/1 without vetting anyone who called in with such specific information.

'This is the office Mark and I share.' Angie pointed into a room as they walked past. Two desks pushed up against each other, both relatively neat, with a potted plant right on the dividing line.

'And here's the briefing room.' Angie swung open the door that anchored the end of the hallway.

Jayne saw Eric bent over a projector while Scott was at a table to the side. Both men greeted them and Angie introduced them to Special Agent Mark Wilson, sitting at a computer. As soon as he stood up, she saw how tall and trim he was, the brush cut he wore contributing to his air of neatness. He came over with a friendly smile and shook hands with a strong grip.

'Good to meet you. Welcome to Atlanta. How you guys feeling?'

Jayne replied, 'Been more awake before but we're ready to help out on this.'

'Great. Help yourselves to coffee.'

They put their bags on chairs and joined Scott, who was spreading cream cheese across a bagel sitting in halves on a paper plate. He winked at Jayne and she surreptitiously grinned back, noticing that he'd traded his blue suit for a black one, though he wasn't wearing the jacket.

She relished seeing his left side after using the waking hours on the flight to study his right side, which was all she could see of him from one row back and across the aisle, as she continually turned over how he'd behaved after his meltdown on the freeway. He wasn't ashamed of the impact Kate Alston had had on him and he hadn't apologized for almost running them off the road while having a flashback. He'd even told Eric what had happened. He seemed to accept that there could be fallout from his work. Could she follow his lead? And if that kiss was just a prelude to what could happen between them, could he accept in her something she hadn't yet accepted in herself?

A bright light in the briefing room behind her brought her to the present and she turned to see the projection screen lit up with an electronic map. She followed Scott and Steelie to sit at the table.

Angie picked up a remote control and pointed it at the projector. The map on the screen switched to a photograph of a smiling woman. Her face was full, her brown hair showing white roots, and she looked as though she was laughing at being teased. Her shoulders were visible around her sleeveless flowered top.

It was Eric who gave the photo a caption. 'Eleanor Patterson.'

Jayne and Steelie simultaneously sat up straighter in their chairs. It was a shock to see a photograph of the woman whose dismembered limbs they were so familiar with, whose surgical plate had led to her identification. Eleanor Patterson, of whom only her arms had been found so far.

264

Scott addressed the room. 'Patterson is the only identified victim we can associate with the perp's van so we need to do two things as a matter of priority: put her with him while she was still alive and determine if how they met will give us a lead on where he is now.'

Eric said, 'Starting with what we know about Patterson: the 32/1 preliminary analysis suggested that she had been the victim of physical abuse but the misper report filed by her husband made no mention of any scars related to that nor was there any mention of the surgical plate we eventually used to ID her. So we had Carlisle PD talk to the husband. They just sent over their report.'

Eric held up a piece of paper that looked like an email print-out.

'OK, the husband admits to the beating but said he didn't report it because he didn't realize it would be helpful. Didn't expect her to be found dead because when she left, she didn't take any of her belongings or clothes and left behind her credit cards. He presumed she'd gone off to start a new life with one of the men he alleged she was having affairs with. Oh, and he told the Carlisle cops that he didn't want to have her body returned to him; that he'd only filed the misper report so she would come back and, quote-unquote, get her shit.'

Eric looked up at the group. 'Apparently, he's still got her "shit" kept perfectly in place in an upstairs room. Carlisle PD has no leads on how Patterson came to be outside of Oregon, let alone dead.'

Steelie cleared her throat. 'I know Jayne and I are here about the body parts at the suspect's house, but I've just had an idea about this woman.'

Eric gestured with his hand, inviting her to continue.

She glanced at the screen. 'OK, you said she left without belongings, not even credit cards, and that you have confirmation that she was being beaten?'

Scott said, 'Yes.' He was looking at her intently.

'OK. Our sense from the healed fractures on her arm bones was that the abuse had been taking place over a long period of time. So I'm thinking that maybe she finally decided to do something about it.'

'What do you mean?' asked Eric. 'She didn't report the abuse.'

'I don't mean reporting. I mean she decided to get the hell out of Dodge. What about checking with shelters for battered women? And not in Oregon. She was probably trying to get as far away from her husband as possible. I don't know that she came out here to Georgia but you already know she crossed the suspect's path somewhere. You could start by looking at shelters here.'

There was a brief silence and then Eric jumped up from his chair. '*That*, my friends, is what I call a lead.' He was at the end of the table in three long strides. 'Angie?'

Angie had pushed back from the table and was gathering her papers. 'I'm on it.' She flashed

Steelie a smile, and then followed Eric out of the room.

Scott chuckled quietly.

'What?' Steelie asked, sounding taken aback by the activity her comment had set off.

He put his hand on her shoulder. 'I was just wondering if you wanted a job.'

Mark got up from the other side of the table and headed toward the food. Jayne joined him so she could get more coffee. She felt good because the agents had made her and Steelie part of their team. She turned back to the room as Scott was advancing the image on the screen.

'All right. Here's our suspect: a janitor at Atlanta Airport.'

Jayne looked over and then had to grab the back of the nearest chair.

It was Steelie who spoke. 'Well, Jee-sus Christ. Or I should say, Gene King.'

# TWENTY-THREE

Tripper understood the catalysts for the physical sensations breaking over his body like waves. One part was nerves and the other anger, but the zing brought on by the thought of that idiot Wayne's sedan going to a police yard before he'd ensured it was clean was fear, pure fear. He clenched and unclenched his fingers. He knew he had to control fear. He must repeat in his mind that there was nothing to fear as long as he wasn't Gene King.

Sure, that was King's license plate on the car but he was Tripper full-time now. Indeed, he'd planned this day; it had just arrived sooner than he'd planned. That made him angry again. Who were the cops to dictate when he made The Transition? Which meant the real question was, did he leave anything of Tripper's in that car? *Zing.* No! Control the fear. Clench, unclench.

'You sure you want me to take Peachtree?'

Tripper looked up to see the taxi driver eyeing him in the rearview mirror. 'Yes.'

'The parkway will get you there in half the time.'

'I said I don't like that route.'

The driver shrugged. 'It's your dollar.' His eyes went back to watching the traffic ahead of them and he turned up the AM radio.

Tripper refocused. The taxi was working. It kept him off both the streets and the public transit system while the cops might be searching for Gene King during the crucial hours before he completed The Transition. They'd only search hard for him if they knew he'd impersonated a cop, and they'd only know about the assault if that bitch he'd pulled over had reported it already. In case she had, he had done three things: run until he put distance between him and the hospital, given his house a wide berth, and waited several hours before hailing a taxi. There would have been no point in getting a taxi near the hospital, and at a time of night when the driver would remember him if questioned by the cops later. And he wouldn't take a taxi to the house. No, he was going to the storage unit.

The Transition Plan called for this, naturally, but it was supposed to be late at night when the front office was unattended and he could enter with his access code. But current circumstances dictated that he go during business hours when the gate was already open. He might be seen but would draw little attention to himself and his code would never be used, so it could never be tracked.

He would ask to be dropped off several blocks before the taxi reached the storage place, so the driver would have no idea of his destination. Then he would walk. Now that he'd discarded the uniform's shirt, he knew he was unremarkable in a white t-shirt and dark pants. If anything, he looked like a waiter who'd just come off of a night shift.

Tripper dug his fingers down into his right sock and felt the money he'd hidden there when he'd dressed in the uniform at the beginning of the night. He was surprised to find the cash damp with sweat. He didn't remember sweating. As he sat up straight again, he heard a police siren start up behind the taxi. It took extraordinary effort to not whip around in the seat as he watched the driver's eyes looking in the rearview mirror to something behind Tripper's head.

Scott was looking from Jayne to Steelie. 'Yeah, Eugene Frederick King. What's wrong with you?'

Jayne couldn't tear her eyes from the screen and absently asked, 'What?'

'You know this guy? Steelie?'

Steelie replied, 'Yeah, we do. You should know him too. Gene was one of you guys, a Fibbie.'

He looked at Mark, who was shaking his head.

Scott insisted, 'Not according to what we know about him. You sure about that?'

She nodded. 'He was FBI ten years ago, anyway. A criminalist in the DC Lab. Worked for the UN with us in Rwanda. And Jayne can tell you where he works now; he's not a janitor, that's for sure.'

Mark gaped at Jayne. 'You're in touch with King now?'

'I saw Gene last week but I'm not—'

'Everything stops.' Scott pushed back his chair

roughly as he stood up. 'Right now.'

Everyone watched him as he brought both hands to his face as though in prayer. Then he pointed at Mark. 'Find out why he's not in our system and go straight to the Director of the Lab to get *any*thing they have. Find out who worked with him and talk to them ASAP.'

Mark nodded, jerked his chair back and headed for the door, which banged shut behind him.

Scott looked at Jayne, then rubbed his lips hard with his fingers. 'You have some explaining to do.'

'But ... I hardly know him.'

'Let me be the judge of that.' His voice had taken on a harsh edge. 'I need to pick up some equipment. Wait here.' He left the room.

Scott stood just outside the door of the briefing room, his hand still on the latch, thoughts and images colliding in his head. Jayne calling King – *their suspect* – 'Gene'. She knew him. She fucking knew this bastard. He envisioned King and Jayne together, the two of them – friends? This morphed into a vision of Jayne in danger, so he pushed it out to focus on King again. A former FBI lab rat; how could they have missed that? Was he such a smooth operator that he'd wiped his own Government record and if so, who were they dealing with? This was no longer a janitor who'd 'just been lucky' to get away with murder all this time. And if King had been in LA last week, then that tallied with their belief that he was the one who had been driving the van when those body parts fell out. Could it be coincidence that he had seen Jayne that same week or had King known she was involved in the case? What had she revealed? He needed to know how she'd been involved with this sick fuck. Anger and disgust made Scott tense up, so he pushed off from the door and strode down the hall.

Jayne fought the nausea, repeatedly swallowing the saliva that was welling up in her mouth. She stared unseeing, her mind skittering over the night she'd met Gene in LA, recasting him as a murderer, hardly able to believe it, then fully rejecting it. He's an *alleged* murderer only, she told herself, and then felt her stomach twist. I spent an evening with him; he was in my apartment. I let him touch me! Was he sizing me up the whole time? No, no. This is just an allegation. They need proof. I need proof. Jesus, do I *have* some proof and don't even know it? What is Scott thinking? What is he ... what must he think of me? It's over, isn't it? It's over between us and it had barely even started.

Steelie watched Jayne and could imagine what she was thinking. Steelie herself had no trouble casting Gene as a killer, but she couldn't imagine him being creative enough to spend an evening weaving whatever false stories he'd told Jayne about his life. She also couldn't see him taking a janitorial job unless there was some benefit to him beyond the paycheck. Most of all, she had trouble picturing him pursuing any endeavor where he couldn't get right in front of any kudos that might come his way for being a part of it.

Scott signed out the recording equipment from the supply room and then walked to Mark and Angie's office, holding the case in both hands. He put it down at the doorway and gestured with his head to Eric. Eric left Angie's desk, where she was on the phone with a list in front of her. Mark was across from her, also on the phone, a hand over his free ear as he listened to the instrument.

Eric stepped into the hallway and kept his voice low. 'Mark told us. They know King?'

Scott nodded, his lips tightly compressed.

Eric registered the case on the floor. 'You're going to interview them?'

'Jayne saw him just last week.'

'Christ.'

'She could have told him something. Inadvertently, of course.'

Eric's eyes widened and he dropped his voice to a whisper. 'You are *not* thinking that, man.'

Scott gave a tense shrug.

'Let me do the interview,' Eric almost pleaded.

'No. I know they might be the best lead we have on where this asshole is right now – I'll have my kid gloves on.'

'That's not the reason to wear them, Scott. This is Jayne and Steelie. Look, if King is Tripper, he's leading a double life and there's no way in hell he told Jayne. If she knows anything useful, she won't realize it. She doesn't know

273

Tripper; she knows King.' Eric paused and watched Scott closely. 'Don't do an interview. Just ask questions. And make it clear they're not suspects.'

Angie approached. Eric abruptly stepped back from his huddle with Scott. She didn't appear offended by this nor did she ask about the recording equipment on the floor. She held up a sheet of paper.

'With the help of Health and Human Services, I've got a list of battered women's shelters in the metro area. It's recommended that we go in person so we can show ID, otherwise, forget it.'

Just then, Mark got off the phone and called them all into the office.

'The Lab confirms that King worked for the Bureau doing trace evidence and photography for seven years. He was loaned to the UN International Criminal Tribunal for Rwanda on a nine-month agreement in '96, going into '97. Official title: forensic expert. He resigned from the Lab in 1999, stating personal reasons.'

Eric interrupted: 'Nothing precipitated it?'

Mark shook his head. 'Nothing disciplinary in his file. The only thing that stands out was a psych debriefing after the UN mission that came back with a recommendation for further appointments. He never made them but he wasn't required to, either. Speaking of his file, there's no explanation for why it isn't in the Bureau's General Records because it's there in the Lab's database at the Administration level.'

Scott responded thoughtfully. 'That's smart. He doctored it so anyone who knew him from the Lab would find his records as expected but he's not in the system that the rest of us use when we're checking a name against government employee lists. Did the Lab think he had the tech skills to do that?'

'The Director of the Lab didn't know King well – came on just before he resigned, but said King was known as a jack of all trades. He'd been in the Bureau long enough to gain some working knowledge of everything. Blood spatter, geology, entomology, forensic accounting, you name it.'

'They got an address for him?'

'Same one we've got crime scene officers at right now.'

Angie looked at Scott. 'Are we going to have a problem taking Steelie and Jayne over there?'

'I don't know yet. What I want you to do is keep on the shelters, and see if we can find out where this guy frequented besides his house and the airport. Mark, see if you can get on to whoever was the director of the Lab while King was working there. We need leads on friends, anything on what he was planning to do when he resigned. We need some hidey hole he might be at right now, nursing his wounds from last night.'

The team broke up.

# TWENTY-FOUR

Jayne's mental review of possible signs of violent tendencies on Gene's part had quickly run back to Rwanda. But the only thing she could think of was metaphorical violence.

Steelie said, 'I remember when Gerrit called Gene combative, particularly in regard to you.'

Jayne was staring at the tabletop. 'He didn't miss a thing. For whatever reason, Gerrit had my relationship with Gene down pat.' A movement caught her eye and she glanced at the door. Scott was standing there, watching her.

She started to get up. 'Scott, I—'

He launched into the room. 'Whatever you have to say about King is going on tape.' The case he was carrying hit the tabletop with a thud.

Jayne froze, half standing, half sitting.

He spoke again, less roughly. 'So just hold that thought and we'll get to it on tape. OK?'

She nodded and sat down.

Steelie was eyeing the contents of the case he'd now opened. 'What's the deal, Scott? I'm getting the feeling you're about to read Jayne her rights.'

He continued to busily pull out equipment as he replied. 'She's not a suspect.'

He set up a microphone on a stand in the

middle of the table. 'Neither are you, for that matter. You're material witnesses. I'm recording this because I need it to be available for the whole team. You're going to give us background on the suspect. You're not under oath.'

He yanked tangled wires free and bent down to plug into the sockets on the table's edge. He caught Jayne's eye. 'But it would be helpful if you told the truth.'

He turned on the recorder, pulled over a legal pad, and looked squarely at her. 'Who is Gerrit?'

Jayne opened her mouth, closed it, then started again. 'Gerrit? Aren't we supposed to be talking about Gene?'

'Yeah and it sounds like this Gerrit is a mutual friend of you and King so I'll want to talk to him.' He dropped his eyes to the pad, jotted something on it and added, 'For background.'

Scott repeated his question, directing it at Steelie. 'So, who is Gerrit?'

Steelie calmly replied, 'He was the UN Tribunal's lead criminal investigator for the sites we exhumed in Kigali in '96, when we worked with Gene.'

'Surname?'

'Leuven.'

'Seconded or...'

'Seconded.'

'One year or two?'

'He was into his second year.'

'From?'

'Government of the Netherlands. *Politie.*'

'Do you know his current title?'

She looked to Jayne, who replied, 'Chief of

277

Police.'

'You've got contact information for him?'

Jayne nodded and pulled her bag from the chair next to her. She dug around for her cell phone while Scott pushed the legal pad toward her, a fresh page uppermost. She wrote down Gerrit's email and direct telephone numbers as stored in her phone, then pushed the pad back across the table. 'He continued working with Gene after we left.'

Scott turned to the next page of the pad. 'You stated that you saw King last week?'

'That's right.'

'Which day, what time?'

So much had transpired since that night, Jayne had to think for a second. She felt the pause made it seem like she had something to hide so she met Scott's gaze directly. 'Wednesday evening. I picked him up around seven and he left my place at about eleven.'

She saw his pupils dilate and the start of a frown in the moment before he looked down at his pad. It felt like an entire minute passed before he looked up from his pad.

'So, did he contact you for the meet?'

'I wouldn't call it a meet. It was just dinner. He contacted me – us, really. Sent an email to the Agency on Tuesday and—'

'Meaning last Tuesday, the day before you met?'

'Right.'

'So you were in regular contact?'

'No—' She threw her hands up. 'You don't understand.' She looked to Steelie.

278

Steelie's tone sounded conversational compared to Jayne's. 'Scott, we hadn't heard from him since we worked with him in Rwanda. This was a one-off.'

'Uh-huh. So you get this email out of the blue. What did he say?'

'Just that he was flying into LA the next day and could we meet up,' replied Steelie.

'Just Jayne or both of you?'

'Both of us.'

'But you didn't attend the meet, Steelie?'

'Gene was never my favorite person. Even before you alleged he was a serial killer.' Steelie gave him a thin smile.

He made a note. 'OK, we'll get to that.' He looked to Jayne again. 'How many more emails did you have from him?'

'I wrote back, said I'd be meeting him, then he just wrote one more time to tell me that he'd be staying at the Omni and what time I could pick him up.'

'That's it? Nothing about what he was doing in LA?'

'No.'

'And you're sure he said he was flying in the next day, the Wednesday?'

'Yes, positive.'

'Flying in from...?'

'I presumed DC because that's where he used to live.'

Scott tapped his pen against the pad. 'We'll need to see the email traffic between his account and yours, track his account.'

Jayne bit back the words *I'm not lying*. 'Fine.

We can get into the Agency account from here.'

'Have you had any more emails from him since you met?'

'No...' Jayne paused, remembering the message she'd sent Gene on the day the half-empty filing cabinet had depressed her. She realized that Scott would probably see that message now.

'You sound unsure.'

Jayne noticed Steelie looking at her curiously, so mustered herself. 'I'm sure. He hasn't written again.'

The door opened and they all looked up.

Mark Wilson walked in and addressed Scott. 'You want this now?'

Scott nodded and turned off the tape recorder.

'There's almost nothing on this guy. Two people say they were friends of his when he worked at the Lab but they haven't been in touch since. They understood he was resigning to take care of his mother down here, who was getting sick; one of them thought it was Alzheimer's—'

Jayne cut in. 'That's right. He told me she died a few years ago, after living with Alzheimer's.' She looked at Scott but he only indicated that Mark should continue.

'King's friends only ever socialized with him at their local bar in DC or at professional conferences. He used to have a DC-area code cell phone. I called it and also checked with the phone company. He dumped the number four years ago.'

'When his mother died?'

'Around the same time, yeah.'

'Find out if it was before or after and by how much time.'

'You want me to check on the Alzheimer's business?'

'Yeah.' Scott flipped back to another sheet on his pad, ripped it off and handed it to Mark. 'And get a hold of this guy in Holland; get him out of bed if you have to. He was the lead investigator when King was working with Jayne and Steelie in Rwanda. He may have worked with King even longer than they did. Find out if anything happened out there. And his name's pronounced *Herrit*.'

Mark nodded and left the room.

Jayne opened her mouth to speak but Scott was already restarting the tape recorder.

'OK, let's go back to Wednesday night. Did you ask for King at the desk inside the Omni?'

'No, he said he'd meet me where the taxis pull in.'

'Did you see him come out of the hotel, through the doors?'

'No...' Jayne felt sudden surprise. 'I was scanning the area but he spotted me first and met me at the truck.'

'What was your impression of him?'

'Like, his behavior or what?' Jayne knew she sounded distracted.

Scott frowned at her. 'Are you getting tired?'

Jayne shook her head. In fact, her brain was busy fast-forwarding her memories of that night, now alerted to how much she'd taken for granted with Gene's visit to LA and how little she'd actually learned from him.

281

Scott sounded more solicitous. 'Just think back to the first moment you saw him. Close your eyes if that helps.'

Jayne dutifully followed this direction. She thought back to Gene jumping in the passenger side of the truck, the hug he gave her once in the cab. 'I didn't recognize him at first; he looked older than I'd expected even though we're all older. His skin seemed grayer and it was as though his cheeks were being pulled down by gravity but he was energetic, lively, funny, and it was ... nicer to see him than I'd expected.' She opened her eyes and shrugged.

'Good. OK. Was he clean shaven? Moustache? Beard?'

'No. No facial hair.'

'What was he wearing?'

'All beige. A zip-up windbreaker, golf shirt, slacks. I don't remember his shoes. No logos.'

'So he got in the truck. It's about seven p.m. and then what?'

'I drove to Little Tokyo.'

'His choice or yours?'

'Mine, because it was close.'

'He pick the restaurant?'

'No, I'd suggested we see what looked good once we got there.'

'During the drive, what did you talk about?'

'Let's see ... he explained that he'd left the Bureau years ago, didn't miss it, and now worked for an electronics company that was expanding to the West Coast and he was the advance guard.'

'Which company?' Scott had drawn a line out

from his notes and was circling something three times, the ink sitting in a groove on the paper.

'I don't know. Didn't ask.'

'And he didn't volunteer? At any point in the evening? Give you his business card?'

'No.'

'Did he say where he was based?'

'No.'

'So you park and walk into Little Tokyo. Where'd you eat?'

'Um, I didn't notice the name. We had stopped in front of it and the host just handed us a menu.'

'He stopped or you stopped?'

'I don't remember; we just stopped. No, wait. I stopped because he'd said something that pissed me off and I couldn't walk and respond at the same time.'

Scott's mouth twitched into a tiny grin and then he became serious again. 'You were arguing?'

'No. He just made a typical Gene statement, sounding supercilious and sure of his facts as he questioned the likelihood that the Agency could make a difference. He was basically saying that our efforts to link up mispers with unidentifieds was just a drop in the bucket.'

Steelie cut in, leaning towards her. 'You never told me this.'

Jayne gave her a quelling look. 'There was no point getting you riled up as well.'

Steelie's protest was cut off by Scott's follow-up question for Jayne. 'Why did that bother you so much that you stopped walking?'

'Because it's the sort of armchair quarterback

statement you might expect from a disinterested person, not a forensic scientist – or any kind of scientist.'

'Right.' Scott almost smiled again. 'So you set him straight. How did he respond?'

'He kind of backed off and we went into the restaurant.'

'Which you don't know the name of.'

'Look, I can describe it.'

'Later.' Scott consulted his notes. 'During dinner, did you learn anything about where he lived or his activities, if he had a rental car or some form of transportation?'

'No. We were reminiscing.'

'And how long did you stay there?'

'About an hour and a half. Something like that.'

'King paid for dinner?'

Jayne had a ray of hope that Scott could be jealous, wanting to know if this had actually been a date. 'Yes, he paid.' She tried to see his expression but his whole face was tilted down to his pad.

'Credit card?'

She deflated. He was just trying to find out if there was a financial paper trail the FBI could follow to investigate Gene. 'Cash.'

'Then you went to your place?'

'No, first we went to the Agency.'

Both Steelie and Scott's heads snapped toward Jayne. Scott held up his hand to stop Steelie from interrupting again. 'Was that *his* suggestion?'

Jayne nodded, beginning to see how strange it

appeared. She wondered what Gene had actually been doing, if indeed he was the person responsible for the freeway body parts. She sat still and tried to think of anything he might have seen or could have discerned about the case while in her office.

'Jayne?' Scott sounded impatient.

'Yes. Yes, OK? He asked to see it.'

'And that seemed normal to you, at, what, eight at night?'

She couldn't help but sound defensive. 'We'd been talking about some similarities between our work in Rwanda and what the Agency does now. It was a relatively natural request in the context of the evening.'

'Fine. You went to the Agency. What did you do there?'

Jayne rubbed her forehead. 'I showed him around. We weren't there very long.'

'Did you show him anything in particular? Any case files, photographs, notes—'

She glared at him. 'No. I think you know me better than that. And I didn't say anything about consulting on an FBI case, if that's what you're thinking. I didn't mention the freeway body parts and he sure as hell didn't ask.'

'Did he show an interest in anything in particular?'

She thought for a moment. 'He seemed interested in the All Coroners Bulletin.'

Steelie's sharp intake of breath was audible. 'You turned on my computer in the lab?'

Jayne rolled her eyes. 'Of course not.' Then she took on an assertive tone, aiming to clarify these issues for the last time. 'Look, I didn't open anything, use any passwords in front of him, didn't let him see the alarm keycode—' She stopped abruptly. *Oh, shit.*

'What?' Scott leaned forward. 'You've remembered something. The alarm system?'

She shook her head. 'No, I just thought of something, a connection. I mean, Gene's the one anomalous person who's been at the Agency as well as my apartment.' Her assertive tone had been replaced with something higher pitched.

'So what?'

'The bugging. The taps on the phones, dammit!' Her voice was rising. 'He said he was in 'electronics', maybe that's what he meant. He's been in both locations and I let him in myself! For Christ's sake, *I let him in.*'

She tried to stand up but the legs of her chair tangled with the strap of her bag, pulling it upside down to the floor. She bent over to untangle the mess, gave up and stepped over it, only to be confronted by Gene's face on the projection screen when she looked up. *No!* She made an about-face, directly into Scott, who'd come around the table.

He stopped her short by gripping her by the shoulders. She looked everywhere but into his eyes as she felt despair come over her. Gene had manipulated her with ease, she'd possibly compromised Scott's case and maybe even Agency 32/1 itself. *What have I done?*

She was aware that Scott was telling Steelie to turn off the tape recorder. She watched Steelie follow the instructions. *Oh, God, Steelie; I'm sorry.*

Scott dipped and weaved, trying to get into her line of sight. 'The wiretaps were *outside* both buildings, not inside. I don't want you thinking about what could have happened or making connections right now. Just tell me what happened that night. We'll deal with whatever comes up.'

Gradually, she realized that if she'd screwed anything for the Agency, then she was going to have to fix it for herself, for Steelie, for their clients.

# TWENTY-FIVE

Eric and Angie waited in a small office that was clearly a later addition to the rambling two-story house used by the second battered women's shelter on their list, Percy Gale. The first shelter, Horizons, hadn't yielded results but they hadn't crossed it off the list because the manager there had simply refused to discuss any of her clients. She had agreed to look at the photograph of Eleanor Patterson, at Eric's insistence, but had said she didn't recognize the woman. Eric hadn't been convinced.

He liked Steelie's theory that Patterson had come to Georgia to get away from her husband for good and it made sense that she would have started with a shelter. He wanted to follow every sniff of a lead and it was Angie who cut off the interview at Horizons by giving Eric a look he recognized from when they'd first worked together in Atlanta a year earlier: she was telling him to back off. He only complied because he knew she wasn't going to let anything drop; that wasn't Angie's style.

On the drive to Percy Gale, she had suggested a new approach to the same theory: get the shelter to explain their methods so they'd get leads on how Patterson might have come into

Georgia, even if they couldn't find the shelter she used. They had agreed that Angie would lead the next interview, so when the Percy Gale site manager walked into her office, it was Angie who moved forward first.

The woman who introduced herself as 'just Dora' looked about sixty. She wasn't exactly over-weight but looked as though she had been, then lost some and there was still enough skin to contain the old bulk. As she passed them to reach her desk, she left a fresh floral scent behind her.

She picked up a paper fan decorated with flowers and leaned back in the chair to cool herself with practiced flicks of the wrist. 'Please sit down, both of you. It's much too hot to stand.'

Angie began. 'Dora, we're looking for information on a woman who went missing while she may have been seeking assistance from a battered women's shelter.'

'Is there a missing person report out on her?' Dora's eyes were shrewd.

'Yes.'

'Put in by the woman's husband?'

'Yes.'

Dora leaned forward and snapped the fan shut, placing it on the desk. 'Can't help you.'

Eric's impatience led him to fidget but Angie continued seamlessly. 'We believe you can, in fact.'

'We don't reveal information on any of our clients, not even to the police, unless there's a warrant out for their arrest. And it doesn't sound like that applies here.'

'She's not a wanted person, she's a missing person. And as I said, we believe she went missing while seeking shelter. It would be helpful to us if you could at least give us some information on how Percy Gale's clients find the shelter.'

'We're in the phone book, we have fliers at libraries, we're listed with all accredited counselors. Women who need our services find us.'

'What about women from outside of Georgia?'

'Same process. Now, I really must get back to the main house.' She got up from her chair.

Neither Eric nor Angie rose.

Eric spoke. 'The woman we're searching for information on has actually been found. She's dead.'

Dora looked away as she pursed her lips. She fiddled with some papers on the desk, then sat down. 'Husband killed her?'

'We're investigating that now.' Eric gave Angie a slight nod.

Angie continued, 'We're trying to trace her movements and we would appreciate it if you could at least tell us if she was a client you were expecting. Her name was Eleanor Patterson.'

Eric was surprised when Dora laughed. 'My dears, you could give me any name you like but I wouldn't recognize it. Didn't you know that battered women's shelters don't use names?'

'Wait,' said Eric. 'How do you know a client is who she says she is when she arrives here?'

'We use code names, for everyone's protection.'

'How do they work?'

Dora opened her fan and cooled herself again.

'When someone contacts us to seek sanctuary, we assign a code name to them, ask them to guard it safely and then use it when they arrive here.'

Eric looked at Angie with an expression of frustration.

Angie asked, 'Would you look at this photograph and tell us if you recognize the woman in it?'

Dora lifted some papers and retrieved a pair of glasses from underneath. She cleaned the lenses and put them on, their silver frames highlighting her feathered white hair.

Angie handed over the photograph of Eleanor Patterson and Dora studied it before removing the glasses.

'I don't recognize her. And I'll confess that I just looked at it out of curiosity. You see, we wouldn't know what any of the women look like before they arrive here. We've never seen them before and as I said, we don't know their names.' She stood up and this time, she moved toward the door and held it open for the agents. 'I wish you luck and I hope you get the bastard.'

It hadn't taken long for Mark to get through to Gerrit Leuven on the telephone. First Mark had had to leave a message at the direct number Jayne had given them but, while he was tracking his way back to a main number at Leuven's station, Mark's own phone showed an incoming international call. Leuven's accent was clipped and his tone open but Mark could barely believe his ears when he heard Leuven's account.

*  *  *

Jayne sat at the table, feeling jet-lagged as she let Scott take her thoughts back to the minutes she had spent at the Agency with Gene.

'You said he was interested in the All Coroners Bulletin?'

Her voice was quiet. 'Yes.'

'Did he say anything in particular?'

She sighed. 'He said that it was something we could be legitimately positive about. He said that he understood how I handled the work, that I'd broken the big problem down into little ones.'

'And you said you left him alone for a minute?'

'When I went to the bathroom. I left him in the lab but when I came out, he was in my office, in my chair.'

'Did you notice anything disturbed or moved on your desk or anywhere else?'

Jayne shook her head.

'So you left and went straight to your apartment? What did you do there?'

'Um, he used the bathroom. I made coffee. We sat on the deck, talked a bit more.'

'Anything come up about your work or his?'

'No, it was more ... personal topics.'

'Personal?'

Jayne fixed her eyes on the table between them. 'He was wondering if I was involved with anyone.' She felt as though a weight was on her chest as she anticipated Scott's next question but none came. She looked at his face and saw he was staring at the recording equipment, rubbing his chin.

He didn't look at her. 'And you again left him alone at some point?'

'I just went to get a photograph from my storage room downstairs. A photograph from Kigali that he wanted.'

'About how long were you down there?'

'A couple of minutes. Probably less than five.'

'And then?'

'We looked through a bunch of photos and he left.'

'How did he leave? He say anything about staying in touch? Give you his number? Talk about getting together again?'

'I never had his number. He said he'd keep in touch but he hasn't been in touch yet. I understood he was flying out of LA in a day or two. He just left after giving me a kiss goodbye.'

Scott's pen hovered over the page but he didn't write down what she'd just said. 'You didn't drive him back to the hotel?'

'No...' Jayne now remembered how odd it had been at the time, that Gene had disappeared down her residential street into the night. 'I thought he got a taxi.'

'Did you see him get into a taxi or did you call a taxi for him?'

'Neither. In fact, I ran out to get him so I could call a taxi but he was already gone.'

'You get a lot of taxis on your street?'

Jayne shook her head firmly. 'No.'

'OK.' Scott leafed back to an earlier page in his notes. 'Steelie. You said Gene was "never your favorite person" and you didn't meet up with him last week. Why didn't you like him?'

Steelie assumed a more relaxed position in her chair, legs crossed and one arm slung across the back. 'Ten years ago, he was arrogant. Smart, but arrogant with it. Self-important. And he had a tendency to act like a white settler in colonial-era Rwanda, which is never a good look thirty years after Independence. I thought he made the UN look bad.'

'Was there something in particular? How'd you manage to work with him for so long if you felt that way?'

'One, I'm a master at disguising my feelings – note my witty banter despite the grilling you've just given my best friend here. And two, he was good at his job once he got over the fact that he wasn't in charge of everyone else's job as well. The straw that broke the camel's back was when he—'

'Guys.' Mark Wilson slammed the door open and crossed to the computer hooked up to the projector. 'Guys, listen up.'

Tripper pulled up the roller door and surveyed the storage unit in the sunlight slanting in around the corner of the concrete and steel building. He looked up and down the access lane he was in; no one. He'd chosen this particular unit when he'd signed the contract with an alias because it was at the farthest corner of the storage center. Most people didn't want to drag their belongings any further than they had to once they were in the front gate, so his comings and goings were usually unobserved.

He walked in, turned on the light, and pulled

the roller door down behind him, slotting into place a temporary lock. The items he'd left inside looked undisturbed: select pieces of his mother's faded slip-covered furniture, the pile of old curtains with their hooks still attached, the aquarium whose ferns now resembled miniature ocotillo, and, right at the back, the motorcycle. He went to the motorcycle first.

He prized off a spoke and inserted it into the left exhaust pipe to retrieve a plastic bag. Out of the bag, he brought a knife and went to the sofa. He pulled off its slip-cover and began cutting through the stitching on its back. He worked without concern about any noise he was creating or with hiding the destruction. As soon as he'd opened a foot-long section, he dug within the stuffing and retrieved two more small plastic bags as well as a much larger padded one.

He pulled on the edges of the padded bag until it formed a box. He attached this to the motorcycle's rear rack, ensuring its label faced out: *Joey's Pizza – We Deliver!* He put the smaller bags in the false bottom inside the pizza delivery box.

He moved on to the slip-covers on the two easy chairs and repeated his actions, retrieving scalpels, tweezers, surgical gloves, telephone wire, twine, and duct tape. From the bottom of the aquarium, he pulled out bags holding the false driver's license and insurance cards, license plates for the motorcycle, the cell phone pack, and the one grenade. Then he cut the lining off the curtains and peeled out a change of clothes, several Tyvek suits still in their plastic covers, and his motorcycle leathers.

Tripper changed clothes, stuffing the remainder of the cheap cop costume into the back of the sofa before putting the slip-covers back on all the furniture. He put on the leathers and turned on the cell phone to check its charge. The manufacturers had been good to their word; it had held its charge since he'd last been at the unit. He typed in a text message and pressed *Send*. When he saw it had gone through, he smiled and put on his helmet. He lifted the door and began to wheel out the motorcycle.

# TWENTY-SIX

Mark Wilson plugged the flashdrive into the computer. He spoke as he tapped keys. 'I just got off the phone with Gerrit Leuven. I think I know where King got his inspiration for the killings. Check this out.'

The projection screen at the end of the room switched to an image of a streambed bordered by tall reeds whose color was washed out to a pale yellow by bright sunlight. The clear sky above them looked almost white. Amongst the reeds was a black photo board. It looked out of place. Beyond it on the ground, a fluorescent orange plastic arrow pointed toward a plastic letter N.

Mark looked at Jayne and Steelie. 'After you two left Kigali in '96, Gerrit and King were called in by the Civilian Police to assist on a homicide investigation. At first, CivPol had thought it was related to the genocide but then they realized it couldn't be because the body was fresh. So then they thought it was a retribution killing; like, a witness for the Tribunal killed so she couldn't testify about the genocide. That was when CivPol called in Gerrit and he in turn asked King to photodocument. All right, look at this. Here's the overall scene and the photo board's right near the body parts.'

'Parts?' Scott asked.

'She was dismembered.'

Scott muttered something but Mark continued: 'Hang on. Look at this. I'm putting it on slide show.' He pressed a button and the slide dissolved and was replaced by another, which stayed on the screen for a time before dissolving and being replaced. Each photo brought them closer to the reeds, but in the third shot, a body part was slightly visible. In the subsequent photographs, someone was holding back the reeds with a flat tool, exposing the body parts like eggs in a nest. Two feet, the brown skin mottled by decomposition and the soil beneath them darkened with dried blood. Two hands, each finger separated from the palm. Then a single body part that it took Jayne a moment to recognize as a neck.

Mark came to sit by Scott. 'Remind you of anything?'

'Yeah, the first body parts we found on the outskirts of Atlanta. The neck especially.'

'And I don't think it's a coincidence. I think that when King was called in to photo these BP's, it gave him ideas.'

Scott sounded doubtful. 'But if he worked in the Bureau Lab, he'd have seen all kinds of stuff during his career. Why this particular case? Did they ID the body? Did they find the head?'

'No, never. And they only made a probable ID – turns out there aren't that many new missing persons in Rwanda. Most cases date to the spring of '94 when the genocide broke out. So the list of new mispers was small and most of the women on it were sex workers – and most of them weren't even Rwandan. They came from elsewhere to cater to the peacekeepers and internationals. For this body, they liked a young woman from the Ivory Coast. She'd only been in Kigali for a short time but was already known to pick up johns at a club called...' He consulted his notes. 'The Cadillac.' He looked up interrogatively at Steelie and Jayne. 'Heard of it?'

Steelie addressed Jayne. 'Um, maybe now would be a good time to tell them.'

Scott held up an index finger as his cell phone rang.

Jayne could tell he was talking to Eric and the news wasn't good. She looked back at the screen, where the slide show was progressing automatically. As she watched, she began to think, *Something's here ...what is it?* She went closer, pulled by that familiar professional curiosity again, which was quickly displacing the self-doubt that had put her on the back foot earlier. She only gave part of her attention to Scott as he relayed Eric's news that the shelters used code words for clients and, therefore, Patterson's name and photograph wasn't getting them anywhere.

Scott concluded by asking Steelie, 'Now, what is it you were going to tell us?'

Jayne spoke without turning from the screen. 'Hang on a sec. Mark, can you run the slides back and pause the show?'

He got up and punched a few keys at the computer. 'How far back do you want to go?'

'Go back two.'

The photo she was interested in was a close-up

299

of a foot but it hadn't been taken *in situ* at the streambed. It had been taken on a table covered with a green surgical drape. Lighting had been used to illuminate the cut portion of the ankle. A ruler was placed in the photograph for scale, along with a label that read *UNCP #7-0193*.

Steelie got up to join Jayne at the screen. 'Can we see the others in this section? Did Gerrit say where they took these shots?'

Mark replied, 'He said that all the material came back to UN HQ and they did the detail shots there, at your guys' temporary morgue.'

They looked at the photographs; separate ones of each dismembered finger, then the group placed in rough anatomical position to the palm. There were images of all surfaces of the hand and each shot was lit perfectly to show the cross-section of the cuts.

Jayne reached up, pointed at one of the cuts, and looked at Steelie, who nodded. They communicated silently like this two more times before Scott said, '32/1, there are other people in the room. What are you seeing?'

Jayne replied, 'Gene wasn't inspired by these cuts.'

Scott threw up his hands in exasperation. 'You can't rule out that he photographed them, came back here and copied them.'

She shook her head. 'No, I mean ... or at least, I think I mean that he wasn't inspired by them. He made them.'

Both agents stared at her and she looked to Steelie for back-up.

Steelie elaborated, 'We've seen these cuts

300

before. We saw cuts just like this at Critter Central. Patterson's arms. Same going between the joints, same careful approach toward not nicking bone. Dismemberment with hand tools – fine tools – not just going in with a bone saw.' She drew breath to say more but Scott interrupted.

'Are you seriously telling me that King *killed* this woman in Rwanda and then photographed her for the investigation?'

Steelie appeared to be choosing her words carefully, sounding more like a lawyer than ever. 'All we're saying is that there's a strong possibility that the same person who was responsible for cutting off Patterson's arms also dismembered this woman in Kigali. We don't know who that person is and it could be that it's actually two killers ... though they'd be two peas in a pod.'

'What, the woman was killed by some other perp King met over there, who then taught him how to do this kind of dismemberment?'

Steelie shrugged.

Mark had been flipping through his notes. 'This is making sense. Listen to this: Gerrit knew that the cuts were precise, particularly compared to trauma inflicted during the genocide with a machete or scythe. He said he later developed some suspicions about people with access to the UN HQ because when they went to open a new supply kit for the morgue, about half the blades for the scalpels were missing, plus a few handles. Let's see.'

He scanned a page and then pointed at it.

'Yeah, here. He said he questioned the Logistics guys but they confirmed that the supplies had arrived from the European Union boxed up on a pallet.' Mark looked up at Scott. 'But Gerrit stressed that his suspicion that someone had stolen from their supplies was just a personal opinion and he didn't have any proof.'

Scott questioned Jayne. 'Could King have accessed a pallet?'

'Easily. If you were UN personnel, you could get access to almost anything that would be legitimate. Of course, we had to sign in and out and list how much of whatever item we took.'

'Was someone guarding the pallets or controlling the sign-in sheet?'

'The Logs guys had way too much to deal with to be able to guard anything. The sign-in sheet hung on a clipboard at the edge of the supply area.'

Scott swung his chair toward Mark, putting his back to the women, and lowered his voice. 'What do you think?'

'I think we gotta get them over to King's house ASAP, Houston. They can see things we can't.' He gestured at the slide on the screen.

Jayne called out: 'What's the problem with taking us to the house? That's why you flew us out here.'

Scott swung around again. 'The problem is that now, we know that *you* know the suspect. We need to make sure our case isn't screwed by taking you to his house.'

'Oh.'

'Mark, check on whether it's going to be a conflict to have them over there. And if you find a conflict, make it go away.'

# TWENTY-SEVEN

Eric felt like he was being garrotted by his seat-belt as Angie brought the Crown Victoria to a lurching halt in front of a building in a suburb of Athens. He glanced at her and saw her grin as she put the car into park.

'Soft brakes,' she said, mock-defensively. 'Gotta stamp on 'em like that or they don't work.'

He released his seatbelt and twisted to lower its anchor point on the car's frame. 'I don't remember you doing any "stamping" earlier.'

'And I don't remember asking you to comment on my driving.' She leaned forward to look out of his window. 'Looks like this one has a security system at the door.'

Eric turned to look and saw that the only feature differentiating the façade of the brick row house from its neighbors was the discreet metal panel encompassing a doorbell and key-pad alongside holes for a speaker and micro-phone. He got out of the car and looked up at the building, noticing the small camera mounted above the door but beneath the windows of the second story. Railings painted a glossy black flanked a staircase that led up to the front door and down to a basement. The brick on the building looked clean, as though recently sand-blasted.

They mounted the stairs together and Angie pressed the bell. A woman's voice came through the speaker.

'Yes?'

Eric instinctively looked up at the camera above them and Angie held her badge open toward it.

'Special Agents Nicks and Ramos, Federal Bureau of Investigation. May we come in?'

'Just a moment.'

They heard the lock turn and a person who reminded Eric of the nuns who had run his elementary school opened the door. This woman wasn't wearing any religious adornment but there was something familiar in the cut of her grey dress and her air of friendly rigidity. As she inspected their badges and identity cards, he noticed a streak of white hair just to the left of the midline of an otherwise very dark brown bob. When she looked up from their badges, he saw brown eyes that were neither impressed nor curious about why they were there.

'Come in.' She held the door open, then closed it after them.

Eric knew that the front door of most row houses would let into a hallway that would run to the back of the house, but this one had been remodeled to put them into a reception room that prevented further entry. There was a window to an office-like room that could be reached through another door flanked by its own access panel.

The woman in grey said, 'I'm Aviva Gold-smith, co-director of Sanctuary House. How may I help you?'

Angie spoke. 'We're trying to ascertain whether you, at any time, have had a resident or visitor by the name of Eleanor Patterson. She would have come to you from Oregon.'

Aviva Goldsmith shook her head. 'You may not be aware that at Sanctuary House we don't know the names of the women who seek shelter. This is done for everyone's protection so that if their abusive partner comes here looking for them, we can protect them without deceit.'

Angie resumed. 'Ms Goldsmith, we're in the midst of a manhunt for someone we believe may have harmed Eleanor Patterson. Could you look at this photograph and tell us if you recognize this woman?'

'I can look at it but I won't be able to tell you if it's the person you're looking for.'

Angie brought out a copy of the photograph Eric had used in the briefing room that morning. Eric watched Aviva Goldsmith closely as she looked at the photo and thought he detected relief under her calm exterior.

She said, 'I don't recognize her.'

Jayne spent the duration of the drive from the FBI building to Mead Street training her brain to think of their destination as a site, not Gene's house. But when Mark parked the Suburban and she looked out the tinted back window, she just saw a house. A two-story Victorian building covered in siding that was supposed to look like bricks but didn't succeed, topped with a chimney and an attic window in the peak of the roofline. A small porch above three concrete steps fronted the house and a large police tent dominated the unkempt yard.

Jayne got out of the car and waited for Steelie to come around from the other side. She looked down the street and saw a television crew and a small crowd of people on the other side of some yellow tape. She and Steelie joined Scott and Mark to cross the street toward the house.

Inside the tent, a police officer and an FBI agent logged them into the Site Visitor books, then gave them protective gear to put on over their clothes and shoes. Once everyone was suited up, Mark led the way from the tent to the front porch of the house. He greeted a police officer standing sentry on the door and then he addressed Steelie and Jayne.

'The electricity was turned off here. We're working on having it restored but take these flashlights. Use them. We'll be going straight through the house to the back; the side access is barricaded. You'll meet the Medical Examiner and it'll be easier if you don't make a reference to ever having met King.'

He handed them the flashlights and they entered the house.

On stepping over the threshold, Jayne felt like she'd walked into another climate zone. Where it was warm and humid outside, the house was cool and smelled of old carpet. Boxes and debris crowded a narrow hallway that led past a staircase. At the top of the stairs, voices and light emanated from a room off of the landing.

Mark called back, 'The evidence techs are working off a generator upstairs.'

Past the base of the stairs, rooms came off to the left of the hallway but it seemed even darker. Jayne swung the beam of her flashlight across the floor and up the walls to make sure she didn't bump into anything, until they emerged out the back door into the sunlight and a strong smell of decomposing tissue.

The back yard was narrow but long, and bare in the middle. Rangy bushes hugged the tall wood fence that separated it from the neighbors on each side. There was a concrete path leading to a clapboard garage whose double doors stood open, and Jayne could see floodlights set up on stands, their extension cords running to the generator humming on the path outside. Scott was going toward the garage but the decomposition smell was coming from the open section of the yard.

Mark said, 'Let me introduce you to the doc and his team.'

Over by the right fence-line, there were four people working in different sections of a grid marked out by fluorescent pink twine suspended between stakes hammered into the ground. They were all wearing Tyvek protective suits and rubber boots. Beyond them were three more Tyvek-suited people standing at waist-high sifting trays suspended over large plastic buckets. A table near the sifting station was laden with plastic bags, paper bags, evidence labels, photograph markers and other tools needed to document evidence emerging from the excavation.

A man was walking across to them by following plastic squares placed on the ground like stepping-stones. He pulled his mask down as he approached, revealing a lined, olive-colored face. His protective suit was baggy and slightly twisted off the mid-line of his slight frame but his voice was strong.

'You must be the anthropologists. I'm Leonard Penman, the ME.'

Mark introduced Steelie and Jayne to the Chief Medical Examiner. They shook gloved hands.

'We're not completely backwards out here,' Dr Penman said with a smile, 'but we're honest enough to say that we haven't had to deal with multiple sets of buried remains, let alone mostly skeletonized remains. Even our biggest recovery effort – the commuter jet crash last winter – was fleshed remains and we had DMORT's help on that one.'

Jayne nodded. She and Steelie had enormous respect for the regional Disaster Mortuary Operational Response Teams that were made up of forensic scientists and dispatched to scenes of mass fatalities to provide immediate human identification services.

Dr Penman waved a hand to indicate the yard behind him. 'As you can see, the criminalists have already put a grid over the area where we started. We're working over there by the fence first because it's where the soil was recently disturbed – by a dog, most likely – which exposed the remains that are putting out the stink. We've got Dr Greg Parker from the university here.

He's the archaeologist and it's his grad students from the Anthropology Department over there sifting the soil. I've been told that you two can advise on strategy? If so, you've arrived just in time because we're reaching the bigger body parts now.'

Steelie said, 'I guess the best thing at this stage would be for us to have a closer look at what you're dealing with.'

'Follow me,' said Dr Penman, with something like relish.

Scott emerged from the garage and called out, '32/1. I need you for a second.'

They looked to Dr Penman, who said, 'Go on. We're not going anywhere.'

Scott held a clear evidence bag with something inside it. He pointed inside the garage.

'You see that cabinet against the back wall?'

Jayne saw a metal wardrobe. A criminalist was collecting and documenting items that were on the labeled shelves.

Scott continued. 'OK, next to it is a huge chest freezer where King probably kept body parts. But he used that cabinet for a different bunch of mementos. This was in there.' He held up the bag to show the large cream-colored purse inside. 'There wasn't much in it, but one thing it did have was an Oregon driver's license for one Eleanor Patterson.'

Steelie let out a low whistle.

'What else is in the purse?' Jayne asked.

'Like I said, not much.' He glanced at it. 'An empty coin purse, an empty wallet, a powder compact, a tube of lipstick, and a, ah, sanitary pad.' He hurried on. 'Looks like he kept belongings from other vics on the shelves.'

He started to go back inside but Jayne said, 'Wait.'

He stopped and looked at her.

Jayne was thinking about the contents of the purse and about Patterson's arms as they'd seen them at Critter Central. In her mind's eye, she could see the sunspots on the forearms. 'You told us you'd ID'd Patterson from the surgical plate on her arm. How old did they say she was?'

'Fifty-one when she went missing. Why?'

She ignored his question and held out her hand. 'Can I see that purse?'

He hesitated.

She turned her hand and flicked her fingers toward her palm. 'I know it's evidence but you haven't sealed the bag yet. I'm gloved.'

He handed over the bag.

She reached inside and pulled the purse so its open top was aligned with the top of the evidence bag. Looking inside, she could see the lipstick, compact, and the two wallets. Then she used her finger to expand the small compartment in the lining. She could see a maxi pad in there, still folded in its wrapper but the glue at the edges wasn't holding it closed. She handed the evidence bag back to Scott.

'You're going to want to look inside the pad.'
'What?'
'You should section it – carefully.'

He only paused for a moment longer before gesturing for them to follow him. He called out to the criminalist working at the far end of the garage. 'Tait.'

Scott put on surgical gloves to pull the purse from the evidence bag and put it on the table in front of the young man. 'Doc this inside and out.'

The criminalist labeled the purse and photographed the exterior and interior. Once he was finished, Scott pulled the maxi pad from the inner pocket and put it on the table.

'OK, now open this up.'

Tait gave Scott a look like he thought this was a joke.

*'Now.'*

Tait instantly composed himself. 'Yes, sir.' He picked up his camera and photographed the item with an evidence label before touching it. Then he used a pair of tweezers to peel off the thin plastic wrapping.

The pad was folded into thirds and he eased it flat before looking at Scott for direction.

Scott turned to Jayne. 'You said section it?'

She nodded.

He looked back to Tait, who used a scalpel to begin an incision on the side of the pad. Then he stopped, picked up a magnifying glass, and used it to look at the pad again. 'There's already a cut here, sir.'

Scott leaned down and looked. 'OK, peel it back from the existing cut.'

Tait carefully pulled back several layers to reveal an object that had nothing to do with moisture absorption. It was a small piece of paper, folded many times and pressed flat as though with an iron.

The criminalist photographed the item with a ruler and an evidence label before opening it with his tweezers. Then he stepped back to let the others see. Visible inside the folds of the paper was something written in faint pencil:

*793 Cobb /Agapanthus*

Jayne spoke. 'You said the shelters gave the women code names. That might be a code she was trying to keep hidden.'

Before she even finished speaking, Scott pulled his cell phone from its holster, his eyes fixed on the piece of paper. Jayne and Steelie started to leave and heard him say, 'Eric. Is 793 Cobb an address on your list? You're there right now? OK, check this: Patterson's code may have been Agapanthus.'

Just outside the garage, Scott caught up with Jayne. 'How in hell did you know to look in the pad?'

'You said Patterson was at least fifty-one years old. She was likely menopausal. So the pad didn't fit. It was possible, but not probable.'

# TWENTY-EIGHT

Eric hung up from Scott's call and regarded Aviva Goldsmith carefully as they stood in the reception area of Sanctuary House.

'We have reason to believe that you would have known Eleanor Patterson as Agapanthus.'

Instead of looking at the photo again, Aviva Goldsmith's eyes stayed on Eric's and he saw her left eyelid twitch. She steadied it with a finger.

He said quietly, 'Please look at the photo again.'

'I don't need to. Agapanthus never arrived.'

He pounced on her use of the past tense. 'What do you mean, "never arrived"? So you expected her? How was she supposed to get here?'

He felt Angie's hand on his arm so stopped shooting questions at Aviva Goldsmith, who had been trying to get a word in.

'Let me explain,' she said. 'Our system here is that when we're contacted by women who need sanctuary, we don't ask any questions of them. We only give them our address and instructions on how to get here. We don't know their names, anything about them, or where they're coming from, other than if they're out of state or will be arriving with children ... oh, and which day. We need only enough information to determine if we have enough space to accommodate them. If they're coming from out of state, like Agapanthus...'

She paused and only then looked again at the portrait in Angie's hand. 'We instruct them that on arrival at the airport, they should take the bus to our nearest stop at the Naval College. We tell them which number bus to take and to walk here to the house. This makes it harder for their abusers to track them because it reduces the number of people they interact with, particularly by not using taxis, and it gives them a way to get here that makes them appear to be local. They're instructed to travel without baggage so they don't appear to be visitors. All of this is designed to reduce their vulnerability while in transit. The bus also provides some safety in numbers.'

Eric caught Angie's eyes.

Aviva Goldsmith must have noticed the exchange because she asked, 'Is that important?'

Angie asked, 'You instruct them to use a bus from Atlanta airport?'

'Ye-es.' She looked at them, her eyes questioning.

Angie said, 'I'm afraid that those instructions may have put Eleanor Patterson directly in the path of a predator.'

Eric thought Aviva Goldsmith was looking upset and he wanted to get information from her before that rendered her useless. 'We need to know what day Eleanor Patterson was supposed to arrive at the airport. And we need to know if you've got any other women who didn't show.'

She looked into the middle distance.

'Are you all right?'

'No, I'm not all right.' She blinked back the wateriness in her eyes and focused on him. 'I'm damn angry.' She turned on her heel, went to the inner door, and punched buttons on the security panel, the noise a staccato tattoo. Watching her, Eric wondered how he could ever have mistaken her for a nun.

The agents went to the window and watched her open a file drawer to pull out some manila folders. She put the items on the window ledge for them.

'There are only three women who haven't arrived at Sanctuary House after making first contact. That's three women since we opened in 1990. In these files are the records of our contact with them and you'll see what dates we expected them.'

Angie immediately began going through the files, her notebook and pen at the ready.

Eric looked at Aviva Goldsmith. 'Were you ever concerned about why these women never arrived?'

She smiled at him wearily. 'Human beings are complex creatures. Women being abused by the person they love or the father of their children have yet another layer of complexity. Even after they've decided to leave the abuser, they can change their minds and stay, or they leave but decide they don't need a place like Sanctuary House to assist their transition. To exercise choice is a woman's right and it's a crucial one. It has been our practice to assume that a woman

316

who didn't arrive after first contact with us has exercised choice. We know there are alternatives...'

Her hand strayed to the roots of her streak of white hair and he noticed fine scar tissue on the backs of some of her fingers.

'For example,' she was saying. 'We know that it's possible that in the act of leaving, abuse victims face an even greater danger from their partners. But I must say that we had not thought that, having left the abuser, they would encounter someone yet more dangerous.'

She stopped touching her scalp and looked directly at him. 'May I ask how you knew this woman's code word? They're instructed to avoid writing it down or sharing it with anyone.'

Eric was limited in what he could say at this stage in the investigation but he wanted to give her something.

'I think she didn't trust herself to remember something so important. She wrote it down but hid it well. But the fact that she wrote it down may help us find her killer.'

'Her killer?' She echoed him. 'You only said she had been harmed by this person.'

'Yeah. He harmed her by killing her.'

This time, he recognized Aviva Goldsmith's expression; she was angry, damn angry.

Angie closed the last file. 'Got it. Let's go.'

Tripper waited until the electronic display came up, acknowledging the cash he'd fed into the machine: 'Go pump at #4'. He walked to the motorcycle and began to pump the gas. Through

317

his helmet, he could hear a newscaster's voice coming from the small television screens mounted above the pumps. The man's tone was breathless.

*Back to our breaking story. We're just now getting the vision we promised you from Northside where it's understood that police and FBI officials have made a break in the case of several unsolved Atlanta homicides. Teri is live at the scene. Teri?*

Tripper's grip relaxed on the pump and he turned to look at the screen. The camera was focused on the field reporter's heavily made-up face as she lowered her finger from where she'd been covering her ear.

*That's right, Don, but I should add that, so far, neither the police nor the FBI have made an official statement as to what is taking place in the house that is just about halfway down the block on this quiet street, but it's widely believed to be related to the discoveries of female body parts around Atlanta, all still unidentified. As you can see behind me, law enforcement vehicles are continuing to arrive and they have put up crime scene tape to keep us some distance away.*

The camera shifted from her face to the street behind her and attempted to focus on a house partially obscured by one in the foreground. In the corner of the screen, a box materialized with a view of the same street with a subtitle: *Earlier Today*. Several people were visible emerging from an SUV and crossing the street. Tripper raised the visor on his helmet and stared hard. Jayne Hall and Steelie Lander were unmistak-

318

able as they walked behind Special Agency Houston.

*... and although we have no official word on the case being investigated, the families of women missing in Atlanta are already beginning to congregate here, hoping for some word on their loved ones. Back to you in the studio, Don.*

Tripper's anger was so great that it outweighed the zing of fear that shot through him and made his toes tingle. His plan to go back to California and cause those bitches as much trouble as they'd caused him was no longer enough. They had interfered one step too far now. He had to eliminate them – all of them, including Houston. It could mean taking his chances by going back to the Mead Street house, which was in violation of the Transition Plan. But he would have to take that chance.

Tripper lowered his visor with a snap and turned back to the motorcycle.

As Angie drove them back to her office, Eric made a series of calls. First, he confirmed that King was indeed working at Atlanta Airport on the day that Eleanor Patterson was due to arrive there. Then he contacted the relevant Transport Police units to track down any CCTV footage from in and around the airport. Without a time frame for Patterson's arrival, they would have to scan through all the footage from that day and hope to see some contact between Patterson and King. They needed a strong link to solidify the case against him because they didn't have proof that he was driving his van when her dismembered arms fell out of it on the freeway. Nor was her purse in his garage proof that he actually killed her.

By the time Eric and Angie walked into the briefing room, the airport's Closed Circuit TV tapes were waiting for them. The Transport Police had sent a note that Eric could thank the increased camera coverage and extended CCTV storage requirements that came into effect after September 11, 2001, otherwise the footage would have been wiped by this time.

Angie corralled a television and playback machine from someone's office and wheeled them into the briefing room while Eric brought sandwiches and sodas from the cafeteria. They had Eleanor Patterson's photograph illuminated on the projection screen to assist them in identifying her if she turned up on the video and they kept each tape on fast-forward as they ate while watching the screen.

The stationary camera had only picked up the part of the room that showed the information desk and about fifteen feet of tiled floor in front of it. Many people passed back and forth in the room and the fast-forward made them appear to be involved in some complicated dance, sometimes appearing to twirl in the center of the floor when they were consulting monitors mounted around the room.

Angie stopped the first tape several times for false alarms; women who looked like Patterson on fast-forward but then were revealed to look completely different once the tape was put on play. There was no sign of a man cleaning the

320

floors as King was alleged to have been doing that day.

Then Angie exclaimed, 'Whoa!' and rewound the tape. 'You said Houston described a big off-white handbag in the shed at King's house? I think I just saw one.' She pressed *Play*.

At first, the image was just the floor, the desk, and the man working behind the desk. Then a woman came into the shot from the right, the airport terminal side, and she stood in the center of the floor, turning slowly as if deciding which way to go. Angie paused the tape while the woman was turned toward the camera. The time marker read 16:22:12. Eric looked at the portrait on the projection screen and then back at the frozen CCTV footage.

'That's her,' he stated.

'Yeah, definitely. Same square jaw, same features, same type of hair. Big, pale bag.'

'Play it, Angie.'

As they watched, Eleanor Patterson turned and walked to the information desk. She kept her handbag tucked under her arm as she stood talking to the attendant. It was while she was doing this that another man entered the shot from the left at time marker 16:26:34. His head was tilted down and he was walking backwards slowly, which was confusing until it became clear he was mopping the floor, shuffling backward so that he wouldn't walk on areas he'd just cleaned.

'Shit,' Angie hissed.

The man with the mop passed close behind Patterson while she was leaning into the counter to look at something. He paused as though to

321

stretch his back and pulled a kerchief from a back pocket. As he wiped his forehead, he glanced at her. At the moment he put the kerchief back in his pocket, Eric pressed *Pause*.

'That's him. That's King, the sonofabitch.'

'She doesn't even know he's there.'

'He means nothing to her at this stage. If she even noticed him. He's just the guy cleaning the floor. We have to see how he gains her trust.' He restarted the tape.

King carried on mopping until he was out of the shot to the right. Patterson finished the conversation at the desk and walked out of frame to the left, toward the curb pick-up and bus stop area. The time marker read 16:31:02. Then King was back, now entering from the right and working backwards. He seemed to be mopping faster. At 16:40:36, he was no longer visible on the CCTV footage.

Angie exchanged the tape for one that showed the exterior of the same area. They would examine the rest of the interior tape later. She fast-forwarded the tape to time marker 16:30:00 and they saw Eleanor Patterson walk out of the building at 16:31:01, cross a few lanes for other buses, then stand at the third island across. They had a clear view of her. Over a period of 24 minutes, four buses came and went and Patterson didn't get on any of them. Once, she waved at someone on a bus who may have spoken to her and she held up three fingers as if to suggest she was waiting for the Number 3.

At time marker 17:03:00, she appeared tired of standing and sat on the bench, keeping her handbag close to her body. And at time marker 17:07:20, a van pulled up to the bus stop. It was pale but it was otherwise a match to the gold van Eric had spent two days watching in Mesa, Arizona. In the passenger window was a neat, hand-lettered sign: *Athens*. The town where Sanctuary House was located.

The agents watched her go from waving the van off to shrugging to scanning for the bus again ... and then someone opened the passenger door from the inside. Eric lunged forward to hit *Pause*. In the freeze-frame, the driver's wrist was visible. They would get the tape enhanced. He let the tape begin again.

Eleanor Patterson got into the van and closed the door behind her. After exactly three seconds, at time marker 17:08:10, the brake lights on the back of the van went off and it pulled forward, its Georgia license plate clear. It accelerated at a sedate pace until it was out of the frame.

Eric fast-forwarded the tape until they saw the Number 3 bus arrive at the stop four minutes later, belching exhaust and canting to one side. He didn't know how late the bus was but it was too late for Mrs Patterson.

# TWENTY-NINE

When Greg Parker, the archaeology professor, hailed them, Jayne and Steelie came over from where they had been training his graduate students to discriminate between human and non-human juvenile bone. Greg was using a trowel to expose a partial, skeletalized hand. The arm it was attached to still had some tissue adhering to the bones and it disappeared into the wall of the depression Greg had created in accordance with the grid pattern laid over the yard. When he had the hand sitting on a pedestal of soil, he leaned back on his heels, holstering the trowel on his tool belt. 'Take a look.'

Jayne got on her knees and peered at the bones. 'Can I borrow a brush?' He handed her a small paintbrush. She gently brushed the cut edge of the bones and confirmed what she thought she had seen: a bright, dry cross-section and a general absence of fractures radiating from the cut edges. Then she let Steelie take a look.

In short order, Steelie said, 'Postmortem cuts.'

Jayne nodded and they all pulled down their masks, sitting back on undisturbed soil.

Greg launched in. 'As you can see, I came at that hand from this side of the grid, so I know the fingers aren't here. They're gone. And this isn't the first area of the yard where I've come across this.'

Jayne asked, 'You're thinking someone dug through this body when digging another hole?'

'Maybe he wasn't paying attention where he buried previous bodies and he hit things with his shovel as he buried someone else?' Greg offered.

Steelie weighed in. 'This actually reminds me of some of the graves around Zvornik.'

Jayne knew what she meant. They hadn't worked directly on the Drina River flanking Serbia but it was common knowledge that mass graves there had been 'robbed' of the bodies of people killed near Srebrenica. Someone had attempted to remove the bodies and hide them in a second location but, because the exhumations were done hastily, perhaps at night and with the clumsy broad strokes of a backhoe bucket, body parts or fragments of clothing were left behind.

Jayne looked back at the hand in question. She could see that there was nothing beyond their cut edges, just soil all the way to the fence-line. Greg Parker had done a nice job of isolating the feature.

Steelie explained to Greg, 'I don't think this is someone accidentally cutting through previous interments. I mean, *some* of it may turn out to be just Gee ... the perp double-digging in one spot but not this. This is someone taking out parts.' She looked across the yard. 'And they may not all be here.'

Dr Penman had joined them. 'Are you saying we might dig up this whole yard and not find all the parts of a single body?'

'I'm saying it's a possibility,' she replied. 'I'm not up on serial killer behavior but I'm not sure that the person who wants to kill and dismember is the same person who wants to go back and move already-buried decomposing parts around his backyard just for fun.'

'Yeah,' said Greg with a little laugh. 'The latter sounds more like what you guys are known for.'

Jayne glanced at Steelie and they stood up. An uncomfortable silence followed that Greg tried to fill.

'Like the Body Farm,' he said uncertainly. 'At UTK...'

Dr Penman was staying on topic. 'What do you recommend?'

Jayne looked around the site. 'Look, you were always going to have to grid off the whole yard. I'd suggest that you carry on with that process but be alert to any remains that show disturbance or fragmentation from postmortem damage, then carefully go from the known to the unknown wherever you see it. Since you're likely dealing with already dismembered bodies, it's going to take just that much more attention to whether the cuts are peri or post.'

'So, I'm looking for the usual perimortem signs; radiating fractures, lifting and bending?'

'Yes.' She looked at Greg, who was getting to his feet. 'And Greg can cover what's familiar to him with postmortem breaks from the archaeological setting.'

Steelie said, jovially, 'You guys are a dream team.'

'Actually,' he replied. 'I've just realized it

takes two of us to do what just one of you can do.'

'Perhaps, but neither of us can tell what's a stone tool and what's just a battered rock, nor could we analyze stomach contents.'

'Nor would you want to,' Greg commented, as he slapped Dr Penman on the back.

Just then, Scott walked over on the step stones. 'What's going on?'

Dr Penman explained the apparent disturbance of the burials.

Scott looked serious. 'Do you know how many people you've got so far?'

'A minimum number of three, based on the fifteen body parts we've exhumed so far. We've had two right clavicles with the sternal end fused and one left clavicle with a fully unfused sternal end.'

'In English?'

Steelie answered him. 'Collarbones. Two right collarbones, so that's two people, and they're both fused at the business end, so both people are probably over twenty-five years. Then one left collarbone from someone under twenty-five, which makes three. Minimum. Though only one cranium so far.'

'OK,' replied Scott. 'From the garage, we've got ID cards or driver's licenses from eight different people, all female. We're going to be working on cross-checking to see if any of them have missing person reports – besides Eleanor Patterson and the two names I recognize of local missing prostitutes. Not all the trophies may be from women he killed; there could be some

327

assault victims we don't know about yet. But I came over here to tell you to keep looking.'

'Say no more,' said Greg, who went to give instructions to his graduate students.

'And I'm afraid, Doctor Penman, that I've got to take away these two ladies. They've got a plane to catch.'

The ME shook Jayne and Steelie's hands as though they'd known each other for years and then the women gained the concrete behind Scott. He turned and spoke under his breath. 'Look at this.' He was holding a set of clear evidence bags, which he fanned out in his hands. 'King made copies of those photos from Kigali.'

Steelie flicked on her flashlight and concentrated it on the corner of the top photograph. 'Look at the photo board, though. The others had a UN CivPol case number. These are different.'

He turned the photos toward him. The board read *EK-001*. Scott whistled softly before translating. 'Eugene King: first victim.'

'A perfect trophy,' Jayne muttered.

'Yeah,' agreed Steelie. 'These aren't copies; they're fresh photos and anyone seeing them thinks they're legit crime scene or case photos. He can explain them away; after all, he worked for the FBI and who knows what you weird Bureau employees carry around.'

Scott dropped the photos to his side. 'All right, I've got your ride out front. He'll take you back to your motel, drop you with some dinner, then we'll be sending an Agent Carter to take you to the airport. He'll have your boarding passes.'

Steelie detoured to say goodbye to Greg's

students while Jayne preceded Scott into the house. As she mounted the back stairs, she noticed it was getting dark. She turned on her flashlight and felt the chill of that house go into her bones again. She could barely believe she actually knew the person who lived here or was responsible for what was in that yard. That partial hand bothered her. Where was the rest of that person?

She came out the front door of the house and was halted by the scene in the street directly ahead: men, women, and children, dressed in exercise clothes, school uniforms, suits. They were holding lit candles and something else ... Jayne gradually perceived that they were photographs but only photos of women. Some portraits were big, while others were snapshots; women holding children, women laughing, women looking dubiously at the camera, women in graduation clothing. Women who were alive. Alive but missing.

Then Scott was in the doorway next to her. 'They already know, Jayne. Or they suspect. I recognize some of the relatives of the women who went missing on my watch.' He set off for the tent.

Jayne looked at the relatives one last time. She felt they were identical to a group who'd waited for the bodies strapped down in the back of their UN truck in Kigali in 1996 after an exhumation. *Everyone is the same, everywhere.* Jayne followed in Scott's footsteps, feeling like she could be in Kigali, walking into the UN's old morgue tent, then stripping off mask, booties, gloves –

just like this. Putting everything into red bio-hazard bags – just like this. Movements so familiar, she could have done them in her sleep back then. Now, inside this tent, she couldn't tell where she was, what year it was. She could go out and find that it was 1996 again and Gene would be there; everything was the same and the families were waiting.

She hesitated and Scott said, 'Follow me. When I stop to talk to the relatives, keep going to my right. The black Suburban down the street has an agent in it, waiting for you. Just get in.'

Jayne followed him out into the deepening darkness. She noticed a television camera when a bright lamp came on to focus on Scott. She heard Scott announce his name and title and tell them that there was no official information yet. She kept walking, focused on the dark bulk of the Suburban in the distance. Then a hand pulled her to the side.

# THIRTY

Half-empty pizza boxes sat in the middle of the conference table in the FBI briefing room. Agent Mark Wilson chewed anti-gas pills as he watched the CCTV tape of King's van pulling away from the airport with Eleanor Patterson in the passenger seat at 5.08 p.m. He had lost track of how many times he'd examined the footage but he kept doing it in the hope that he would glean some clue as to where King was now.

Agent Angela Nicks watched Mark from her seat at the head of the table as she tapped a pencil against the papers in front of her. She had drawn circles around King's name and the names of the missing women and what they knew about each. She was looking for ways the circles might overlap and give them a lead on where King could be hiding now. So far, it wasn't working too well. The modus operandi that King had displayed at the airport with Eleanor Patterson appeared to be the only time he had used it. They didn't know how he might have adjusted the MO when he wasn't at the airport but he had got the women back to his house somehow. Angie switched to tapping the eraser end of the pencil against the tip of her nose. She knew that sometimes worked.

Agent Scott Houston was temporarily not thinking about King as he used the computer to connect to the Internet and check on the status of the return flight Jayne was due to board that evening with Steelie. The Internet connection was slow and he waited, emptying his brain as he stared at the screen. He was about to ask Angie and Mark if the connection was always this slow these days and then he realized something.

'Did anyone check the Agency 32/1email account for the messages from King?'

He was met with silence, which was enough to get him to bail out from the airline website and switch to the Web-based 32/1 account. Mark came over with the password that Jayne had left with them and Scott typed it in. After a pause, the inbox appeared.

'Jesus.' Scott sat up straighter.

'What time zone is that stamp?' Mark pulled up a chair.

Angie and Eric immediately came over.

Mark explained, 'King sent them a message today. Depending on what time zone the account's set to, he might have sent it just a few hours ago.'

Scott had clicked on the message, whose subject line was, 'Hi from SF.' They read the message on screen.

*Jayne: bk yr way nxt wk. Dinner? GK*

Angie leaned in closer to the screen. 'That's not an email; it's a text message.'

Scott gestured at the screen. 'It's an email. It

came on email.'

'But it came from a cell phone,' she persisted. 'Look, hit *Reply*. See what happens.'

Scott followed her instructions and the 'To' field was filled with an email address made up of letters and enough numbers to resemble a telephone number.

'Angie, can you—' Scott turned but she had already put her cell phone to her ear.

'Tech Unit? I need a check on a cell number. This is Priority One.'

Standing at the dressing table in the motel room, Jayne placed the candle in her briefcase and thought about the woman who'd stopped her in the street by Gene's house. She hadn't looked very old but her skin had made Jayne think of parchment. She'd been holding a photograph, its subject obscured by her fingertips, and she'd smiled at Jayne but kept a hold on her arm until another woman joined them.

The second woman was the color of chocolate and held an unlit candle, which she offered to Jayne. She'd accepted it with a nod. Then the two smiled and turned away as though their work was done and in that moment, Jayne had no longer felt confused about what year it was or where she was. It was where she always was and where she always would be: halfway between the living and the dead, helping to work a link that transcended time and space because the need for it was timeless and crossed all borders. It existed wherever the living searched for the missing and wherever people died deprived of their names. Jayne had held the candle on the ride to the motel and now she would carry it home to Los Angeles.

She heard the knock at the door that she and Steelie had been expecting. Agent Carter had arrived to drive them to the airport. She glanced at Steelie, who was zipping up her own bag, and crossed to open the door.

The man standing there was dressed in motorcycle leathers and helmet, which was unexpected. He raised the visor and said, 'Hello, again.' Even before she heard his voice, she recognized Gene's eyes.

She abruptly and belatedly shoved the door closed but it bounced back at her fast and she was pushed off balance. As she stumbled backwards, she was aware of Steelie charging Gene with a cry that sounded far away and of him coming across the threshold, and then her vision went gray at the edges, closing down further and further, until there was nothing.

Scott had ceded his seat in front of the computer to Mark, who'd navigated into the Settings page of the Agency 32/1 email account.

'There.' Mark pointed to the screen. 'The account is on Pacific time. But incoming messages could still be stamped with the time at the sender's location.' He looked up at Scott. 'Do we believe this? That King's in San Francisco?'

Scott was standing with his arms crossed, watching Angie on the phone with the Technical Support Unit. 'No. No way. I don't know what game he's playing but he's here in Atlanta. We tracked him here in Wayne Spicer's car.'

Eric said quietly, 'We don't have a firm ID from the EMT's or anyone else who saw the driver of the Spicer car.'

Scott gave his partner a withering look and Eric put his hands up in surrender. Just then, Angie turned toward them, a hand raised with a finger in the air as she listened to her phone. They turned toward her expectantly.

'OK, OK,' she said, then covered the mouth-piece of the phone as she addressed the three men. 'The text message was sent from a cell phone today at 1:07 p.m.'

Scott walked up to her. 'Is it turned on right now? Can they track it?' He all but took the phone from her hand.

'It doesn't need to be turned on – hang on.' She listened to her phone, thanked the person on the other end and then cut the call. 'OK, the cell doesn't need to be turned on for the phone company to ping it and get a location within one hundred feet. But first we gotta get a warrant out to the phone company.'

'This is bullshit!' Scott fumed. 'This is high priority, did you tell them that?'

'We might have another way.' She exchanged a glance with Mark. 'Look, the D's in Missings at Atlanta PD have the technology to ping cells.'

Scott looked at each of the agents in turn. 'Missing Persons? You know any of those detectives?'

Angie's mouth was set. 'I've got a couple of favors I can call in. It might not be enough.'

'If they're like other detectives I know, they'll

scratch you this time if you're ready to scratch them next time. What's it gonna take, Ange?' Scott implored.

'Let me make some calls.' She turned to leave the room.

Eric was hard on her heels. 'I'll start the warrant process in case we need it.' The door slammed behind them.

Scott gave Mark a questioning look.

Mark responded, 'She's got some history with the head of that unit.'

'Personal or on the job?'

'Both, but that's not where the favors are. She helped them out on a case so she's going to be calling that favor in. But because there's some personal stuff, she's not going to like doing it. You know Angie.'

'She left him, then?'

'Hey, I didn't say anything.' Mark gestured at his own chest as he got up. 'Did you hear me say something?'

'She's not going to forget it was me that had her call in the favor, is she?' Scott grimaced to himself as he followed Mark out of the briefing room.

# THIRTY-ONE

Jayne blinked her eyes open and felt total confusion about where she was. Her head hurt and her mouth was dry. She tried to swallow and felt cloth – *a gag?* – holding her mouth open and wicking her saliva away. She instinctively raised her hands to remove it but discovered she was lying on her arms and they were bound behind her. She looked up and saw a doorway she didn't recognize. And then it all came back. *The motel, Atlanta, Gene. Oh, God.* She shivered convulsively and raised her head to look down the length of her body. She saw duct tape binding her ankles and then noticed movement across the room.

Gene was dressed entirely in white Tyvek with the hood pulled over his hair and surgical gloves on his hands, eyes staring wide as he bent over Steelie – *Steelie!* – stomach-down on the bed, arms tied behind her back, her face turned away from Jayne. And then she registered the sounds. Gene grunting with exertion, the noises coming from lips thinned with effort, interspersed with higher-pitched sounds that had to be coming from Steelie as he tied a gag at the back of her head.

Suddenly, Steelie kicked out at Gene with her

bound legs and managed to connect with his lower back. He muttered something and stepped away from the bed to yank at her legs, pulling her backwards. As she slid off the mattress, she twisted to avoid landing on her face and the movement allowed her to see Jayne. They locked eyes and when Jayne saw tears in Steelie's, her own instantly welled up but the connection was quickly lost as Gene yanked Steelie up to her knees. She bucked and twisted, so he clamped her against him as he groped her body roughly, his fingers spread wide.

Jayne screamed but the sound went nowhere, trapped by her dry throat and truncated by the gag. She frantically rolled to the left but couldn't get past her own shoulder to get up. She cried out once more in desperation, heart pounding, and craned her neck again. Steelie was trying to slam her head backwards into Gene's face as he bent over her. Jayne felt a surge of hope. *That's it; get him, get him.*

But Gene just strode forward, pulling Steelie on her knees until she was against the edge of the bed. He pushed her over easily, using one hand to keep her head buried in the covers as he used the other to pull open all the snaps on Steelie's cargo pants. Jayne's eyes widened. *Christ!* She had to get him away from Steelie. She looked around wildly and saw the bathroom window was open. Hoping he would follow her if he became afraid she could raise the alarm from the bathroom, she started pushing backwards over the threshold, making as much noise as she could.

She looked back to see if Gene had noticed her and almost stopped breathing when she saw that he was smiling to himself. But then she saw why. He'd located Steelie's cell phone in one of her pockets. He'd been frisking her – violently – but he'd found what he wanted and had stopped. Dragging her by the neck to the head of the bed, he began tying her to the frame, keeping her face to the wall.

Jayne felt her lungs start to function again and she threw her energy into rolling to the right this time, hoping to get all the way over on to her stomach, but her knees smacked into the side of the bathtub with a loud thud before she completed the revolution. Almost immediately, she felt a foot on her ribcage, rolling her on to her back again.

She tried to yell 'Get off me' but it came out as unintelligible noise so she was left simply glaring at Gene. There was a large bruise between his eyes that had leaked blood into the whites, making his pale irises yet more preternatural.

He smiled down at her, a bag in one hand. 'Thanks for getting yourself in here. This is exactly where I want you.'

He closed the window and opened the bath taps to full blast. When the water hit the empty tub, the initial noise was deafening and she had a frightening image of Gene drowning first her, then Steelie. But he sat on the tub's edge, keeping a foot on her while retrieving an object from his bag. Jayne couldn't see what it was because his hand was clasped around it but the glimpse between his fingers suggested a grenade.

He leaned toward her and held the object to her ear, pressing it to her skin. 'I will remove your gag. If you start yelling, I pull the pin on this baby, which gives me time to leave and you time to die. Got it?'

The object was cold enough to be metallic but it could have been hard plastic and 'pins' only meant grenade to her. She tried to look at what he was holding to her head but he wouldn't let her. Now she understood that the faucets were blasting in order to cover some conversation he intended to have with her; to get some piece of information from her before killing them like he must have killed all the others. She wanted to cry, to give up. She closed her eyes.

'I said, got it?' He jammed the object even harder against her ear.

She forced her eyes open and nodded.

He pulled her gag down and in so doing, leaned his foot hard on to her diaphragm, making her convulse as her stomach muscles tensed. He looked at her like she was a specimen in a dish and then tut-tutted her. 'Jayne Hall. I'm surprised you didn't recognize my MO the second you came to the freeway in LA.'

She actually felt her eyes darting around in their sockets as she took in the implications of his words. She tried to produce some saliva and swallow. 'How did you know I was there?'

'I was watching you. And I must say, for an "expert", you didn't put two and two together at all because I haven't changed my cuts since

Kigali.'

*Jesus. He really did kill that woman in Rwanda.* 'I didn't know about Kigali.'

Gene cocked his head. 'You surprise me. I was sure Gerrit would have sent you the crime scene photos. It was such an unusual crime for Rwanda at the time. Quite evolved compared to all the other killing.'

Jayne couldn't hide her disgust.

He rolled his eyes. 'You've always been too soft, Jayne. I listened to you talking to your so-called clients—'

She felt her cheeks flush. 'What are you talking about?'

'Why don't you just tell them that if their daughter's missing, she's already dead?'

'You're the one who bugged my phone?'

'You shouldn't give them false hope like you do.'

'Was it you? Why did you come and see me? I don't understand.' Jayne knew she sounded needy and plaintive but couldn't help her tone. Details from the past two weeks were jostling for position in her mind.

'I wanted to know what you knew.' He gestured with the object clasped in his hand and Jayne was finally sure: it was a grenade. Small, dusty, lethal. 'I needed to know how much time I had before I had to go to ground. And everything I heard put me at ease. You suck at your job as bad as Houston does. And I would've left you alone, given how incompetent you are, but then you told Houston about me. Now you have to pay for that.'

Jayne felt a frisson of fear. *What was he talking about?* 'I–I didn't tell him anything.'

'You were never a good liar, Jayne. I saw you at my mother's house. You were there today, leading Houston right in.'

'But I wasn't! He found you and your house himself!' She was almost shouting over the noise of the open faucet.

'Spare me. He's an *agent*. He can't find his own asshole without help.'

He suddenly sounded petulant and Jayne saw a way in. Gene wasn't crazy, or maybe he was, but there was some logic behind it. She tried to push down her fear and changed her tack, her sole focus keeping Gene talking long enough for the FBI driver to arrive and end this before Gene did something even worse. She didn't know what time it was, but the airport pick-up had to be any minute now.

'You've got some issue, don't you?' She was trying to sound conversational, as though she wasn't lying on the floor trussed up in twine and duct tape, but her underlying fear was making her shiver and her voice was uneven and trembly. 'Some kind of grudge against agents. What, did you apply and they wouldn't take you? Too old, were you?'

She wasn't ready when he lunged at her and slapped her face, his hand open, the rubber of the surgical glove burning her skin. Tears stung her eyes but she knew she'd hit a nerve. She didn't let the topic go. 'That's it, isn't it?'

'Shut up!' He was clenching and unclenching the hand he'd slapped her with.

'So you applied.' Jayne pressed on. 'And you didn't make it – for whatever reason. Though I'm surprised they didn't take you, what with your postgraduate degree, obvious intelligence, previous Bureau history, plus you're active and athletic.' She was almost gagging on her words but her voice was getting stronger. 'I would have thought you were perfect agent material. You know you're good, right? No matter what they say.'

She watched the compliment take its effect. Gene's back straightened perceptibly, his mouth relaxed.

She went further. 'You were already a Bureau employee in the lab. Why was it so important to become an agent?'

He didn't respond initially but when he did, his eyes were fixed on the grenade. 'I wanted to stay in Rwanda another year but the Bureau said extensions were only open to agents.'

Jayne hadn't expected this and couldn't immediately think of a follow-up question. 'So?'

His eyes bore into her. 'If you hadn't noticed, not a single one of those "special" agents can investigate their way out of a paper bag. Not only does the Bureau prevent me from carrying on my work in Rwanda, but, two years later, they decide to send a team to Kosovo for the UN and what happens? They send that stupid piece of shit *rookie* in my place. *My* place.'

Jayne frowned. 'What rookie?'

Gene rolled his eyes at her like she wasn't keeping up. 'Houston,' he sneered. 'There I was, with all my forensic experience as well as a

343

previous UN mission – I even advised them on who to get for the team – and who gets passed over? Me. And who goes? Scott Houston. I don't think so. No, uh-unh, the Bureau was only going to fuck me over like that one time. I resigned immediately, deprived them of my talents, and I've been making sure they know what a mistake they made on Houston ever since. I've taken my time but I'll see that dirtbag stripped of every accolade he's received. I've shown he can't even solve a couple of homicides, that he's a fantasist who sees serial killers around every corner. He can't even close a couple of local missing person cases, for Chrissakes!'

Jayne heard that familiar, superior tone, now applied to Scott like he was a target. To her knowledge, Scott didn't even know Gene. She stared at him, struggling to understand how she had missed the signs that he was a sociopathic killer in the time she'd been side by side with him in the graves. She was suddenly assaulted with the images from the photographs they'd seen in the briefing room. The technicolor of Rwanda bleached out by midday sun, the rich soil wetted anew with fresh blood, and then she remembered further back. Gene at The Cadillac, dancing out of rhythm with a young woman who followed him back to the bar, her suggestive smile fading when he didn't buy her a cold drink despite the crush of heat and noise and twirling disco-ball light. That young woman had been dancing with death and hadn't even known it. Not only that, the rest of them hadn't seen it and so hadn't protected her.

Jayne was mortified to feel tears springing to her eyes unbidden as she said, 'So you murdered that girl in Kigali? And in a place that had just survived a *genocide*?' Her voice trembled audibly.

He fed off her display of emotion. 'But even you understand why it was the ideal place to do it: what was one more dead body in Rwanda? People were too busy with eight hundred thousand other corpses to pay attention.'

'But ... but you were a forensic scientist. You were supposed to be helping people, not victimizing them. Why, for God's sake, did you kill that woman?'

He shook his head. 'Still such an idealist, aren't you, Jayne? Let me tell you the truth about these victims you put on such a high pedestal. The cases we got at the Bureau were *all* about stupidity. The vics were stupid to get themselves into a situation where they were killed and the killers were stupid enough to leave behind trace. After a few months of scraping dried shit out of people's underwear after they'd voided their bowels, I knew the world was a better place without people like them but I had no intention of being caught getting rid of 'em.'

Jayne gazed up at him in wonder, forcing herself to skip over his obviously wilful misunderstanding of the way bowels can sometimes relax upon death, leaving feces free to flow into anyone's underwear, regardless of their IQ. 'You're saying that you think some people deserve to die? You think that young woman in Kigali *deserved* to die?'

'I'm saying I don't want stupid people in the gene pool.'

Jayne almost spluttered. 'Who the hell are you to say who's stupid?'

Gene pulled a ball of twine from his bag as he spoke, leaving the grenade inside the bag. 'Hey, I give people the opportunity to make a choice: go with an instinct for survival or go with the social fiction of Trust in Others. If they can't make the choice to survive, they shouldn't be allowed to live, let alone reproduce. It's the same choice our ancestors had when they came face to face with a lion in the savannah. I give them that choice, they usually make the wrong one and I get to clean up while I simultaneously drag Houston down.' He flashed a grin at her. 'Who said men can't multitask?'

Jayne pictured Eleanor Patterson meeting a man like this when she was at her most vulnerable. Gene was justifying his murders with some kind of perversion of evolutionary biology when, really, he had victimized women, first out of career frustration and then out of misplaced revenge. But his reasons didn't change anything. She couldn't fake a plaintive tone any longer; Gene was deeply wrong and he needed to know it.

'You haven't been giving people choices, you've been giving them bait-and-switch. All you've done, Gene, is *betray* people's trust.'

He put a loop of twine through the pin on the grenade and then stood up, towering over her as he placed a foot on either side of her waist. 'You and Steelie have always had a way of sounding holier-than-thou.'

He dropped down on to her, trapping her with a knee on each side of her waist. 'We've talked enough. You're going to lay here in this bathroom, Jayne, the lure on a hook for Houston, and when he comes through that door looking for you – and I know he will because he likes the chase and you've been giving him one hell of a chase for quite a while now. Unh-unh, don't try to deny it. Now he's going to walk in and trip the line to this grenade I got specially for you.'

He leaned down toward her face. 'I lied when I said I hadn't kept up with where you went after Kigali. I heard about Kosovo and the mine your team blew, so you should enjoy this. You'll get to watch Houston and Steelie bite it. You'll probably survive it with a few limbs intact. Now, you start the show by calling Lover Boy to reel him in. If you tip him off to the grenade, I pull the pin the second the words come out of your mouth. You don't mind if I frisk you now, do you?' He began going through her pockets.

Jayne panicked. She didn't want to die and she knew Scott wouldn't be the one to come through that door. It would be the FBI driver. Another innocent, just like Benni in Kosovo; there because she was there. She had to stop this. Gene had located her phone and rocked back as he held it aloft, compressing her tailbone against the tile floor. And suddenly all the fear and pain mixed with his weight on her hips to trigger an old, old memory – she'd been young, on a mat, in a class, being taught – *defend yourself.*

She screamed with all her might and Gene reacted just as she'd hoped, lunging to push the gag back into her mouth, his weight now forward and, crucially, off her hips. Using strength she didn't know she had left, she thrust her hips up as hard and high as she could, sending him head-first toward the cold, hard toilet bowl, shutting her eyes a millisecond before his knees smashed into her face.

Scott attempted to be patient as he watched Angie from the doorway of her office.

When she finally slammed down her phone, she shouted, 'We got it! Guys, we got it.' She looked up at Scott in triumph.

He felt warmth spread across his chest and went to her, his hand up for a high five. She hit it and merged it into a down low, followed by one of their old handgrips.

Eric popped his head in from the hallway. 'You got the location?'

'Not yet,' she replied, breaking free from Scott and grabbing an FBI windbreaker from the back of her chair. 'It's in Northeast. We can go mobile and I'll keep in cell phone contact for them to give us the one hundred-foot radius.'

'OK, I got the warrant underway, so I'm coming with you.'

Mark was out of his seat. 'I'm driving.'

The four agents ran down the stairs and out the back of the building to the motor pool. Mark shouted, 'Four-eight-six' and the others diverted course to the black Suburban with the corresponding license plate. 'It's got the flak jackets

348

and shotguns.'

Within seconds, Mark had reversed out of the parking space and activated the red and blue flashers in the front and rear windows. They entered the roadway at speed.

Angie's cell phone rang and she listened, then said, 'OK, head southeast. We're keeping the line open.'

Mark swerved around a double-parked delivery truck and then braked hard as a taxi veered into their lane. 'Come *on!*'

Angie's voice came loud. 'We got him! Last ping is from near Eden and Forty-Fifth. We're almost there.'

Mark slowed as they approached that intersection and turned off the lights. He halted at the corner so they could scan the cross street and take in the buildings.

Scott looked out the front window, saw the motel across the street, dismissed it, and then did a double-take. 'Holy shit!'

Mark followed his gaze, and then threw the vehicle into reverse, parking it out of sight from the motel. Scott dialed a number on his phone as the other agents jumped out and opened the rear doors.

Scott joined them a moment later, his phone still in his hand. 'This is the motel where Travel put Jayne and Steelie last night. Carter's here, in the parking lot. He arrived early to pick them up, was able to hear water running, assumed someone was bathing, so was waiting until the appointed time to go back and knock.'

Eric cut in, 'King's got to be in there with

them; no way one of 'em's having a bath when they're due to leave.'

Scott nodded. 'Get your gear on. We're going in on the presumption that he is armed. We are *not* waiting for further backup. Got it?'

The others assented and they ran to the building, splitting into two pairs to take the separate exterior staircases up to the second floor. They positioned themselves on either side of Jayne and Steelie's door, guns drawn as Mark held a small battering ram. Scott nodded at him and he rammed the door. It slammed open with a crack and they all shouted, 'Federal Agents! Drop your weapon!!'

They were met with silence so they charged the room.

Scott saw Eric rush to the bed, where Steelie was on the floor against the wall, but his eyes were taking in the emptiness of the rest of the room. He felt rising panic as he imagined King taking Jayne away with him. Then he heard a shout from his left.

'Call a medic!'

He spun around and Angie's concerned expression gave him a stab of worry. He pushed past Mark to get to Angie in the bathroom doorway, then heard a squelching noise and looked down. The threshold was soaking; his eyes followed a film of bloody water across the floor. He saw two bodies by the toilet: a man collapsed around the toilet, his knees obscuring the head of someone contorted underneath. *Jayne.* Scott figured the water was coming from the overflowing bath. That left the blood. He desperately hoped none of it was coming from her. He stepped into the room and got down on his knees. He was going to get her out.

# THIRTY-TWO

Scott stood next to Jayne's hospital bed, looking at the clipboard he'd removed from the door of her room. She murmured and he looked at her, but her eyes remained closed. She was semi-reclined under a blanket and her forehead looked discolored. He could see abrasions on her arms where the short sleeves of the hospital gown ended. When he heard footsteps in the hallway, he darted out in time to stop a nurse, who gave him a polite, interrogative smile.

He held up his Bureau badge and the clipboard. 'What does all of this stuff mean? Why is she out cold?'

'She's not out cold. She's sleeping.' She took possession of the clipboard and slotted it back into the holder on the door. 'There's nothing to be concerned about, sir. She took a knock on the head that had a mild concussive effect and the doctor wanted to keep her in for observation. He cleared her half an hour ago and she is now sleeping. Please don't disturb her.'

Scott sighed and ran his hands through his hair. 'What about Lander? Steelie Lander? They would have come in together.'

'Around the corner in 808. I believe one of your colleagues is already there.' The nurse continued down the hall.

Scott turned to look at Jayne again. Her mouth was hanging open slightly and the fluorescent bar above the bed was shining bright on her forehead. He walked back in to lean over her and switch off the light, half hoping the noise would wake her. He wanted to ascertain that she was really all right, to apologize for putting her in danger.

He reached down to her cheek but remembered what had happened when he'd picked her up off that bathroom floor and pulled the gag from her mouth. She'd opened her eyes but hadn't been able to focus on him. Even when he'd repeated her name, she hadn't recognized him and then the paramedics called in by Agent Carter had arrived, pushing Scott aside while castigating him for moving someone without first establishing the nature of their injuries.

He had been forced to stand on the sidelines, watching them tend to both Jayne and an unconscious Eugene King, and he hadn't even thought about the effect the same sight would be having on Steelie, who was standing just behind him, supported by Mark and Eric. He should talk to Steelie.

Scott stepped away from Jayne's bed and saw that Angie was watching him from the doorway.

She looked him up and down as he approached. 'You got a chance to change clothes?' She kept her voice low.

'When I logged the evidence at HQ.'

'Any sign of Franks?'

Scott shook his head.

Angie's eyes went to Jayne. 'How's she doing?'

'Nurse says she's fine. Just sleeping. What's the word on King?'

'The Doc won't let us have him yet. Seems he's experienced two separate traumatic "events" involving his head in the last twenty-four hours. He won't be out of the woods for a day or two.' She paused. 'She's tough. Wouldn't think it to look at her.'

Angie made to leave, then turned back. 'Don't let that one get away.'

Scott tried to acknowledge this suddenly personal directive with a casual response but only succeeded in producing a strangled noise.

Angie regarded him with a smile for a moment, then set off down the hallway.

Scott took a final look at Jayne before going in search of Steelie's room.

When he looked in her door, he saw Eric sitting on the side of Steelie's bed, his hand closed over her fist. He was saying, 'Keep the thumb on top. That's key.'

Scott took in the bruise coming up on Steelie's chin. Her hair was unruly, making her head look huge over a thin body lost in a voluminous hospital gown.

She noticed Scott and said, 'Welcome to Fight Club.'

She raised her fist. 'The first rule of fight club is ... know how to fight.' She pointed at Eric, *'That's* key.' She leaned back against the pillows.

Scott sat down in the chair just inside the door. 'Eric giving you lessons?'

'Yeah, which beats him giving me medical tests. A minute ago, he asked me how many fingers he was holding up. It was just the one – the middle one.'

Eric smiled as he stood up. 'I don't get to run that joke too often.' He crossed to the door. 'I'll be back in five.'

Steelie regarded Scott for a moment, then asked, 'Is Gene here as well?'

He nodded.

'You've got him under guard, right?'

'He's not going anywhere.' He cast around for something to say. 'I just came from Jayne's room. She was sleeping. She's going to be fine.'

'The doctor told me.'

They fell silent. Scott leaned his elbows on his knees and looked at the floor. He was uncomfortable but spoke anyway. 'Steelie, I owe you both an apology. I should have known—' He broke off to see why she was groaning.

Steelie had sat up. 'Should have known what?' she challenged. 'That Gene was lying in wait for us? That he's got a mean right hook? What are you, a mind reader?' She sank back on to the pillows.

He had never seen her look so angry. 'Point taken.' Waiting for her to compose herself, he averted his eyes and took in the IV stand next to her bed. The nametag appeared to read, *Lander, Sandra*. He frowned and tried to focus on the name and then quickly looked over at her, hoping she hadn't clocked him reading it, which he was almost sure had her name as Sandra. She wasn't looking at him. He got up and came to the

355

side of her bed.

'Look, Steelie, when I was driving back from Phoenix with Jayne, I had a ... situation.'

'Yeah, I heard.'

'Right. Well, then you'll know she bailed me out. Which made me wonder who bails her out, when she needs it. Is it you or is there someone else?'

She didn't respond.

He continued. 'Because I think she needs it. At least to deal with the seriously bad dreams I think she's having.' He waited. 'I'm only asking because I care. No one should be alone on this ... or groping in the dark. In the Bureau, we don't even get a choice about getting debriefed. So who do you guys talk to?'

She seemed to assess him. 'We never got debriefings. But I don't think Jayne would have these repercussions if it weren't for one particular incident, which jumbled up some of her reactions to other, normal things. That's my opinion, anyway.' She exhaled. 'Look, she was in the wrong place at the wrong time, though not as wrong a place as our escort. His name was Benni, a French soldier, all of twenty years old. We were looking for a gravesite in Kos. He tripped a wire, a mine blew, and he bled out a few feet from Jayne, who was on orders to stay put by the de-miners, who were trying to get a handle on the situation.'

She paused. 'I've heard you've got a good six hours to intervene before a traumatic memory fixes itself like fucking concrete in your brain. No one got to Jayne, or anyone else, for three

356

days. So,' she reached for her bedside control and began reclining the mattress, 'you know anything that can break up concrete?'

After a moment, he met her gaze. 'Freeze-thaw usually works.'

She gave him a slight nod before she closed her eyes and settled back on the pillows. 'Now, I'm an invalid and I know my rights, so stop harassing me. Sheesh.'

He took a chance and looked at the name on the IV bag again from much closer. Then he pulled the covers above her shoulders, looking at her bruised chin one more time. 'It's good to have you back, Steelie.'

'Yeah, I'm great,' she mumbled.

Outside the room, he saw Eric emerge from the elevator at the far end of the hallway. His partner shook his head as he walked.

'What's happening?' Scott asked, assuming the worst and that King had managed to die in the last half-hour.

'You won't believe this,' Eric murmured as he drew him back toward the elevators. 'You know the cell phone SIM cards the criminalists found at King's house?'

Scott nodded.

'Tech Support's pulled the numbers off them to cross-check against those suspect numbers on our missing prostitutes' call records.'

'He called the vics,' Scott deduced.

'Nope.' Eric glanced at him. 'He called our old boss Franks.'

'*What?*' Scott halted.

Eric pulled on his arm to get him into an

elevator and pressed the button for the ground floor. 'One of the SIMs shows a call to our anonymous tip line and two show a call each to Franks.'

'Direct to Franks?'

Eric nodded. 'They date to after you started the media campaign for information on the van. Each call is about six months apart. We don't know the content yet but Franks is going to have to give up his own phone log. My bet is that King was the anonymous tipster Turner referred to when he quizzed me in LA – the guy whose tips Franks was relying on to crucify you and get us transferred out of here.'

Scott felt anger and vindication in equal measure.

Eric looked at him. 'King was playing him like a violin, man.'

They left the elevator and walked out to the Crown Victoria Scott had left parked in an area for emergency vehicles. 'You think Franks will go down for this?'

'If he doesn't go down, he'll at least go sideways. It'll be up to OPR. They'll decide how much more Franks should have done to verify the information in the tips before he used it to make operational decisions. You want me to drive?'

Scott hesitated at the car door and looked back at the hospital, where only every third light or so was still on at this late hour. He tried to work out which one was Jayne's room and then realized he didn't even know which side of the building it was on.

Scott turned back to his partner. 'Who's on King's door?'

'We've got two guys on loan from Atlanta PD.'

'Do they know he's dangerous?'

'Houston, he's concussed. *And* handcuffed.'

'Do they know he's dange—'

'They came personally recommended by Angie.'

'OK, then.' Scott threw his partner the keys over the roof of the car. 'You should have said that first.'

When Scott woke in the hotel room to the sound of his cell phone ringing next to him, he felt like he'd just gone to sleep. He saw it was Eric calling and answered in the dark.

Eric didn't bother with preliminaries. 'King's awake and talking.'

Scott sat up. 'Who to?'

'Whoever'll listen. But he's made it clear that he refuses to talk to someone he calls "Special Adversary Houston". That would be you.'

'Oh, I'll get him to talk to me.'

'No, I think we need to use this, Scott. Keep you out of there, to start with.'

'I don't think I can do that, Eric. I need to get this guy.'

'He's more likely to confess if he thinks he's getting us to jump through hoops at the start. We can show him our good faith.'

'This is bullshit.'

'This is tactics,' countered Eric.

Scott lay back down and thought for a

moment, stretching his mouth and running a hand through his hair. 'OK, but we review how you're going to do it. You've gotta start with Patterson because we've got an evidentiary link with her personal effects at his house and then you want to get corroboration with Spicer's evidence, so we can nail King with the biological traces from the van ... sorry.' He sighed. 'You know what to do. Who are you going in with?'

'We'll start with Angie, see if he wants to boast in front of a woman. If that throws things, we'll switch in Mark.'

'OK. They both know the case.' Scott paused. 'I want ears in the room.'

'You'll get 'em. You can be next door, down the hall, whatever you want.'

'Fine.' Scott tried to switch into support mode. 'What else are you going to need?'

'Well, if he doesn't confess straight off, I need whatever we can get from his property that rules out someone else using his backyard as an abattoir. But I think we'll get a confession. If he'll spill it to Jayne—'

'Wait, what?'

'Angie interviewed her.'

'When?' Scott strained his neck to see the clock on the bedside table. 'It's the middle of the night, for Christ's sake! Are you at the hospital? Have you talked to her?'

'Scott, I'm right here at the hotel. I can practically hear you shouting from down the hall, in fact. No, Angie talked to her while you were at HQ.'

'Why didn't anyone tell me?'

360

'We were just doing the routine. Jayne was lucid, so gave her evidence.'

Scott recollected Angie's comment that Jayne was tougher than she looked. So Angie would have already heard Jayne's account of whatever King did to her in that bathroom. Scott felt he was being left out of his own investigation but knew that wasn't happening.

Eric began again. 'So ... if you can liaise with the ME's office on the ID's of whatever body parts are coming out of King's yard and take over my link to the criminalists?'

Scott exhaled. 'You got it.'

'I'll drop you at HQ. See you at 08:00 out front?'

'Done.'

Scott hung up and let the phone rest on his chest as he lay in the dark, listening to the climate-controlled air conditioner kicking on. He hated sleeping in air-conditioning and had never become used to it even when he had lived in Atlanta. Now here he was, sleeping in it again, dealing with the same case, and he wasn't even going to get to interrogate their suspect. He felt immensely irritated. He put the phone on the bedside table and lay on his back, drawing in deep breaths and letting them out slowly, willing a few more hours of sleep.

# DAY ELEVEN

## FRIDAY

## THIRTY-THREE

Scott pulled into the hospital parking lot at 11.30 a.m. He'd finished his morning punch-list and was supposed to be on his way to the room neighboring King's, where Eric had set up a station for Scott to hear the interview. But he was taking a detour to see Jayne. He turned into her room and almost collided with a cart of cleaning supplies. The bed was empty, didn't even have bedding. He went back to the desk he'd sailed past a moment ago when ignoring staff who had asked if he needed assistance. He got the attention of one of the nurses.

'I'm looking for Jayne Hall. She was in 813. Just admitted yesterday.'

The nurse consulted a sheet of paper taped to the wall. '813 was discharged.'

'When?'

The nurse looked at the sheet again. 'Nine thirty this morning.'

'But I ... who authorized that?'

The nurse answered slowly. 'Doctor Reid, the

attending. Is there a problem?'

Scott told himself not to shoot the messenger, so shook his head and set off toward Steelie's room. It was also empty. He backtracked to the elevator and ascended to the police-protected area where King was being held. He showed his badge to the Atlanta PD officer in the hall, who directed him to the room with the listening station.

Scott found Mark already inside, sitting at a table and wearing a headset that was plugged into an audio playback device. Mark held out a second headset toward him. Scott shook his head and indicated that he wanted to talk.

Mark removed one earpiece. 'You haven't missed much.'

Scott held up his hand. 'Where are Jayne and Steelie?'

Mark glanced at his watch. 'Probably in the security line at the airport.'

Scott rolled his index finger over, as if spooling a tape backward.

Mark got the message. 'They were cleared by the doctor and had no reason to – or interest in – staying around, especially with King upstairs here. Carter org'd their flights and took them to the airport. He's escorting them right up to boarding.'

Scott swallowed an expletive.

Mark put a hand on his earpiece and then pointed at Scott. 'Here we go.'

Scott got his headset on and sat down. He didn't recognize the voice he heard. It had to be King.

*King: I didn't need a uniform back then. And I was using the van.*
*Eric: How'd you get them to go with you, then?*
*King: It's the red light district. How do you think I did it?*
*Eric: You were a john?*
*King: I wasn't a john. I posed as a John. Two different things.*
*Eric: So you asked the women to get in your van. Then what?*
*King: You don't have to ask them to get in! They ask you. Or haven't you cruised the district, SA Ramos? Houston'll tell you; they're desperate to get in. Isn't that right, lady?*
*Angie: It's Special Agent Nicks, Mr King. Answer the question.*

Scott pulled off the headset. He couldn't focus but he knew what he would have to do to get back on track. He indicated to Mark that he'd be back in a few minutes and went in search of the hospital's post office.

When Scott returned and resumed listening, he could tell the interview had moved on.

*Eric: The garden and the garage. Why did you use them?*
*King: First rule they teach us Bureau criminalists, something a lowly agent never learns: every contact leaves a trace. So I had to hang on to the bitches. Took 'em up the garden path. Literally. Ha!*
*Eric: Why the dismemberment?*

*King: Running out of space. Easier to transport from the back of the van. You ever move a dead body? It's heavy. Because of the water or the bones, or both.*

*Eric: But you didn't just dismember. It looked like careful cutting.*

*King: I'm flattered that you noticed. Yes, for show pieces, I took great care.*

*Eric: Show pieces?*

*King: The ones I've been scattering across the country in one long love letter to Special Adversary Houston.*

*Eric: You mean the ones you left in Los Angeles?*

*King: [Laughter] Uh, no, SA Ramos. He's a bit slow, isn't he, lady? Let's ignore him. You, lucky lady, will find body parts everywhere between here and California.*

*Angie: These are people you killed in other states?*

*King: No, they were not people I did in other states. The body parts are from the same pros I picked up on Atlanta's fine boulevards. I've dumped them along the interstate.*

*Angie: Why did you do that?*

*King: The glorious day finally arrived when Special Adversary Houston went public with his warning that a serial killer was loose in Atlanta and he gave a decent description of my van. I seem to recall he was flanked by you, Ramos, but you stayed silent like the good little partner that you are. And that was the signal for me to start making it look like those bitches were killed elsewhere. I had some body parts frozen solely so I could dump them in places where they'd defrost in time to look fresh to the cops who'd find them. I left clues that different truckers came through Atlanta with regularity, picked up pros, took them interstate, and killed them while on the road. Houston would have been following that trail, with me leading him by the nose. And that would have been the end of the serial killer theory, the end of the interest in my van, and the end of Houston.*

*Angie: We're not aware of body parts being found outside Atlanta, besides the ones you lost in Los Angeles.*

*King: Yeah, well, the cops are stupid. First they have to find the stuff, then they have to scratch their asses. It would have worked, in time.*

*Angie: Mr King, if you're going to do a deal with the prosecutors, you're going to have to give up the locations of these women's bodies.*

*King: I am, am I? Listen, you don't tell me how it's done. I tell you how it's done. [Unintelligible muttering] Bitch.*

*Eric: Watch your mouth, King. Agent Nicks is right. They will not deal with you unless you give us locations.*

Scott pulled off the headset to answer his cell phone, which had begun vibrating and displaying the Los Angeles number of his boss, Craig Turner. He walked into the hall as he answered.

'Morning, sir.'

'Houston. I've got your fax from this morning. The suspect's declined legal representation?'

'That's correct, sir.'

'Is the interview underway?'

'Yes, I'm at the hospital now and Ramos and Nicks are in with him.'

'And?'

'It's going well. They're stringing him out, taking him round corners.' Scott didn't refer to how often his own name was coming up in the interview because he didn't understand it yet.

'Good. What have you got for material to ID the bodies coming from the suspect's back yard?'

'I spoke to Atlanta Missings this morning. They're going back over the misper reports for cases that fit the suspect's activity period. They will transmit any biological information direct to the Medical Examiner's office. But we've got another issue. The suspect has just alleged that he dropped body parts along the interstate between Atlanta and LA. We need to find out if any of the material's been recovered and why it hasn't been ID'd yet. If we can get proof on those ones, we can charge him on each count.'

'I'll call Cates at CJIS; he'll get you an NCIC liaison.'

'Sir.' Scott could hear his boss switch the call to speakerphone and he waited for him to continue. He thought about how the head of the whole Criminal Justice Information Services Division might not be too pleased to get a direct call about an NCIC issue, but he couldn't help it if Turner wanted to show off.

'OPR interviewed me last night.' Turner sounded more casual now, as though leaning back in his chair. 'Never liked internal affairs myself but I try not to hold it against the rank-

and-file.'

Scott smiled as he imagined the cross-grilling tactics Turner probably used on the agents trying to question him.

Turner stated, 'I made it clear that my assessment of the situation is that, during the course of this investigation, you have not displayed activity that warrants disciplinary action.'

'Thank you—'

'Now, Houston, the only way I could do that was to *actually* assess the situation. I see now why you chose this Agency 32/1. Why is it called *that*? Do you know?'

'Uh, it's named for the Geneva Conventions, Article 32, Protocol 1.'

'Geneva? As in the laws of war?'

'Yes, sir. I understand that the part it's named for deals with the right of families to know what happened to their relatives – where their bodies are buried, and so on.'

'Huh. Well, your fax this morning shows that 32/1 led you to the firm ID that's become crucial for building the case against the suspect. Is that correct?'

'Yes, sir.'

'And now you tell me we've got body parts strung across the Bible Belt, the Corn Belt, *and* the Rockies?'

'Yes, sir.'

Turner went from the speakerphone back to the handset and Scott quickly ran down a mental list for what Turner could hit him with next.

# THREE DAYS LATER

## Monday

## THIRTY-FOUR

San Fernando Road, Los Angeles: 2.00 p.m. Carol was having a vacation day so when the mailman came in the front door, Jayne went to meet him. She gave him the outgoing mail, which consisted of one piece, a checklist for the Ledbetters of Wisconsin, now that they'd decided to do a profile of Amy at 32/1, combining it with a road trip to Disneyland for their other two daughters. The mailman handed over the incoming pile and Jayne heard Steelie call out to her, so she diverted down the hall, mail still in hand.

Steelie was sitting at the light box, looking at a rectangular X-ray that measured about an inch and a half on each side. She turned when Jayne walked in and said, 'Can you look at this?'

Jayne put the mail down, checked out the bruise on Steelie's chin for new color changes, then focused on the X-ray. It showed several upper teeth in a human jaw.

'Got anything besides a bitewing?' she asked.

369

'This isn't a buffet,' Steelie parried. 'Would you say that's a root canal plus a post or just a root canal?'

'Got any dentist's notes?'

'No. When they archived these they lost all the paper notes. The only things left were these bite-wings, probably because they were stapled on to the folder itself.'

'OK, I'm leaning toward root canal but I'd put a note about the possibility of a post. We simply don't have enough information to do more than that.'

Steelie pulled a magnifying glass from a jar on the counter. She used it to look at the X-ray again. Jayne walked to the end of the room and started rummaging through a drawer.

After a while, Steelie turned on her stool. 'What on earth are you looking for?'

'Didn't we have some candlestick holders in here from when the power was always going out?'

'Oh, you mean in the days *before* a generator?' Steelie was expansive. 'Who even remembers those days?'

'Seriously. And where did you move that candle the women in Atlanta gave me?'

'They're both in the top drawer of the other cabinet.' She turned back to the light box.

Jayne pulled open that drawer and brought out a holder. She put the candle in but it was too narrow to stand up on its own. She lit a match to warm the wax so that it would stick to the holder and she could see the wick inside. Then she re-membered Scott saying something about the wick going all the way through.

They had been in the Sunkist parking lot – that first reunion. He had been right, both about the wick and about how the two of them were at opposite ends of the same effort. They were all identifying people, whether starting with a body or a missing person. Watching the wax melt, Jayne decided Scott was right about a lot of things and the memory of their embrace on the side of the road surged forward in a rush – his hands in her hair, her mouth on his, the desire.

And the desire was now only part of it. When she'd become aware of Scott lifting her up from that disgusting, bloody motel floor, she'd felt truly alive. But she hadn't been able to make any words come out. Later, when she'd asked Angie where Scott was, she'd explained that he was logging evidence and offered to take him a message. But by then, Jayne just wanted to show him how she felt. They'd talked enough. She'd held off calling him, just waiting – in excruciating, deeply pleasurable anticipation – for him to return to LA.

The telephone rang and Steelie called out, 'My turn,' as she rolled over on her stool to answer it.

'Scott!'

Jayne turned around, half expecting to see him in the doorway. But Steelie was listening intently to the phone and gave her a thumb's up sign. 'Hang on, Houston, let me put you on speaker.'

Jayne put the candle down and came to stand by Steelie, who pressed a button and turned up the volume while telling Jayne, 'They're still in Atlanta. You gotta hear this.'

'Scott?' Steelie called out. 'Tell Jayne what you just told me.'

After a pause, Scott said, 'Jayne.'

It gave her a jolt to hear his voice. 'Scott, hi.'

'Hi. So, what I said was, we've got a full confession from King on the Georgia cases, plus the BP's on the Ventura Freeway.'

She and Steelie called out questions simultaneously. Scott used broad brushstrokes to describe how King had preyed on the women who worked in Atlanta's red light district and posed as a shuttle driver to pick up Eleanor Patterson. 'He had also stopped a woman while dressed as a cop. But not you, Steelie. At least, he denies it so far.'

Jayne stared at Steelie, who looked suddenly anxious. 'I never thought it was Gene...'

Jayne said, 'And if it wasn't, that means there's someone else out there posing as a cop and assaulting people.'

Scott replied, 'We've checked in with LAPD and the Sheriff's Department on this and it turns out that people posing as cops happens in LA County more than you might think. Most of the time, the ruse is part of a shakedown for cash. Sometimes sexual assault. But it doesn't generally result in murder and the local guys have caught a fair few of the perps. Then there are a few cops who've abused their badges. But Steelie? Don't worry about your guy right now. They'll catch up with him eventually. As for King, the prosecutors are dealing with him by rolling some charges together in exchange for getting locations on body parts he's dropped across the country.'

Jayne immediately thought of how she and Steelie were bruised but alive while the families waiting outside Gene's house might soon have answers of a different sort.

Jayne asked, 'What's he said about Kigali?'

'Nothing yet. He won't be drawn on the details. I'm sure he doesn't want to see the inside of a prison overseas. So we're talking to Gerrit Leuven, seeing if he can get the UN involved.' He paused. 'Leuven's got a lot of good things to say about both of you. Of course, I cautioned him that his information was ten years out of date.'

She laughed and was rewarded by hearing a laugh come back through the speaker. She pictured his lips curving into his usual half-grin and said, 'Thanks for giving us the low-down, Scott.'

'Well, we owe you ... for a number of things on this case.' He cleared his throat. 'Bringing me to the next point. Let me get Eric over here.'

Eric's enthusiasm was in his voice when he came on the line. He intoned, 'Ladies...' like a DJ in a hazy nightclub.

'You sound good, Agent Ramos,' Steelie remarked, starting to go through the mail, which Jayne had dropped on to the counter.

'Just a little demob happy.'

'When are you guys actually demobilizing?' Jayne asked, simply wanting to know when Scott would be back in Los Angeles.

'Good question,' Eric replied. 'The Bureau won't spring for us to stay out here for more than

373

a week—'

'You gotta be kidding me,' exclaimed Steelie as she slid a square envelope addressed to Jayne in her direction.

'Actually, they would, but Houston and I would have to double up and trust me, no one wants that.'

Scott cut in. 'Can we get back on point? Jayne, Steelie, our supervisor, Craig Turner, has asked us to draft an MOU with your agency, for this and future cases.'

Jayne paused in the act of opening the envelope and saw that Steelie's eyebrows were raised about as high as her own. She clarified, 'You're saying the FBI wants a Memorandum of Understanding with our nonprofit organization so we can help you again?'

'Yes, as you just did on this case, minus the personal endangerment. This is on the up-and-up. It would be an official agreement for implementation on an ad hoc basis. And Turner's already got a request for you in the hopper. We need better antemortem info on our missing prostitutes, since King's ensured that their remains are going to come in as separate bones from different places. A couple of the family members out here are already asking after you. They were pretty surprised to see two women and such quote-unquote, young women, walking out from the crime scene at King's house.'

The sound of the bells jangling on the Agency's front door traveled back to the lab. Jayne addressed the phone. 'Look, someone's at the door and Carol's off, so we gotta go. We'll ...

get back to you on that offer.'

'All right, 32/1,' Scott sounded amused. 'Sounds to me like you're playing hard to get, but you should know that two can play that game.'

Jayne had to bite her lip to stop from smiling as she hung up.

Steelie made for the hall, asking, 'Who's that from?'

Jayne finally looked at the envelope she was holding. No return address, an Atlanta postmark, and something with a shiny border inside. Her heart started to pound. *Scott?* She slid out the card. It was a gilt-edged invitation to dinner with him at In-N-Out Burger that Friday.

This time, her grin was so broad and came on so quick that she couldn't hide it from Steelie, who rolled her eyes and set off down the hallway. Jayne enjoyed the bursting-with-happiness sensation for a full thirty seconds. Then she went to join Steelie and meet the next client of Agency 32/1.

# A NOTE FOR THE READER

Although Agency 32/1 does not exist, it should.

It is based on the Missing Persons Identification Resource Center, a California non-profit founded by the author to link families of missing persons with coroners holding thousands of unidentified bodies.

The plot and characters of this book are fictional.

The statistics on unidentified bodies are fact.

Forensic profiles of missing persons are hope.

www.mpid.org

# ACKNOWLEDGEMENTS

The first draft of this book was written in September 2004. Yes, that long ago. The only way you can be reading these words on this page or that e-reader is because of the people who made sure I didn't give up on *Freezing*, or myself, for more than six years. This was a tall order at times. Some of these folks fed me, others bought the new computer I couldn't afford on my own, almost everyone had to see me weep (both kinds of tears), and too many of them had to endure me quoting Jayne and Steelie like they were friends of mine, not just words on the page. I would like to name these very important, very real people.

I am indebted to my constants since 2004: David, Msindo, and Kimera Koff, Sam Brown, and Suttirat Anne Larlarb. In ways unique to each of them, they propped me up, often literally. Between them all, they read every draft. Yet at every turn, they put the manuscript on a pedestal and illuminated it with the intensity of their conviction, keeping the light shining for as long as it took for me to stand up and reach for it again. Thank you.

For 2005, I thank Isobel Dixon and Deonie Fiford, whose first impressions of *Freezing* sent me back to the keyboard with the transformative knowledge that what I had written could become a book. I was tremendously lucky to have two experienced people to whom I could entrust my long-held, private dream of becoming a writer of mystery novels.

Early readers of *Freezing* in 2005 and 2006 were key. In those days, the manuscript was known as *Freezing: The Pamphlet* but Peter 'In the shops in time for Christmas!' Brown and Victoria 'There's a scary Portland connection!' Bodell's enthusiastic but considered responses remain a touchstone for me to this day. I also thank my grandmother, Geri Koff, for reading everything I had one magical weekend in Santa Barbara. It was her birthday but I was the one who received the gift.

In 2007, George Lucas shared the important rules of crime fiction with me while Amy Uyematsu took me to Little Tokyo so I could meet a real, live writer of crime fiction. I dined out on that combination of education and inspiration for the whole year and thank Naomi Hirahara for encouraging me, both in person and through her mystery series.

If a manuscript could have a pulse, 2008 was the year to call for a really experienced medic to check that *Freezing* still had one. The manuscript was post-op with an organ transplant that wasn't quite taking and the surgical scissors might have been left inside. I was living in LA and didn't have health insurance, so calling a medic was out. Then I had a conversation with Paul Crowther who told me in no uncertain

378

terms, and not for the first time, to stand by my convictions: my book, my characters, my dream. His words were the right ones at the right time; my laptop became a triage unit and *Freezing* lived to fight another day, which was essential, given what happened next.

I will be forever grateful to Michael Ondaatje for his unquestioning assistance and generosity of spirit in 2009. He changed the future of this book. Conrad Ketterer provided a refuge where I could write myself into that future; thank you for being sure of me and it. And I thank Pat LoBrutto for insisting I consider life, death, *and* the life to be had after death.

Finally, I am still buoyed and emboldened by my agent Ellen Levine's original, immediate, unwavering 'Yes' in 2009. Thank you for bringing me together with Severn House, of which I'm so proud to be a part. 2010 and 2011 are now inextricably linked with Ellen, Monika Woods and Trident Media Group, along with my publisher Edwin Buckhalter, editor James Buckhalter, and all at 'Team Severn', including the visionary Tony Mulliken of Midas PR. Thank you for talking about my characters like they're real people, thereby letting me finally stand, in fact, through fiction.